I[illegible]NG

Short Sharp Shocks!

Book 0: Dirty Paws - Dean M. Drinkel
Book 1: Patient K - Barbie Wilde
Book 2: The Stranger & The Ribbon – Tim Dry
Book 3: Asylum Of Shadows – Stephanie Ellis
Book 4: Monster Beach – Ritchie Valentine Smith
Book 5: Beasties & Other Stories – Martin Richmond
Book 6: Every Moon Atrocious – Emile-Louis Tomas Jouvet
Book 7: A Monster Met – Liz Tuckwell
Book 8: The Intruders & Other Stories – Jason D. Brawn
Book 9: The Other – David Youngquist
Book 10: Symphony Of Blood – Leah Crowley
Book 11: Shattered – Anthony Watson
Book 12: The Devil's Portion – Benedict J. Jones
Book 13: Cinders Of A Blind Man Who Could See – Kev Harrison
Book 14: Dulce Et Decorum Est – Dan Howarth
Book 15: Blood, Bears & Dolls – Allison Weir
Book 16: The Forest Is Hungry – Chris Stanley
Book 17: The Town That Feared Dusk – Calvin Demmer
Book 18: Night Of The Rider – Alyson Faye
Book 19: Isidora's Pawn – Erik Hofstatter
Book 20: Plain – D.T. Griffith
Book 21: Supermassive Black Mass – Matthew Davis
Book 22: Whispers Of The Sea (& Other Stories) – L. R. Bonehill
Book 23: Magic – Eric Nash
Book 24: The Plague – R.J. Meldrum
Book 25: Candy Corn – Kevin M. Folliard
Book 26: The Elixir – Lee Allen Howard
Book 27: Breaking The Habit – Yolanda Sfetsos
Book 28: Forfeit Tissue – C. C. Adams

Book 29: Crown Of Thorns – Trevor Kennedy
Book 30: The Encampment / Blood Memory – Zachary Ashford
Book 31: Dreams Of Lake Drukka / Exhumation – Mike Thorn
Book 32: Apples / Snail Trails – Russell Smeaton
Book 33: An Invitation To Darkness – Hailey Piper
Book 34: The Necessary Evils & Sick Girl – Dan Weatherer
Book 35: The Couvade – Joanna Koch
Book 36: The Camp Creeper & Other Stories - Dave Jeffery
Book 37: Flaying Sins – Ian Woodhead
Book 38: Hearts & Bones – Theresa Derwin
Book 39: The Unbeliever & The Intruder – Morgan K. Tanner
Book 40: The Coffin Walk – Richard Farren Barber
Book 41: The Straitjacket In The Woods – Kitty R. Kane
Book 42: Heart Of Stone – M. Brandon Robbins
Book 43: Bits – R.A. Busby
Book 44: Last Meal In Osaka & Other Stories – Gary Buller
Book 45: The One That Knows No Fear – Steve Stred
Book 46: The Birthday Girl & Other Stories – Christopher Beck
Book 47: Crowded House & Other Stories - S.J. Budd
Book 48: Hand To Mouth – Deborah Sheldon
Book 49: Moonlight Gunshot Mallet Flame / A Little Death – Alicia Hilton
Book 50: Dark Corners - David Charlesworth

Murder! Mystery! Mayhem!

Maggie Of My Heart – Alyson Faye
The Funeral Birds – Paula R.C. Readman
Cursed – Paul M. Feeney
The Bone Factory – Yolanda Sfetsos

Garland Cove – Deborah Sheldon
Death In The Dugout – Bruce Harris

Beats! Ballads! Blank Verse!

Book 1: Echoes From An Expired Earth – Allen Ashley
Book 2: Grave Goods – Cardinal Cox
Book 3: From Long Ago – Paul Woodward
Book 4: Laws Of Discord – William Clunie
Book 5: Fanged Dandelion – Eric LaRocca

Weird! Wonderful! Other Worlds

Book 1: The Raven King – Liz Tuckwell
Book 2: The Wired City – Yolanda Sfetsos

Horror Novels & Novellas

House Of Wrax – Raven Dane
And Blood Did Fall – Chad A. Clark
The Fallen – Anthony Watson
The Underclass – Dan Weatherer
Cheslyn Myre – Dan Weatherer
Greenbeard – John Travis
Tower Of Raven – Kevin M. Folliard
Welcome Home Natalie – Reyna Young
Little Bird – TR Hitchman
Society Place – Andrew David Barker
Axe – Terry Grimwood

Science Fiction Novels & Novellas

Odyssey Of The Black Turtle – Paul Woodward
Sons Of Sol – Kevin R. Mcnally

The 'A QUIET APOCALYPSE' Series

A Quiet Apocalypse – Dave Jeffery
Cathedral (A Quiet Apocalypse Book 2) – Dave Jeffery

The Samaritan (A Quiet Apocalypse Book 3) – Dave Jeffery
A Silent Dystopia – Edited by D.T. Griffith

General Fiction

Joe – Terry Grimwood
Finding Jericho – Dave Jeffery

Science Fiction Collections

Vistas – Chris Kelso

Horror Fiction Collections

Distant Frequencies – Frank Duffy
Where We Live – Tim Cooke
Night Voices – Paul Edwards & Frank Duffy

Anthologies

The Darkest Battlefield – Tales Of WW1/Horror

SONS OF SOL

To Sandy,

SONS OF SOL

A NOVEL BY
KEVIN R. MCNALLY

See you in NM!

First Published 2022

For further information, please visit:
WEB: www.demainpublishing.com
TWITTER: @DemainPubUk
FACEBOOK: Demain Publishing
INSTAGRAM: demainpublishing

To Mum and Dad - whose gift was imagination...

CONTENTS

PROLOGUE

Gagarin Space Station.

Two hundred and fifty miles above the coast of Morocco.

Its three, quarter mile diameter hoops of human living space turning, stately, across the edge of the Sahara and on towards the Indian Ocean below. Attached to one of the thirty docking ports at the station's hub, a huge space ship, like a sleek infant suckling at the behemoth's breast. The Earth emblem: five planets against a blue background, emblazoned on its hull beneath the Presidential crest.

Security Officer Harlan Lewis floated alongside the door of Space Force One, listening intently to his uplink, peering down the flexible umbilical corridor joining the Presidential transport to the space station. The Chief of Security's voice sounded directly in the centre of his frontal lobe.

"Lady One approaching."

Harlan Lewis tapped his smart finger to his thumb, switching the secure link to send.

"Space Force One clear."

Harlan braced himself mentally and physically in preparation for the Great Person's arrival. A flutter of excitement in his gut brought a smile which battled with the inscrutable, unreadable stare he had long practiced in the bathroom mirror of his tiny cabin in the security wing of the wheeling space station. A tough, serious look he'd been honing since his years in the Academy. How far he'd come, he thought, how high he'd risen. Literally. He peered out of the porthole next to him and watched the Earth turn below until the sun appeared over the azure crest of the planet and sensors blackened the clear window. His smirk widened, utterly defeating the hard man stare.

Two officers appeared at the space station's airlock and glided down the tunnel, the diminutive figure of Ji Quang, Earth President and self styled Lady One, floating serenely between them. It was Harlan's first glimpse of the great woman in the flesh, she having been holed up with her ministers and advisers in the Gagarin's state rooms since her arrival the morning before and a slight pang of disappointment descended upon him as she passed without so much as a glance in his direction. Perhaps for the best, he thought with a thump of embarrassment hitting his cheeks, as he'd probably been grinning like an idiot as she went by.

When President Quang had passed through the door of Space Force One, Harlan shook off these musings and became businesslike again sending an 'all clear' to the Chief who appeared from the airlock with the Presidential entourage. These technocrats had little experience of orbital transfer and tumbled in an ungainly clump along the passage, their gravity reliant muscles overcompensating for their new found freedom.

Once the group had been safely passed through the doors of Space Force One, the Chief turned to Harlan Lewis and barked an instruction.

"Retract the umbilical and get back on station."

"You're making history today, sir," said Harlan, in a reverential tone, looking wistfully into the plush interior of the world's most famous space vehicle. "You'll be there when Earth finally makes peace with the Centauris. I wish I could join you."

The Chief regarded his junior officer with a barely contained look of derision crossing his craggy features.

"Let the grown-ups do their work, son," he said. "Now get this umbilical stowed."

Dang, thought Harlan, but the Chief could be a real jerk. He turned, hand-over-handing along the guide rail as he floated back to the Hub and retracted the umbilical tunnel. With it safely stowed he made his way up to the observation port to see the President's ship, already five miles out, glistening over the arc of the Earth and turned on the ship-to-ship radio link to hear the Space Force One captain addressing his prestigious passengers over the ship's intercom.

"Good afternoon, Ma'am. Welcome back to Space Force One and your historic flight to the Aldrin Lunar Centre."

Harlan could hear a ripple of applause break out among the passengers and he imagined President Quang nodding graciously, her right hand rising slightly and describing a small circle in her familiar regal wave.

"Please fasten your harnesses in readiness for Push."

The ship began to hum as the nuclear engines came on-line in preparation for Trans Lunar Injection.

"Push in t-minus..."

The speaker above Harlan's head crackled momentarily and, now some ten miles out, the ship's lights appeared to flicker.

"Please bear with me for one moment, Ma'am, we seem to be having a slight..."

The ship, now glinting and tiny in the vast blackness of space shuddered slightly. Harlan Lewis, his face pressed to the plexiglass porthole, widened his eyes and his jaw dropped as Space Ship One expanded to a huge, silent ball of plasma which faded as quickly as it had appeared leaving a spherical vacuum a mile in diameter.

1. ALMA MATER

Percival Prendergast, tall and slim, a wave of blonde hair drooping across his slate blue eyes, sat in the Goddard Lecture Hall of Edinburgh's Space Propulsion Academy, surrounded by the entire third year body of students, looking for all the world like a decent chap who you could trust with a family heirloom and your darkest secret. Which you could, because he was. A decent chap. And a genius to boot.

Doctor Mungo McNeal, a bulky man in his sixties, gray of hair and complexion, stood before the students, delivering his key note lecture in advanced propulsion in a voice that could by no means be called riveting. Because it wasn't. Quite the opposite.

Doctor McNeal did not have Percival Prendergast's undivided attention but not for his lack of charismatic delivery. Percy was entirely unaware that McNeal was even in the room, his attention being fully focused on the back of a shapely head, cascading with blonde curls. It belonged to Doris Pilbrow, the Siren of Southshields with whom, after a few visits to the peak of Arthur's Seat and an intimate dinner-a-deux in Stuffers, the revolving restaurant atop the Castle, he believed he had 'an understanding'.

Despite Percy's attentions Doris had become distant of late, preferring to keep company with a succession of the more sporty element among the post graduates. As she was today. Darn close to canoodling, thought Percy, with a rower called Simms. And in the front row too. Now no-one who knew Prendergast well would call him a man of boiling passion but it could be said he was at a low simmer.

Percy was on the verge of definitely deciding to say something at lunch time, if Doris could spare a moment, when his train of thought was broken.

"By the Laws of Physics!" hissed the young man on Percy's left, a little too loudly. Several students looked round to see who had had the nerve to disturb the air of reverent silence demanded by McNeal and the Doctor himself broke off his lecture mid-sentence, giving a momentary respite from that familiar drone which had earned him the nickname, Mogodon. After a brief bout of peering over his bifocals, he picked up where he had left off.

"Whatever is the matter, old boy?" Percy hissed at Anthony Smith who had crouched down in his pew, two hands over his mouth, eyes darting from side to side.

Smith was a shorter, stockier make of student than Percy, with a close cropped shock of jet black hair and what many described as a shifty look about him. He had a barrow boy demeanour - in stark contrast to Percy's genteel air - but was nonetheless the engineering genius behind Prendergast's theoretical brilliance in their finals' space propulsion project.

Smith leaned in close growling in a hoarse stage whisper.

"The entire government, including President Quang, has just been wiped out in an explosion on the way to the Lunar Conference, that's what's the matter."

"Who? What conference?"

"Keep up, Percy. The President of Earth."

"Oh, him?"

"Her!"

"Quite. Not really a political animal. Wiped out you say?"

"Obliterated, the lot of 'em."

Prendergast tut-tutted regretfully. Then frowned deeply as a thought struck him.

"How do you know?"

Smith tapped the side of his head and grinned broadly.

"I'm uplinked to Gabble."

"On the Innernet?"

"Exactly."

Prendergast shook his head. Anthony Smith was simply making no sense.

"Setting aside the fact that Doctor McNeal would throw a fit if he knew, he blocks all his classes magnetically. You just can't uplink in a Mogodon Sleepover."

The dour Doctor's lectures were aptly named. McNeal had long ago realised that he could not hold a classes interest for very long and had found his students drifting off into the Innernet. So the attention he could not command was demanded by the simple expedient of having his lecture room built around a Faraday Cage thus cutting his prey off from the rest of humanity. The result? A fair approximation of snuggling down with friends under a duvet after a handful of downers. The famed Mogodon sleepover.

Smith looked saddened and hurt.

Percy, Percy. He may not've had your privileged upbringing but who by the sweat of his own brow's become the greatest engineer at Edinburgh SPA?"

"You have, old chap."

"And what can any system be?"

Prendergast nodded again, wisdom dawning.

"Overridden."

Smith held up a cube of blue plastic, an inch on each side, which throbbed gently with an inner light.

"Thank you. So let's have no more of the Doubting Thomas please."

"Sorry. Silly of me. So this government thing. Terrorists, was it?"

"Accident they're saying."

The Mogodon drone stopped once again.

"Gentlemen!" McNeal's face had reddened considerably and his right hand was clenching and unclenching in a rather worrying manner.

"Something you would like to share? Am I boring you?"

Prendergast smiled at the man and gave him a genial wave.

"So sorry, Doctor. How rude of us. Do go on. Absolutely riveting."

The drone started up again and the breathing of the students in the back row began to slow once more as they drifted back to a dreamless sleep. Smith looked at Prendergast scornfully.

"You are a little crawler, Percy."

*

An hour later, in the concrete courtyard of the Theory Wing, Smith once again returned to the accident and the demise of the President. By now everyone had heard and the campus was abuzz with the news.

"The way I see it, Percy, this is the third Push Drive accident in as many years. Not surprising really. Here we are in the twenty-fourth century and we're still flying around space on nuclear bombs. It's medieval and outdated and our little beauty is the way forward."

"Yes but, Tony, you're always telling me how the industry is so short sighted. And how it refuses to invest adequately in new technology like ours.

And the rant usually ends with you giving me a graphic description of what you would like to shove up them."

"Was short sighted, Percy. Past tense. But these new victims are so high profile the industry can't ignore the problem anymore. They're gonna have to sit up and take notice. This disaster is a massive opportunity for us!"

"Steady on, old fellow. People died up there. Human tragedy all round and whatnot."

"Yes, yes, heartbreaking. A bloke simply doesn't have the words at a time like this. But, Percy. With HENRIE we're going to graduate next month, winners of the Von Braun medal and then we can write our own ticket. Research and development jobs with any of the major players in space propulsion. Maybe even the finance to start our own company. We'll be trillionaires before we're twenty-five."

"And do a lot of good for humanity."

"Yeah, yeah, whatever."

Prendergast paused for a moment, a fixated on a head full of blonde curls across the courtyard. Doris Pilbrow was sitting astride a bench with an ice cream cone in one hand and the thigh of a rather beefy looking chap in the other.

"Would you give me a few moments, Tony?"

Smith followed Prendergast's stare, spotting the girl and the jock.

"Testing Lab. Ten minutes," he ordered in a disapproving grunt.

*

It was half an hour before Prendergast rejoined Smith who was quietly fuming at the entrance. Percy had a sheepish look on his face and the mother of a shiner starting to swell around his right eye.

"Sorry, Tony old chap, got into a bit of a pickle."

Smith raised a dignified hand.

"Keep it to yourself. I've more important worries than your sickening infatuations. Viz. Problems with HENRIE."

HENRIE was an acronym. It stood for Hydrogen Energy Nuclear Reactive Impulse Engine. Hydrogen Energy because hydrogen atoms were its power source and Nuclear Reactive because it generated a nuclear fusion reaction for its power output. Impulse Engine didn't really mean anything but naming it HENR seemed a bad idea and they couldn't think of anything else starting with IE. This wasn't the first name they tried. Smith had suggested HYDRA, an abbreviation of hydrogen with an 'A' stuck on the end but Prendergast vetoed this as intellectually unrigorous if not downright sloppy. He had suggested HER for Hydrogen Energy Rocket but Smith insisted that the machine was in essence a masculine one. Solar Hydrogen Impulse Thruster hadn't flown as an idea with either of them.

They walked the length of the testing facility to Bay 16. Smith turned on the lights and there on its mounting gimbals was HENRIE under a pristine nanoplas sheet. He pulled back the cover and stroked the machine tenderly.

HENRIE was an experimental prototype. Exactly congruent in all but size and power with the actual thruster that they hoped would one day push liners and cargo vessels all around the solar system. Smith regarded it reverentially.

"We're not getting the best Hydrogen take-up, percentage light speed ratio. Until we do, what we have here is just a top-notch, safer version of a standard Push Thruster. Not the revolution in interplanetary travel that we envisioned and frankly that won't do. If we want to win the Von Braun medal you're going to have to do some serious number crunching Percy or we won't have diddly for the finals assessment in three weeks."

Prendergast nodded gravely and patted HENRIE's onboard input port.

"Very well, old boy. You want numbers crunched then crunched numbers you shall have. By morning."

*

An hour's calibration, and a small test run later, HENRIE was safely stowed back under the nanoplas. Smith and Prendergast left the building and went their separate ways. Before heading to his room, Prendergast paused. After a moment of conflicted consideration, turned on his heels and strode off purposefully in the direction of the women's dormitory. He had unfinished business in his romantic affairs. He wanted them settled before he could bring the full weight of his mighty intellect to bear on HENRIE's hydrogen sweep factors.

*

The next morning Smith rose early, uplinked to the news channels and waited for Prendergast to show. But show Prendergast did not so at ten o'clock it was an irritated, muttering Anthony Smith who set out in search of his theoretician.

He discovered Prendergast in the refectory just after eleven and sat down in front of him, ready to tear him off a strip. He noticed Prendergast's smart finger tapping on the plastic table with the far away, Innernet look in his eyes, both of which were now darkening purple and yellow around the cheek bone.

"Did you enjoy your evening?" Smith asked with a forced bonhomie.

"Not really," responded Prendergast as he gingerly touched a cheek and winced.

"So I see. Are you working now?" Smith asked quietly.

Prendergast shook his head.

"C-mail," he replied.

Smith slapped Prendergast's hand and clicked his fingers in front of his face.

"Save it to draft and pay attention to me."

Prendergast tapped out a save and turned his attention to Smith, a pleasant smile on his face.

"Fire away, old thing."

Smith took a deep breath.

"Percy. Why am I here?"

"To talk to me, old chap?" ventured Prendergast.

"At the academy, Percy. Why do I attend this academy?"

Prendergast furrowed his brow. If his engineering colleague wished to talk in riddles, who was Percival Prendergast to stop him.

"I don't get you."

"Why am I slogging my guts out in this glorified septic tank, toiling away day after day, working with morons and instructed by sadists?"

"To learn advanced engineering..."

"No."

"...to build better Space Drives..."

"No."

"...and benefit all humanity?"

"I'll tell you, mate. To learn advanced engineering to build better Space Drives to benefit all humanity and become incredibly rich."

"Ah."

"So I can go out with beautiful posh women, drive dangerously fast cars and drink ridiculously priced wine. That's why I'm here, Percy and to do that I need to build the best engine that's ever been built and I can't do that without the figures mate, without the maths which I rely on you to provide."

Prendergast nodded sagely, a look of concerned understanding on his face.

"Yes, quite. Perfectly understand, Tony but you must understand that these things take time. We are at the very edge of the theory here and at the frontier things move a tad slower."

"Nadgers! Who were you c-mailing?"

"Erm..."

"It's Doris, isn't it? That dozy tart from Metallurgy."

Prendergast deflated slightly, a shifty, guilty look playing hide and seek in his eyes.

"Here we are, our final project due in a month and you're mooning around like a love struck antelope after a woman destined for a career in scrap metal."

"Now steady on, Anthony."

Smith was on his feet.

"No, you steady on, Percival. You may be content to throw the last four years away and play kiss-chase with Doris-bloody-no-hope-cant-tell-her-arse-from-an-alloy Pilbrow and have the cheating little vixen's boyfriends use you as a punch bag but I'll tell you this free and for nothing. You'd better extract your head from your fundament sharpish matey-boy or I'll find some other Aspergers geek to do my sums for me and leave you well and truly in it, up the creek without a finals project. Comprendez? Mush!"

Smith stood, panting slightly. Prendergast lifted his reddening face and eyed Smith guiltily.

"Alright, old bean. I'll get right on it. There's no need to raise the temperature of the whole thing."

*

Prendergast prepared himself for the night's work. He placed his favourite chair next to an open window which looked out over the college's south quad and doused the lights, save for a single, bright, angled lamp which bathed him in a pool of illumination. Ordering a beaker of coffee from the kitchen module, he took a deep breath and closed his eyes.

Shapes tumbled and shifted, their surfaces rippling with oil-slick rainbows in the reaches of Prendergast's mind. The metallic flickering of colourful motion, like the wings of crystalline insects, became more frantic as the imaginary objects attracted and repelled each other, probing and exploring, vibrating in geometric ecstasy.

Slowly, a subtle change occurred. One or two of the twirling forms merged and as they did so their colours settled and their loci stilled in the centre of Percy's perception. More and more of the congealing geometries joined in a chain which soon stretched to his inner horizons and as their colours intensified, the still jangling, jagged, morphing objects around them faded and disappeared.

A faint smile twitched on Percy's lips as he held the stream of shapes, undulating behind his closed lids. He breathed deeply. As he let the air out of his lungs, some of the shapes expanded. The first, the second, the third, the fifth, the eighth, the thirteenth...

Prendergast opened his eyes. They watered softly in the evening breeze and his pupils shrank to a point from the bright lamp before him.

He tapped his smart finger on the arm of his chair, marking down his unique, idiosyncratic mathematical notation onto a virtual scrap of paper on file in his DNA.

Percy Prendergast: the most highly developed grapheme to colour synaesthesiac to ever walk the face of the earth.

*

The next morning, after putting in his all nighter with the metaphorical pencil and slide rule, it was a pale faced, bloodshot and puffy eyed Percival Prendergast who presented himself at the rooms of Anthony Smith. Tony was uplinked and working at a large engineer's plexiscreen upon which he projected a 3D image of his current working model of HENRIE from the HD contact lens he wore in his right eye.

"You got my hydrogen sweep algorithms?"

Prendergast cut off a yawn, mid-way.

"Yes, of course, Tony. All done."

"Right. Let's have 'em then."

Prendergast sleepily uplinked to the Innernet and started shooting over the figures.

"Coming your way. Mind if I make coffee?"

"Help yourself," said Smith as he closed the virtual model and started downloading Prendergast's work to the DNA in the cells of his neck. Prendergast wandered dozily over to the kitchen module and gave it a good blast of the morning stares.

"Coffee. Black," he said. The machine gurgled and a cup of hot black coffee slid from its vending hatch. Prendergast took a deep slug and settled into the comfiest chair.

"You know, Anthony, I did some pretty stiff thinking last night."

"Hmmm?" Smith was deep into the work now and scarcely gave Prendergast half an ear.

"Yes, I did. Pretty stiff thinking I can tell you. And I had a thought. About benefiting humanity and all. You see HENRIE is going to be darned powerful. We've reached such levels of efficiency for it, sweeping up all that interplanetary hydrogen, that it's going to cut journey times round the solar system by a factor of three."

"Give or take, mate, give or take."

Prendergast nodded and furrowed his brow.

"Yes. But that's it. Dashed effective planet to planet but useless on interstellar runs for obvious reasons."

"Absolutely. Hydrogen atoms are down to as near complete vacuum in interstellar space as to make no odds. Not enough to fuel our little beast. It'd be like trying to run an old fashioned rocket on water."

"And that wouldn't get you very far!"

"It certainly wouldn't, mate," Smith chuckled at the thought. "It certainly would not!"

"Yet that's where improved travel times are most needed. I mean the wormhole sections of the journey are instantaneous. It's the travel to and from the hyperspace ports that takes up the time. Alpha Centauri is presently...what?"

"Four months," said Smith, "Eridani ten. Sirius eight. Not that anyone's allowed to go there of course. Bunch of superior, stuck up bast..."

"But there is fuel in the interstellar regions and if we could tap it I estimate that with an interstellar drive based on HENRIE we could quarter those times. Centauri one month. Eridani two and a half!"

Smith came out of the Innernet and turned his full attention to Prendergast.

"What's the fuel?"

"Why the very thing you find most of in the spaces between stars. Dark Matter."

Smith pouted derisively.

"It's never been done."

Prendergast raised a finger and slowly rotated it in the air by his temple.

"I've already started on the Physics."

Smith moved away from the plexiscreen and pulled up a stool alongside Prendergast. He rubbed his chin thoughtfully and narrowed his eyes.

"Percy, me old mucker. If you could pull this off and I could build the bugger, cutting those journey times and stimulating trade between the colonies like that would certainly be..."

"...jolly beneficial to humanity..."

"...lucrative!"

Smith rose and padded wistfully around the room. He put his hand on the plexiglass screen, tapping it gently.

"Right! Put that on the back burner for a moment, Percy. Pour yourself another coffee and keep them coming because you are going to work day and night between now and the finals and I am going to rebuild HENRIE from scratch. And when we sell it to the highest bidder we shall hit them with your all new interstellar version and become the most famous men in the history of space travel," he paused and beamed at Prendergast, "and do more good for humanity that you ever thought possible," he added by way of translation into words Prendergast could understand.

"D'you really think so, old chap?"

"I know so, me old china!"

Smith uplinked and the plexiscreen lit up with a rotating model of HENRIE.

"Now clear off so I can incorporate these new figures into the schematic. I'll strip it and rebuild it by the end of Friday and we can run final tests next week. Get to it, Percival Prendergast."

*

Smith was the only other person on the planet who understood Prendergast's peculiar hieroglyphics and he quickly began to incorporate them into the model of HENRIE. Not a model on the plexiglass screen nor even a model which anyone could download internally from the Innernet but the model he kept in his own cellular cortex; created without the aid of any inner, man-made software.

Because Smith's genius was one of enhanced visualisation.

He could hold in his mind complex, three dimensional graphic images enabling him to test design changes at speeds even the greatest engineering computers would be pressed to match, and with the laterality of human thought which computers of his time still had trouble mimicking.

By the time he had put in six hours work, reshaping and re-imagining their engine, he froze the simulation and hardwired it into his memory, sure in the belief that they were going to revolutionise the known universe.

2. MEANWHILE...TWO MONTHS EARLIER

Space.

Black.

A sector of the known universe 500 billion miles from Earth towards Galactic Centre. A chunk of space-time no different from any other. Unless you looked very closely.

And one man was looking very closely indeed. Dallas Bulba had just taken over the Zeta shift as Gatekeeper of the Khyber, a space station monitoring and controlling traffic in and out of SolAlpha, one end of a wormhole which stretched the three and a half light years (though actually no distance at all when you travelled through it) to AlphaSol, the gateway to the Centauri system some 600 billion miles from Toliman, the largest and only inhabited planet orbiting Alpha Centauri B, Earth's closest colony.

Sipping on a bulb of coffee he smart fingered the system and a reflexive tingle in his forearm told him he had control of the Portal. To the untrained eye the view from Bulba's screen was a vast vista of stars in a wide range of magnitudes in the familiar whites, yellows, reds and blues of the main sequence in the solar family. But Bulba's eyes were well trained. He recognised the unnatural green tint of objects that were not stars but human artifacts. Bright discs the size of sports stadia describing the surface of an imaginary sphere with a radius of one nautical mile. It was around this star port that the Khyber described its orbit.

Though highly trained and a Gatekeeper of five years experience Bulba had never got used to the arrival of a ship in the Portal. For anyone fortunate enough to witness such an event, and Bulba was preparing to clock his 6,427th ship, the arrival was a challenge for the eye to convey and the brain to interpret because the word 'arrive' is misleading. It implies a process, a transition from one state to another. A space craft's appearance through a wormhole has none of these qualities. It is *not* there one instant and *is* there the next in a way that always made Bulba feel it must have been there all along and he'd simply overlooked it.

The only warning that the Alpha Centauran ship's presence was imminent was a brief glowing of the stadium sized discs for a few seconds prior to 'arrival'. Bulba was glowing nearly as brightly as the discs but his glow was one of pride. To be the man who opened the gate to the envoy from Alpha Centauri. A man headed for a meeting on the Moon. A meeting that might bring peace to the colonies after years of disharmony. I have, thought Dallas Bulba, earned a small place in history.

*

The man who shouldered a far greater chunk of history's weight was sitting in his quarters aboard the Diplomatist. The Alpha Centauri envoy himself. Commodore Janken Harfu. But the Commodore's thoughts were not ones of undiluted pride. He was plagued by a niggling doubt. One which had been haunting him ever since his audience with the Generalissimo back on Toliman when the great leader had entrusted him with this mission. The Generalissimo's credentials were well known to Harfu. A bellicose, authoritarian dictator whose ascendance had piggybacked a wave of anti-Earth resentment. Isolationist and xenophobic by nature, this enthusiasm for peace talks were a surprising volte face. Still, no matter. His mission was peace and Harfu was a peacemaker, whatever his leader's motives.

The Commodore sat before his communication console and opened channels to traffic control aboard the Khyber. He sent the craft's call signal and an encrypted request for entry to the solar system, all performed manually and by conventional radio waves as the Innernet was only available within low orbit of inhabited planets. Inside ten minutes the ship had clearance. He closed the frequency and hailed the bridge.

"Proceed," he said before flipping off the intercom and turning to a figure in the corner of his room.

"We are on our way."

The man in the corner nodded.

*

Once Home-system security had given clearance, Dallas Bulba gave the order for Clear and Release. The Portal disc hanging in space, a quarter of a mile in front of the Diplomatist's nose, started to slide aside like a hangar door. The ship's Nuclear Push Engine began to glow, edging it forward, out into empty space. Within minutes the engines were at full power with a stellar white intensity that drowned the light of the Portal and its satellite space station. The craft accelerated to one-tenth the speed of light towards the faint star Sol at the centre of the home system, half a trillion miles ahead.

3. TO THE VICTOR...

Finals week at the Edinburgh Space Propulsion Academy was always a fraught time and the week that Smith and Prendergast were making the final preparations on HENRIE was no different. Worse if anything. As Anthony and Percy bustled around the campus making their last minute arrangements, young men and women could be seen openly weeping in frustration at the testing centre. Frequent fisticuffs broke out in the library and there were several attempts at suicide. Most were considered a cry for help by less able students brought to breaking point by the institutions famed academic rigour. But the one success, if that's the appropriate term, came when a boy named Cubbit hid himself in the exhaust escape pipe of launch pad A6 just before the firing of a fourteen ton suborbital rocket burning pure kerosene. This was undoubtedly fueled by a genuine desire to shuffle off this mortal coil and in a pretty decisive manner at that. Sadly there was nothing left of the lad to bury so they named the pipe after him.

For the rest, like Smith and Prendergast they sat their exams, handed in their coursework and waited for their appointment to face the Academy's board of assessors. Smith was pulling out all the stops. Though their only real requirement was to uncover the machine, start it up and let the assessors read its performance parameters, Smith felt they needed to come up with a slick presentation to give them an edge over the competition in the race for the Von Braun medal. Prendergast had demurred when Smith had put the plan before him. He felt that HENRIE's lily was being somewhat over-gilded and when pressed, even went so far as to suggest that its pudding was in danger of being over-egged.

"You simply don't get it do you," berated Smith.

"What do you mean, old boy?"

"This is our moment. Our once in a lifetime. When destiny calls us. Our future rests in that presentation. We can't just chuck HENRIE in front of them and mumble 'Here, have a butchers at this!' We have to impress them."

"Of course, old thing. Quite agree. I just think old HENRIE speaks for himself and that you may be overdoing it. Somewhat."

"What on Earth d'you mean?"

"Well...for example...is the dry ice really necessary?"

"Necessary? It's essential! It creates atmosphere."

"Well, there's atmosphere and then there's just showing off."

"Rubbish. What are you saying?"

"I'm saying no one likes a clever dick."

"They'll realise we're serious."

"They will think we are smartalecs!"

Despite Prendergast's finely honed arguments Smith won the day and on the morning of the presentation, with the help of Mickey's Multi Media System from the Crater and Crescent, Edinburgh's premier music venue, the stage was set.

As the assessors trouped into the Testing Facility they were surprised to find Bay 16 curtained off, with Prendergast nervously ushering them through a gap in the plush velvet drapes and handing them expensively printed brochures as he lead them to their seats.

The assessment team was headed by none other than Doctor Mungo 'Mogodon' McNeal himself.

As his colleagues took their seats, chattering bemusedly, McNeal cornered Prendergast.

"What's all this about, laddie?"

"The presentation, Doctor Mogo...Maga...McNeal."

"Well. Get on and present it then."

"All in good time, sir. If you would just be patient."

"I am running short of both time and patience with every passing second, Prendergast. Do you realise how many assessments we have today?"

"Absolutely. Must run into the dozens but if you could just give us a moment, Smith's got a thing he wants to do."

Prendergast was by now squirming quite noticeably. He didn't find his relationship with Mogodon comfortable at the best of times but the added anticipation of Smith's gala presentation was making him distinctly chilly in the area of his feet. It was all he could do to stop himself making a dash through the curtain and hiding under his duvet until the whole thing had blown over.

"Thing? What sort of thing?" thundered Mogodon.

Before Prendergast could answer the lights dimmed to blackness.

"What the...? We're having a black out!" Mogodon continued, his arms groping the air before him.

In the ensuing darkness the opening chords of *Also Sprach Zarathrustra* boomed through the bay. Mogodon pushed through his fellow professors towards a huge speaker.

"What in blue blazes? There's no music allowed in the testing areas!"

Over the Strauss horn section came Smith's voice, heavily reverbed.

"Since the dawn of time man has striven to conquer new frontiers."

"Eh? Who's that?"

Mogodon spun round and dragged Lionel Parker the diminutive Head of Fuel Research to his feet.

"Find out who is doing this and stop it!"

Parker hurried towards the doors getting tangled in the velvet drapes en route. Dry ice began to pour from vents at the side of the Testing Bay and a bright red spotlight came up on HENRIE.

"Scrivens! We're on fire," boomed McNeal as Smith emerged from the gloom, bathed in a yellow glow, lifting a microphone to his mouth and raising his free arm theatrically.

"Ladies and gentlemen, we present to you the future of space travel. HEN..."

Lionel Parker had by now extricated himself from the curtains and located the light controls. He threw the master switch and the Testing Bay burst into bright neon illumination.

"SMITH!" Mogadon was now doing a fair impression of Vesuvius on one of its more lively days.

"SMITH!" he repeated for clarity. "What the hell are you playing at?" Smith stopped mid-performance and squinted in the bright light.

"Making my presentation, Doctor McNeal?"

"No, you're not. You're making a spectacle of yourself. This is an Academy not a burlesque show. Now let the board see what you've got and have less of your nonsense."

One bog standard, run of the mill, no frills demonstration later, with the judging panel departed, the boys were alone. Smith had his head in his hands and Prendergast was taking down the velvet curtains which had so tested the Head of Fuel Research a quarter hour before.

"I don't wish to appear a Norman Knowall old boy and 'I told you so' would never leave my lips but I have to say...I tried to tell you...that you were seriously misjudging the whole...tenor of the process."

Smith lifted his head from his hands and eyed Prendergast beadily.

"Ooooh...shut up, you whiny little git."

"Steady on!"

"It doesn't matter. Say they didn't like what I was trying to do. Say they are an unimaginative bunch of dinosaurs, stuck in another era and intimidated by my style and panache. Say it was a little racy for them. It doesn't matter."

"Well, it might."

"You said it before. HENRIE speaks for himself. And Mogodon daren't let any personal animosity sway his decision. The engines a triumph and they all saw it."

Prendergast ruminated for a moment or two.

"Yes. Yes, you could be right."

"Of course I'm right."

"Yes. Just because you went at the thing the wrong way doesn't take anything from HENRIE, does it?"

"Course it doesn't."

"You may have come off a bit foolishly but HENRIE's still a winner, isn't he?"

"Exactly."

"You making a total idiot of yourself is a separate matter..."

"Well?"

"Even if you did behave like an utterly idiotic, stupid, moronic..."

"Alright, alright, you've made your point. There's no need to bang on about it."

"I'm just putting it in perspective."

"Well, you have now and you can stop."

Smith rose and after throwing the nanosheet back over HENRIE, walked out of the building.

*

The exam results wouldn't be in for a few months but the winner of the Von Braun Medal for Space Research would be announced the following week. Smith and Prendergast pondered how to fill the time. They would have both preferred to take a little well earned rest and recuperation at their respective homes with their respective parents but Prendergast's, who were geophysicists, were on a hush-hush project with a mining research team in the Kuiper Belt and Smith's, who had recently won a medium prize on the Luna Lotto, were taking an extended cruise around the inner planets. As neither of them had much in the way of credit left by the end of the academic year and Smith owed more around Edinburgh than he had started out the term with, they decided to take Prendergast's battered old scout tent and camp out at Pease Bay, the intention being to breath in the sea air and paddle in the salt water for a few days, returning to take their prize refreshed and invigorated.

Five days later it was a relaxed and tanned Percival Prendergast who strode into the Peenemunde Study Hall, where the name of the Von Braun Medal winner was traditionally posted on a quarter sized replica of a V-1 rocket engine, which took pride of place next to Neil Armstrong's Apollo training suit and the Beagle Space Probe which had been retrieved from the surface of Mars after two hundred years of silence. Students liked to sit around the Beagle and take coffee while they studied which made it the most expensive occasional table in existence.

Following in his wake was a haggard, sick Anthony Smith. While at the beach he had attempted to make the time pass more swiftly by drinking the remainder of Prendergast's meagre purse and taking ill-advised midnight dips in the cold North Sea waters, resulting in a nasty chill and an even nastier skin infection.

A cluster of students huddled around the rocket and at the centre of the group stood a blond, buxom, beaming girl receiving the adulation of her, mainly male, fellow students. It was none other than Doris Pilbrow, Prendergast's femme fatale and the focus of so much opprobrium by Anthony Smith in recent weeks. As the excited gaggle bounced away, taking Doris with them, Smith and Prendergast approached the V-1 and read the citation stuck to its hull. The result they read there could not have been worse. Doris had taken the medal for her 'astoundingly original work in the field of structural reinforcement in the hulls of mid to long range cargo vessels while lowering weight at near light speed.'

Smith was apoplectic.

"Doris bloody Pilbrow?! There was me thinking she spent every waking hour making your love life miserable, flattening grass with all comers in every corner of the campus, when all the time she was secretly strengthening Tungsten, the little minx! Is there no end to her low subterfuge?"

Prendergast seemed lost in Arcadia, the tan flushing deeper on his cheeks.

"Beautiful and brilliant," he breathed longingly.

"Well, we are well and truly stuffed mate. Four years up the spout and no mistake. But mark my words, I shan't take this lying down. I'll fight it to my last breath. I shall sue that troglodyte 'so called' bloody Doctor McNeal!"

"Ah, Prendergast! Smith!" said a familiar sonorous voice, "Just the men I was looking for." It was Mungo McNeal himself, not an imitation.

Prendergast leaped about three feet in the air, vertically, and upon his return to terra firma, started to gabble nervously.

"Ah! Doctor Mogodon. Erm...Doctor Mogodon. I mean...Doctor Mogodon..."

"MCNEAL for heaven's sake," despaired Smith.

"Yes. We were just talking about you. Weren't we? Saying how wise your decision was in re the Von Braun Medal and how we didn't want to sue you at all. Didn't we, Tony?" babbled Prendergast adding a whimper and falling silent.

The good Doctor looked at him briefly, the picture of perplexity then waved a herringboned arm dismissively.

"Be quiet and listen to me."

The boys adopted their attentive poses, Smith slightly more reluctantly than Prendergast.

"Bad luck on the medal, it was a close thing but I had the casting vote and I was very impressed with Miss Pillbrow's superstructure. However, you are one of two honorable mentions and as always these successes are brought to the attention of some of our benefactors who like to get first dibs, as it were, on the Academy's brightest talent. Your propulsion system has most intrigued Mr Canard, CEO and chief engineering scout for Saabre Industries which as you know is the foremost nuclear engine producer in the home system. He will meet you at the Royal Mile Hotel tonight at seven. Don't be late."

And with that he was gone. Smith and Prendergast stared after him for a moment then slowly turned to each other. A broad grin spread across Smith's face and, leaping in the air, he let out an ear splitting rebel yell while pumping the air with his fist. Prendergast raised his left eyebrow half an inch.

"I say," he said.

*

Arriving early at Edinburgh's most luxurious hotel and asking for their host at reception, they were informed he was in a meeting and they were to await him in the bar where Smith ordered a large scotch, charging it to Mr Canard. Prendergast had a sparkling water which he paid for while Smith wasn't looking and helped himself to the complimentary nuts.

Smith sat back in a wide, plump armchair and gestured expansively, rolling the whiskey in its finely chiseled glass.

"Now, Percival, let me do the talking. We need to play this cannily."

Prendergast slumped slightly in his chair.

"Why?" he asked.

"Why what?"

"Why do we have to play this cannily?"

"Well, it stands to reason. We're playing with the big boys now."

Prendergast sipped his water and carefully placed the glass in the centre of a plastic doily on the faux oak table between them.

"Haven't we already agreed that HENRIE speaks for himself? So why don't we just listen to what the chap has to say and not..." He waved his hand vaguely in the air before him.

"Not what?"

"I don't mean to be critical, old boy."

Smith paused mid-sip and held the tumbler of fine peaty malt and inch from his lips.

"Never mind all that twaddle. If you have something to say...say it!"

"Alright. Let's not go in all guns blazing and overdoing the whole thing. Old chap."

It was now Smith's turn to place his glass on its doily and eye his partner.

"I see. That's how it is. Lost a bit of faith in your old mucker's abilities, is it? Alright. We'll do it your way. I leave this captain of industry to you. *You* secure us a deal and ensure our future."

"That IS big of you, old thing."

"Carry on. Good luck."

"Thanks awfully."

"But when you make a complete dog's dinner of it, I'll laugh in your face."

"Perfectly reasonable, dear fellow."

"And kill you."

Prendergast laughed heartily but Smith remained stony. They stared at each other for a moment 'til the spell was broken by a large hearty voice just behind them.

"Boys, boys, boys. Welcome."

Montague Canard was a tall man, long of limb with a shock of black hair atop a rim of steel grey, firm aristocratic features and a robust cut glass voice. Always dressed in the most finely cut suit, the one he was wearing this evening was a navy worsted with a fine chalk stripe. A high collared shirt of vivid pink was set off with diamond cufflinks and a dashing burgundy tie.

"I hear great things. Genius squared they tell me. Is it all true?"

He looked expectantly at the boys. Smith, having handed over the reigns as it were to Prendergast, turned to him with his eyebrows raised and a 'come on, let's see what you've got' smile playing cruelly on his lips. For his part Prendergast stared back at Mr Canard, his eyes wide and his mouth slightly ajar. Montage could take ones breath away at the best of times and Prendergast, of a delicate disposition, was well and truly winded by the man's sheer esprit.

"Come, don't be shy. Another drink? Good show."

Percy decided that spiritous liquor was precisely what was needed if he was to properly represent Smith and Prendergast Limited in the face of this force of nature and a couple of large snifters later he was considerably looser of collar and tongue.

"You see, Montague, may I call you Montague, Mr Canard? You see, sir, your Nuclear Fission accidents are proof, if proof were needed..."

Montague had his hand up like a New York traffic cop at a busy intersection.

"May I stop you there for one moment, Percy?"

Prendergast gave the floor to Montague with a dip of the head and a wave of his hand, the whiskey bringing out his magnanimous side.

"There are a number of words we try to avoid in our industry. Nuclear being one of them. I don't know why but it seems to summon up mushroom clouds and Geiger counters and generally give folk the willies. Another is accident. Mishap, error, logistical oversight, all of these are preferable to the ghastly 'accident'. Once again it's the imagery it conjures in the minds of the uneducated. Deserted East European cities, cooling towers going critical in beloved beauty spots, that sort of thing. Come to think of it we are not too keen on fission either. A cumbersome word for a dirty process."

"Ah, well, that is where we can help you, Monty, may I call you Monty, Montague? Fission *is* a dirty business. Blowing apart those Deuterium atoms, releasing vast amounts of energy that is very difficult to control and all that radiation which it is almost impossible to contain."

"But vast amounts of energy is what's required to push those blessed ships around the solar system and they get bigger every decade and so do our engines which become less and less sa..."

Montague stopped abruptly and narrowed eyes in which a taper of excitement was catching light.

"Do you mean your engine, your..." He groped for its name.

"HENRIE," assisted Prendergast.

"...it isn't powered by fission?"

"Why blow Deuterium dangerously apart..." which he illustrated by flinging his arms asunder nearly knocking the drink out of Smith's hand, "when you can press hydrogen nuclei safely together?" He brought his two index fingers delicately tip to tip, demonstrating his point.

Montague was rapt.

"Fusion?" he asked, with a hushed reverence.

Prendergast nodded the nod of a guru.

"But the energy required renders such a machine uneconomical. Fusion's all well and good for the space factories, manufacturing rare materials from cheap and plentiful ones, but for propulsion energy? You have to put more in than you'd get out."

"In some fusion reactions, yes, but..." he left the thought dangling.

Montague's eyes widened.

"Cold fusion? You have achieved cold fusion?" He made it sound like a state of grace.

"Not cold exactly. Call ours...cool fusion. At any rate the temperature inside HENRIE never rises above 700 degrees and once you've started the thing off the fuel is abundant and free in the interplanetary dust."

Mr Canard sipped his drink, his mind racing with possibilities.

"This would revolutionize space travel."

Suddenly his face hardened.

"If...you can reproduce your results with a full sized engine in the vacuum of space."

Smith could contain himself no longer. The way he saw it, Prendergast had hooked the fish and now it was his job to pull in the landing net.

"With a little seed money we could draw up a few prototypes and in a month or two..."

Montague stood to his full six-feet-four inches. Smith and Prendergast instinctively pressing themselves back into their seats as Mr Canard started his traffic cop routine again.

"You will fly to Gagarin Space Station tomorrow and from there on to our laboratory in geosynchronous polar orbit and begin building HENRIE at once."

He strode towards the door of the bar then turned to Smith and Prendergast.

"Welcome aboard, gentlemen. Oh, and the next shuttle to leave Gagarin isn't for another week so you can have a little R&R at the Vostok Hotel, Casino and Spa. All on Saabre's account, of course. Ever been in a weightless jacuzzi? Great fun."

And with that, he was gone.

*

The Delia Smith Spaceport is England's only such facility and is situated in the Megopolis of Norwich, the second largest in the country. The one thousand kilometer Maglev Vacuum Tunnel stretches across the North Sea, Holland, Germany, Poland and rises to a height of thirty-five kilometers above the city of Pinsk in Belarus where it spits out its space ships at a speed of seven miles per second into Earth orbit. It makes for an impressive sight, reaching out over the Norfolk coastline, the silver tube turning to pastel blue as it tapers to its vanishing point over the horizon. On a clear day, like the one which found Smith and Prendergast riding the East Coast Bullet on the last leg of its journey from Edinburgh, it could induce a giddying vertigo and a crushing sense of existential angst in the dehydrated brain of a newly graduated student who had recently got on the wrong end of an unaccustomed volume of grain alcohol. Indeed Prendergast's transom was already slightly adrift before they passed York and by Lincoln he was feeling distinctly detached in both body and mind.

As the disconcertingly massive architecture of the Space Injection Tube became more clearly defined in the East Anglian sky, the skin on the back of his neck began to crawl, the hairs hackle, and his steadily blanching skin to ooze salt lather, while oscillating between extremes of temperature which tested organic matter's tolerances. Add to this the certain knowledge that he was about to be loaded into the breach of this thing like so much buckshot and he began to unravel.

"I can't do it, d'you hear me? I can't!" he shouted in the packed carriage, turning heads, upsetting drinks and frightening young children. Smith had been lost in the thriller he was streaming on the Innernet and his eyes shot open as he was jolted back to cold reality by the outburst.

"What the...what're you shouting about, you lunatic?"

"That thing. That great big thing up ahead there. I won't be shot out of it. I won't. I'm a human being not a poisoned dart!"

"Percy, Percy calm down. We're men of science. The Maglev Cannon is perfectly safe."

This did not go down with Prendergast as well as Smith had hoped.

"Cannon. There. You said it. I don't want to go ballistic!"

Smith looked around the carriage. Prendergast was, by now, attracting a lot of attention from their fellow travelers and this made Smith uncomfortable.

"Keep your voice down. People are looking."

"I don't care, I don't care." A sudden intensity took hold of him and he thrust himself forward, clutching at Smith's sleeve.

"Don't make me go, it's not natural I tell you. Man wasn't meant to travel at such speeds. I'll disintegrate," he hissed.

"Get a grip man, you're being positively Victorian!"

It was clear to Smith this situation had to be mastered and mastered quickly if they were to achieve earth orbit and their manifest destiny. The first step was to reign in Prendergast's galloping terrors.

"It's very simple, Percy. You're suffering from what's known as a hangover. They're very common. When they're this bad there's a simple procedure. You just add some more of the thing that got you in this state in the first place."

Prendergast blinked and his lower lip quivered like a shrimp in aspic.

"More whiskey? Do you mean more whiskey, Tony?"

"That's right. It used to be called the hair of the cat or something. Think of it as homeopathy."

"But homeopathy is complete bunkum, Tony."

"Not at the dilutions I'm about to administer."

A quick visit to the bar and several stiff scotches later it was a calm and mellow Percy Prendergast who lay sprawled in his seat, gently singing the old disco ballad *How deep is your love?* between whiskey fumed burps.

By the time they had gone through security at Delia Smith and boarded flight VG007 for the twenty minute trip to Gagarin, Prendergast had moved onto a medley of Scandinavian drinking songs he had picked up in his gap year and as he was strapped into his seat ready for Orbital

Injection, the packed flight was being treated to selections from the Wagner's greatest hits album he had listened to with his father as a child. The extra g-forces exerted by the initial thrust as the craft sped up the Maglev Tube proved too much for Prendergast's fragile anima and to everyone's great relief he passed out attempting the high A from Parsifal's *Nur eine Waffe Taugt*.

4. PRESSING AN ADVANTAGE

The Diplomatist was traversing the Kuiper Belt some forty astronomical units out from the sun. Commodore Harfu and his senior officers as they were taking dinner in the mess when news of the Earth President's death arrived.

"It seems we have a long wait before we can complete our mission while Earth appoints a new government, gentlemen."

At a dark corner of the table a shadowy figure held up his hand to quell the murmurs of agreement which had broken out among Harfu's officers.

"On the contrary, Commodore. This makes action even more imperative. Our Great Generalissimo has contacted me personally with explicit instructions on how we are to deal with this unexpected turn of events."

The Commodore stared down the length of the table and arched an inquisitive brow at the man, who stood and continued to speak as he walked around the table.

"The Earth is still enamoured with the concept of democracy, despite history's ample contraindications and shall fret over the 'Will of The People' for some time to come in an attempt to elect new Leaders. During this period they are rudderless and weak. The Great Generalissimo wisely sees this as an opportunity to press an advantage. As of now you are relieved of command, Commodore."

He rolled a small silver disc down the smooth surface of the table. As it spun and rattled to rest in front of Harfu, he could clearly see the Generalissimo's holographic seal. Orders from the

Great Man himself. Though how he could have communicated so swiftly was a mystery. Was it a foreseen contingent, or merely opportunistic improvisation? He kept his counsel.

"I see. You, I take it, will assume control," asked Harfu.

"Precisely. Henceforth this is a military operation."

Commodore Harfu looked grimly round at the faces of his officers. Each in turn, lowered their eyes as the Commodore's gaze fell upon them. He finally turned towards the dark figure who now loomed over him. Harfu nodded gravely.

"We are at your service, Battle Cruiser Commander Zoltac."

*

In the Diplomatist's engine room, Chief Engineer Buckley had a look of deep concern on his face as he ran and reran a simulation of the performance parameters of the Push Engines which powered the giant ship. His engineering computers had, of late, been red lighting against the safety guidance embedded in their positronic templates. As the latest simulation ended, the Chief shook his head and pressed an intercom button on his desk.

*

"Commodore, I have disturbing news," said Captain Philips at the morning briefing of Harfu's officers.

Our engineers tell me they believe firing our engines for deceleration has a seventy-five percent chance of sending them critical and destroying the ship."

A stunned silence descended over the assembled officers and it was a few moments before Philips continued.

"It seems to be the same problem which caused the destruction of the Earth President's ship."

"Isn't that a bizarre coincidence?" asked Lieutenant Jackson a little incredulously.

"It seems," replied the captain, "ironically, we have the same engines as President Quang's ship."

"Oh," said Ratree from Personnel, "And that's not a coincidence I suppose."

"Not really," snapped Philips. "The Saabre company on Earth is the only mass producer of Push Drives in the four systems."

The officers looked to Commodore Harfu for a response but he stared at the desk before him, saying nothing.

"What's to be done, sir?" prompted Jackson.

Harfu remained silent for a moment seemingly turning the problem over in his mind. Eventually he answered.

"That is no longer my problem. Hawkins!"

A junior officer in a slightly baggy suit stepped keenly forward.

"Yes, sir," she barked.

"Report to Battle Cruiser Commander Zoltac and inform him of this new development."

The young Lieutenant's face froze.

"Eh?" she said.

"You heard me."

"I know, but..."

"You heard the commander," asserted Captain Philips.

"Why me?" asked Hawkins.

Harfu's face flushed with indignity.

"Because I told you to!"

"But that's not fair, I'm a requisitions officer. You should get someone from dispatch. Like Jackson."

Jackson stepped forward at the mention of his name.

"Shut up, Hawkins. The Commodore told you to do it."

"I'm just saying. It's more in your line."

"No, it isn't. I'm not senior enough. If anything Captain Philips should do it."

Philips was on this like a hawk.

"Stop sticking your oar in, Jackson."

"I'm just giving my opinion."

"Well, don't. Nobody asked you. The Commodore told Hawkins and there's an end to it."

Hawkins sneered at Captain Philips.

"You're scared."

The Captain gritted his teeth.

"Am not."

"Yes, you are. You're windy."

"So are you," he snapped back.

"Too right," Hawkins responded, "and I'm woman enough to admit it. Zoltac's a nutter."

"Completely mental," agreed Jackson.

"Hawkins is right. Jackson's the man." It was Wardill from accounts.

"Button it, Wardill."

"Well, I think you're all a bunch of wimps and are shirking your responsibilities. If I ran accounts like this, where would we be? Up the creek, that's where. You're a disgrace to the uniform, the lot of you."

The Commodore stepped forward.

"Well spoken young man. Go and tell the Commander..."

"No, no, no, I meant..." Wardill had no time to finish as he was hustled out of the door by Harfu.

"Well volunteered, boy."

"But he's got such a vile temper..."

"Ha ha," gloated Jackson.

"Serves you right," shouted Hawkins at the poor lad's back.

*

Wardill's body was ejected from waste chute three an hour later into the frigid desert of space. The small but dignified ceremony was well attended by the junior officers and it was generally agreed that some consolation could be had from the knowledge that in the lifeless vacuum between the stars, Wardill would look as fresh-faced and innocent in a thousand years as he did today. Though on the downside the look of abject terror that he died with would be plastered on his face for countless millennia.

Zoltac, for his part, had not given Wardill a moment's further thought since he had throttled the life from the boy in the rage that had consumed him. And as soon as the body had been taken away he summoned Commodore Harfu to his quarters.

"Commodore. Give orders that we are to prepare for deceleration immediately. We will put the ship into orbit around Neptune."

Harfu coughed slightly.

"Commander Zoltac. Is this wise?"

Zoltac turned on the Commodore with theatrical surprise.

"You think we should not risk firing our engines? Let our acceleration take us through the solar system and out of the galaxy and onto oblivion, forever?"

"Of course not Commander, we must take the risk, but here? On the edges of the solar system? Once we fire them we dare not try it again. Should we not go on to Earth as we planned?

Zoltac smashed a fist down on his desk.

"NO!" I shall not go cap in the hand to the Earthmen asking for rescue. When I next see Earth, she will be asking for mercy!"

*

The mood on the bridge was grim as Zoltac took his position in the observation bubble at the nose of the bridge. Behind him Commodore Harfu and Captain

Phillips readied themselves with the rest of the crew for the emergency deceleration.

Harfu knew that even if the ship survived the engine ignition this was going to be one rough ride. They had less than two million miles to tame the vessel's colossal forward velocity and shoehorn the mighty craft into orbit around Neptune. It would test the hull to breaking point and put a massive strain on the inertial suppressors which allowed the humans aboard to survive such crushing forces.

Harfu could see Zoltac's right-hand man, Marshal Wittan, at the helm for the firing and orbital manoeuvre.

"Five seconds to firing...two, one. Fire!" shouted the Marshal.

A jolt ran through the ship like a mule's point blank kick to the stomach. Even with the suppressors Harfu could feel his organs move in his body as the nuclear engines powered up. Every man and woman on the ship tensed, awaiting the moment of engine failure, a malfunction that would snuff out their lives. That moment passed as the atomic engines rapidly hit full power without incident. The dice had fallen favourably.

Philips grimaced as he was pressed back in his seat. Turning his head was difficult but he shouted to Harfu who was strapped in beside him.

"We're still here," said Philips.

"But not through this yet," Harfu called back.

Marshal Wittan called out again, louder now as the noise of the ship's metal hull, twisting and fighting the powerful forces acting upon it, become deafening.

"Five seconds to orbital injection...two, one, injection commenced!"

Now alongside the noise, a violent vibration took hold of the very fabric of the ship. Harfu felt his bones rattle and his teeth clattered against each other. His vision blurred as his eyes rocked in their sockets. He could barely see but through his blurred, watery vision he could swear he saw Zoltac, still standing, clutching the rail of the observation deck, throw his head back and laugh. Madman. As the pain in his body peaked intensely. Harfu closed his eyes. Painfully slowly, the clamour and the quaking began to abate.

In contrast, the transition back to normality was remarkably quick. There was a minute or so of unbearable tension as the crew breathlessly waited for the signal that they were through the ordeal. They only breathed freely again when Marshal Wittan called it out.

"Orbit achieved."

A cheer went up around the deck and echoed throughout the ship as every crew member celebrated their salvation.

Zoltac turned and strode from the deck.

"Shut down the engines," he instructed and was gone.

Captain Philips undid his harness.

"We made it. We are here."

"Yes," replied Harfu. "A billion miles from civilization and dead in the water."

*

Zoltac spent the next few days in his cabin turning over the situation in his mind. He needed a course of action that would not involve rescue from home or help from the Earthmen. He desperately sought a way to complete the Generalissimo's grand mission and return home a hero. On the third day of orbiting Neptune, Zoltac summoned Marshal Wittan. As the Marshal entered, Zoltac handed him a printout of a news item he had discovered on the Solar Radio Band.

"I have found our solution," Zoltac said, triumphantly.

5. ...THE SPOILS

"Oh, my Stars! We're famous."

Anthony Smith was sitting at the bar of the Starlight Lounge on the rim of the Gagarin Space Station. Affording spectacular views of the revolving earth two hundred miles below, it was the most exclusive and expensive bar in the solar system and the 'must go' place of the Space Set. Smith and Prendergast had been making pretty darned free with the Saabre expense account for the last few days and had settled into a pleasant routine. After some morning ball games played weightless at the hub of the station and afternoons spent luxuriating in the spa, their evening turned on cocktails in the Starlight before dinner at Ye Olde Mercury Steakhouse in the outer rim of the giant spinning station where the centrifugally induced pseudo-gravity made digestion easier. Smith had been surfing the Innernet while nursing a Tequila Moonrise, when he had chanced upon the article entitled "Wunderkinds snapped up by Saabre are 'Hope for the future' says Rocket boss."

"Famous? How so, old chap?"

Smith pressed his smart finger onto a print terminal by the bar and downloaded the article which glided out on heavily embossed rose scented paper. He handed the sheets to Prendergast.

"Read that little lot, mate!"

Prendergast reached out and took the leaves of paper which vibrated in his hand. Smith looked at the quivering sheaf and shook his head. Prendergast placed the papers on the bar and studied his hand which was in the full grip of the tremors.

"Do you know, Anthony, less than a week ago I was virtually tee-total. Now, what with the night at the Royal Mile, the fiasco of the launch and the three nights in here on Saabre's expense account, I am a shambling alcoholic."

Smith furrowed his brow.

"I wouldn't say shambling."

"An old soak at the very least."

"You've certainly developed a taste for the stuff of late!"

Prendergast shoved his unfinished Martian Mule along the bar towards Smith.

"That's it," he said, straightening his back, "I am, as of now, on the lorry!"

"Wagon," corrected Smith.

"The particular vehicular metaphor is immaterial, old boy," scolded Prendergast. "I eschew the stuff. I forgo it. I am crying off."

Smith put a supportive hand on his shoulder.

"Good for you. Couldn't do it myself."

"I am, henceforth, a stranger to the sauce."

Smith raised both his and Prendergast's drink.

"Here's to you."

"Now," said Prendergast decisively, "let's have a look at this article."

Prendergast leafed through the pages while Smith drained the two drinks in front of him and ordered another Tequila Moonrise. He sipped it, slowly watching Prendergast, whose mouth began to gape as he navigated his way through an extraordinary homage to their genius, courtesy of Montague Canard and the Saabre publicity machine. The article culminated in a photograph of the pair standing proudly beside HENRIE in a pose that Prendergast could not remember striking, in a place he was sure neither he nor Smith had ever been. But, he thought ruefully, most photographs were created nowadays without requiring the presence of even the people depicted in them. He came to the end of the piece, which described their journey to Gagarin and quoted the leader of the advanced propulsion team at the Saabre facility as being 'very excited' about the prospect of working with 'the most talented minds in propulsion theory and technology to emerge in a century'.

Prendergast placed the sheets reverentially on the bar. He looked up at Smith who smiled wryly at his partner.

"Anthony," he said with all the gravitas he could muster, "this is a game changer. We are entering a very interesting phase in our lives."

Smith nodded and giggled slightly.

"We certainly are that, mate."

Prendergast turned towards the bar and clicked his fingers haughtily in the air.

"Barkeeper," he boomed, "a bottle of your finest champagne."

"But, Percy," Smith intervened. "I thought you'd sworn off it?"

"That," said Prendergast with a smack of derision in his voice, "was the old Percival. This one," and he raised the sheaf of rose scented, embossed sheets in the air, "knows how to celebrate."

*

Prendergast's bottle of champagne became two, by which time several of their fellow travellers drifted over to join them at the bar. The second bottle spawned a third as a couple from Arkansas recognised Smith and Prendergast from a news item that morning. Cocktails were ordered and by nine-thirty, ship's time, the entire Starlight Lounge was heaving with punters, slapping the boys' backs and giving the Saabre expense account a kicking it wouldn't forget in a hurry.

Smith recognised an element of hangers-on among the guests. He knew the type well, they were to be found everywhere in the solar system whenever the free booze starts to flow, 'Hail fellow well met, friends for life, you and me buddy,' then the bar closes and you can't find them or a taxi home. Though for the most part there was a genuine atmosphere of celebration in the Starlight Lounge that night.

Smith had noticed a sense of unease and uncertainty amongst his fellow earthmen since the President's demise. Not a sense of sorrow exactly as politicians rarely elicit such feeling from the citizenry, save the occasional fanatic, and President Ji Quang had been considered a particularly cold and distant variety of the breed. But even the most remote of parents can, in their absence, make a child fret and this was how it had been with the people of Earth. Nevertheless, here in this bar, on this night, it seemed that the revellers saw in Smith and Prendergast, 'Sons of Sol' as the article had so publicly dubbed them, a genuine hope for the future. A continuity of human endeavour and a light at the end of one of humanities darker tunnels.

At least that's how it seemed as the wine kept flowing and the spirits kept pouring and the beer steins kept sliding down the bar. Come the morning, as the sentiment abated and the warm glow of newly forged friendship was doused by the cold shards of alcohol withdrawal, very few could remember what all the fuss had been about.

Least of all Prendergast, who Smith found crumpled on the shag pile in the hotel corridor but a few feet short of his hotel bedroom door. Smith had been rendered insensible at around two in the morning and had retired hurt to his room where he fell into a deep coma. Over the next five hours his body had metabolised the vast quantity of drink he had ingested and at seven on the dot brought him painfully back to consciousness with the resultant sugar rush.

Feeling a pang of guilt at having abandoned his partner on the previous evening he dragged Prendergast's inert body back to his room and hoisted him onto the bed. The effort of doing this worked off most of the excess sugar in his system and he too slumped down beside the paralysed body of Prendergast and there they stayed, sleeping soundly 'til noon.

And they would have gone on sleeping, if it hadn't been for the ship's Purser banging on the door and pressing the bell with an annoying insistence. Smith opened the door looking remarkably like the pile of sheets he had just vacated.

"Yes?" he asked groggily, leaning on the doorframe.

"Mr Prendergast?" the Purser probed in a rather soupy, over-enunciated voice.

"Smith," corrected Smith.

"Ah, you will do perfectly well."

Smith raised an eyebrow at the potential slight but on reflection figured the purser's reaction was better than crushing disappointment.

"The Captain requests your presence at his table for dinner this evening. Seven-thirty promptly."

Smith stood with his mouth hanging open for a moment, dribbling slightly, fascinated by the man's plummy accent, then came to, realising it was his turn in the duologue.

"Oh, right."

"Excellent." And with that the Purser turned and slid up the corridor leaving a faint trail.

*

Smith and Prendergast had not yet patronised the Gagarin's large dining room, having eaten in Ye Olde Mercury on previous evenings. They were very impressed. It covered about as large an area as it is possible to get in an orbiting station, space being at a premium in - well - Space. As they threaded their way through the elegantly laid out tables, one or two heads turned in recognition. Saabre had certainly put their publicity machine into top gear, the point being, Smith presumed, to take people's minds off the terrible disaster which had happened a mere month before, not ten miles out from the very station in which Smith and Prendergast were now being feted as the pin-up boys of a new era of safe space travel. Cunning.

The Captain's table was on a raised stage at the far end of the dining room and as they approached, the other guests stood to welcome them. It was the Captain himself who greeted them first.

"Gentlemen, so good of you to join us."

Captain Benjamin Burrows was a barrel-chested man with a voluminous black beard, much favoured by old school space officers. It was a throwback to the pioneering days of space exploration when shaving was an unnecessary luxury. A badge of honour. The bushier the beard, the longer the flight and it looked like Benjamin's had been a marathon.

"Please sit, gentlemen. We are all dying to hear of your plans for the future."

"A rather unfortunate choice of words, Captain," said a rather desiccated woman with the manner of a duchess about her, sitting to the Captain's left, "given recent events."

"Hear, hear," said an old fellow sitting on the Captain's right.

My apologies, Lady Roberts." He inclined his head graciously towards the old relic.

"If reports from Saabre are to be believed we will NOT be dying to hear of your new plans...ha, ha, ha, ha." The rather excitable young man on Tony's right who had so amused himself with this appalling pun was one Harold Rajani, a well known wine critic, bon viveur and if reports were to be believed, utter prat.

A rather willowy blond girl, who Smith vaguely recognised as a crime writer of some repute, leaned intently towards him, cutting out Rajani who sat between them.

"I understand you are going to the Saabre Research Station soon. In polar orbit," she purred. Smith coughed a little nervously and flushed somewhat as he always did when taken with a girl and taken with Susan Silverbirch, author of *Killer Cocktail*, he certainly was. Though who wouldn't be. She being rich, famous and going in and out in all the right places.

"Yes, right, polar...geosynchronous...ha, ha, ha." It seemed the annoying laughter was catching.

"You know," she continued, simultaneously typing a birthday greeting to a friend in Kent with her smart finger, "they have a time machine there."

Conversation came to a bit of a halt at this and all eyes turned to Smith for verification.

"Erm...I don't think they do."

"Yes, they do. I saw a programme about it."

Smith giggled slightly. The very last thing he wanted to do was contradict this woman, as even he knew that was not the way to a girl's heart but he simply couldn't let this arrant nonsense go unchecked.

"Erm...I really don't think so. Given that time travel isn't possible. Yet."

"Oh, wait," said La Silverbirch, as she stared into the middle distance, "why am I seeing Peter Winston?"

The Peter Winston to whom she referred was a popular action hero from the films of the time. Built along the lines of Hercules and Atlas combined and known affectionately as the Physique from Mustique, though in reality he hailed from nearby Bequia Island but that didn't have quite the same ring.

Smith was not unfamiliar with his work and instantly understood Susan's mistake.

"You're thinking of the movie *The Time Traveller.*"

"Oh. And that wasn't shot at the Saabre research centre?"

"I very much doubt it. Probably a movie studio somewhere."

"Ah," she said and went back to her messaging.

"Hear, hear," chipped in the old boy.

Their conversation turned to the latest movies they had seen but with each ill-informed, asinine interjection, Susan's seductive bloom shrivelled before Smith's eyes.

A dark, intense girl to Prendergast's left spoke quietly to him.

"I think it's wonderful."

Prendergast turned. He hadn't really noticed her before. But now he had a chance to drink the girl in as it were, he was struck by her simple beauty. Intense blue eyes looked from under a chalky brow beneath a shock of raven black hair. Her strong but sensitive mouth, glazed in a subtle tone of magenta, parted as she spoke again in her rich, seductive southern states accent.

"Forgive me. Elizabeth Stanton. You're Percival Prendergast, aren't you?"

She held out a delicate hand. Prendergast took it softly.

"Yes. Yes, I am and nothing to forgive, Elizabeth. Please, you were saying?"

"Just that I think it's wonderful when people use their gifts for the good of humanity."

"Oh, rather. Bit of a passion of mine. The good of humanity."

"That's so admirable. All some people do is take, take, take."

"That's a rotten way to be."

"All they can think about is money, money, money."

Prendergast thought he detected a rather impressive echo in the room. Until he realised that, to his left, Smith was holding forth rather volubly

"Money, money, money," he was saying to the others, "they've got tons of it and they're prepared to part with the stuff by the barrowload if you've the ideas and the knowhow."

"Hear, hear."

The old codger was consistent if nothing else.

*

Heading back to their rooms after the lavish state dinner, Prendergast had a distant look in his eyes which troubled Smith.

"You alright, Percy?" he asked, "You look a bit...peculiar."

"Anthony," declared Prendergast, coming to the surface, "I am in love."

"Oh no," said Smith as they reached their adjacent doors, "here we go again."

"Spare me your cynicism, Smith. This is plainly not like the others. They were mere dalliances, infatuations as you have rightly dubbed them in the past but with Elizabeth..."

"Ooooh, Elizabeth," Smith impersonated in a sarcastic falsetto.

"Yes. With Elizabeth I knew from the start that this was it."

"It?"

"Yes."

"It what?"

"The real thing. She has got in amongst me."

"Don't talk rot. You've only known her for five minutes."

The length of time is immaterial. True love is impervious to temporal constraints."

Smith stared at the man.

"I don't know where you get it from, I really don't. You meet some slip of an American bird, all eyelashes and cheekbones. She butters you up and all of a sudden you're talking like the worst excesses of a Innernet soap opera!"

"I noticed you were getting on swimmingly with that novelist woman."

"Don't talk rubbish."

"You were and why not? She's very attractive."

"That may well be mate but I like my women to have at least one foot in reality."

They put their smart fingers to the doors which opened silently. Smith paused before entering.

"Game of floatball in the morning?"

"I can't. Elizabeth and I are going to a zero-g Zumba class."

Smith laughed heartily.

"You? A zero-g Zumba class? Oh dear, oh dear. That I must see."

*

Smith was awakened by an urgent knocking on his door. He threw himself up from the bed and reached for a packet of pills. The revelry was beginning to take its toll and his stomach was starting to rebel. He threw back a few of the antacid tablets and belched loudly.

When he opened the door Prendergast was standing there flanked by a rather nasty looking individual with slicked down hair and a pencil moustache.

"Anthony. There's a Mr Ek here from Saabre accounts who wants to talk to us."

"Come in then," said Smith, with a slight sense of foreboding and they gathered awkwardly in the middle of the room. Before he could say anything more the man from Saabre piped up in a high-pitched Scandinavian accent.

"It's about your bill, gentlemen."

"What about it?" asked Smith defensively.

"It is unacceptable. When we offered you Saabre's hospitality we did not expect such excesses. Daily sports, spa, massages, three course meals in the most expensive restaurant and the drinks bill..." He threw his hands up in bean counter despair.

"Hospitality, mate, be fair."

"It is too much." He handed them a copy of the bill to date and Smith let out a low whistle as he got to the running total at the bottom of the third sheet. They had indeed run up a corker.

"You must pay the extras yourself."

"I don't think so, sir." It was a familiar 'southern belle' voice coming from the doorway. The three men turned to see Elizabeth leaning against the doorframe. The Saabre man turned back to Smith and Prendergast.

"Who is this woman?"

Before the boys could answer Elizabeth shimmied forward.

"That's not your business. You have two choices right now. Either you honour this account, as your CEO promised or I will pay it and my friends here will offer their services to some other party. There are plenty of people who would like a chance to bid for Mr Smith and Mr Prendergast's services and you can explain to Montague Canard how you lost him Earth's most talented propulsion designers."

The threat hung in the air for a moment as perspiration gathered on the three male foreheads in the room. Finally Mr Ek spoke.

"I'll see what I can do," he said in a voice which had risen a full octave. He grabbed the bill and was gone before a farewell could be uttered.

Elizabeth smiled sweetly at Smith and Prendergast.

"Can't let people push you around, boys."

She winked at Percy.

"We have a date. Dance studio. Ten minutes?"And with that, she too was gone.

"Beautiful and so strong," sighed Prendergast as Cupid's barbs dug deeper into his flesh.

*

Smith took a seat in the gallery overlooking the zero-g gymnasium at the heart of the Gagarin Space Station. The gym studios were big enough that the viewing area around the perimeter afforded just enough spin to keep you in a seat at about half lunar gravity but the Luna Colada that Smith ordered had to be in a sealed container. He sipped the drink as the last few stragglers from a pensioner's Pilates class were being rounded up and corralled out of the studio on tethers like deflated carnival balloons.

After a moment the Zumba class filed in and, as a popular Merengue hit came over the speakers, Elizabeth took Prendergast through his paces.

Prendergast took a little time to get with it. His first impression was that Weightless Salsa Dancing was a bit like trying the hundred yard sprint on an ice rink in ballet pumps. For a while you don't get very far. But Elizabeth encouraged and guided him and he began to get the hang of it. Even Smith started to see the beauty of it all. He smiled wistfully at the grace of two young people, gliding and tumbling in the sublime liberation of free-fall.

Oh dear, thought Smith, if Percy wasn't lost before, the sheer romance and proximity of this unfettered pas-de-deux would do for him completely.

*

How right he was. Back in Elizabeth's room when the couple had freshened up after the class, Prendergast still seemed weightless and virtually floated across the carpet towards his seat in the American's suite. Smith resolved to make himself scarce with all due haste. He and Prendergast were bound for the Saabre research facility in the morning where their work would start in earnest, so he could see no harm in allowing Prendergast a little latitude for love. After a decent interval he stood to make his excuses but Elizabeth objected.

"How sweet you are but don't go just yet, Anthony. Sit for a moment. I would like to raise a toast to you and dear Percy."

Smith retook his seat as she reached for a bottle beside the sofa and filled three glasses.

"To Percival and Anthony. May all your dreams come true. And may you have the greatest success. For all humanity."

"Humanity," Prendergast echoed.

"Great success," re-echoed Smith.

They drained their glasses.

"Would you excuse me gentlemen while I go change for lunch?"

"Certainly," said Prendergast and they both stood as she left the room.

"Charming girl," conceded Smith.

"Charming? She's a pippin."

"Oh," said Smith, "think I stood up a bit fast there."

"And that class has taken it out of me somewhat."

Smith and Prendergast fell back in their seats and within less than a minute were unconscious.

6. THE CENTAURIS PREPARE

As Commodore Harfu strode down the corridor linking the control level to the machine rooms of the Diplomatist he marveled at the complexity which was an interstellar space ship. With its powerful (though now he realised inherently flawed) near light speed engines, its huge crew of engineers, physicists, navigators, biologists, geologists, psychologists, medics, soldiers, cooks and cleaners, all working together as one giant organism, could be directed towards good or evil. How sad and stupid, he thought, that the purpose of this great craft was being so surely perverted from the benign to the malignant.

He headed towards the ship's cavernous factory deck where fusion reactors could fabricate any part of the ship to effect repair. In the expansive loneliness of inter-solar space there are no docks or machine shops that can be called upon.

As Harfu walked through the factory's towering hangar doors he could see Battle Cruiser Commander Zoltac striding the length of a gantry, addressing the entire ship's company gathered on the factory floor below.

"My fellow Centaurans," he boomed out across the upturned faces.

"We are on the brink of great change. No longer will Earth dictate its terms to us. For too long She has held our beloved and ancient colony in her iron grip. Our great Generalissimo has decreed that it is time for Alpha Centauri to take its place as the most powerful of the colonies, with mastery even over Mother Earth herself. As you know our grand part in that scheme has been thwarted in recent days. By shoddy Earth technology."

Harfu shook his head. This was, frankly, a low swipe. They only used Earth engines because any the Centaurans had developed had blown up before they could be attached to a space ship and they went to great pains to buy them via the Eridani's to circumvent the strict trade embargoes. However, what Zoltac lacked in accuracy he made up for in oratory because this really got the crowd going. They whooped and stamped as their natural Home Planet phobia was aroused.

"Now I, Zoltac," said the man himself, "have a plan to recover from this disaster and go forward to fulfill our destinies by achieving the Generalissimo's great goal. The last piece of this plan has just now fallen into place and so you, my faithful servants must spare no effort. Go down to the great depths of Neptune and plunder her for everything she's got. Rip out her riches so we can build ourselves anew and go forth, on to Earth!"

The crowd were by now whipped into a frenzy of patriotic fervour and amidst the yells and cheers could be heard the odd voice picking up the cry 'On to Earth'. As more voices joined in, the great cavern of the Diplomatist's factory throbbed to the rhythmic chant. Above, arms crossed and beaming with messianic power stood Zoltac. He lifted a hand aloft to recognise the adulation of his own captive masses.

Commodore Harfu surveyed the feverish scene with a heavy heart. How easy it was to tug at the jingoistic patriotism of these people, turning a fine crew, one of the finest he had ever served with, to no more than a great big uniformed mob, no better than a sport's stadium full of hooligans, their bright febrile eyes turned aloft to the hooligan-in-chief: Zoltac.

But he was one and they were many. Slowly he started mouthing the words, trying to give it as much enthusiasm as he could muster.

"On to Earth, On to Earth, On to Earth!"

Best not to stand out when the pack instinct took over.

*

Later, on the observation deck, Harfu watched in awe as the shuttle bays opened along the belly of the vessel. Light flooded into space and shone all the brighter against the dark side of Neptune, as the mining craft dropped clear of the Diplomatist before firing their topside rockets, plunging them deep into the planet's atmosphere.

He followed their trails as they ploughed their way down through the broiling hydrogen and methane winds, gusting at a thousand miles an hour, buffeted by swirling ammonia slush and sharp shards of water ice. Once down to around five hundred miles below the cloud tops, the shuttles released their long vacuum arms, like huge iron probosci which guzzled up the atmosphere and stored it under pressure in the gas tanks which surrounded the cramped two person cockpits from which the miners controlled the craft.

Back in the shuttle bays the ground crew met each returning ship and connected them to pumps which evacuated the Neptunian gases, feeding them into giant silos ready for transportation to the fusion plants. Once emptied, the mining shuttles dropped back into the upper reaches of the planet to continue their pillage.

Zoltac too watched the ships, as they darted back and forth to the planet's depths, from the observation bubble on the control deck of the Diplomatist. Beside him his second in command, Marshal Wittan, stood still and implacable.

"Are the factories at full power?" asked Zoltac.

"Within the hour, Commander. And the last pieces of the puzzle?" he asked.

"Soon enough, Marshal. Just make sure we are ready when they fall into place."

With that he turned and strode from the bridge.

7. THE BOUNTY HUNTER

Smith was dreaming he was hanging by his fingertips from the very top of the Eiffel Tower. It was a calm, warm day and the air was eerily still as his fingers clutched at the hot, rusting metal which only seemed to make his predicament all the more stomach-churningly perilous. He took a little time out from being terrified to note that the city below was not Paris as one might expect but Edinburgh, and there, nestled at one of the tower's great feet, was his Alma Mater, the Space Propulsion Academy. But this was ridiculous. Everyone knew that Eiffel's great work, the three hundred meter iron edifice, was destroyed in 2089 during the Euro conflict.

Prendergast meanwhile was dreaming that he was floating, suspended in a vast vat of semolina. Equally ridiculous as that particular foodstuff had been banned some six years before by the World Food Administration for being 'revolting'.

Smith woke and for several seconds could make no sense of his surroundings. He seemed to be floating in the middle of some kind of storage space either horizontally, on his head or right side up. Whichever it was he was handcuffed by his right wrist to an iron girder on the floor, ceiling or wall.

Boxes were attached to hooks here and there. Space food judging by the brand names. Powdered potato, steak, broccoli and the like. Popular with those who lived and worked in space as it was cheap and took up little room, even though it tasted blander than the semolina Prendergast was still dreaming he was suspended in.

Smith used his free hand to reach over and grab Prendergast's sleeve, his feet waggling like a frogman's, and shake him awake.

"Percy, Percy," he said.

Prendergast moaned and muttered in his sleep.

"Mnnn? No...no...spit it out, it's illegal!"

"Percy! Wake up, mate!"

Prendergast came to and his eyes rolled in their sockets taking in the room, trying unsuccessfully to find reason in what he saw.

"Tony! What on Earth is going on?"

"I've no idea. But I don't think Earth has got anything to do with it."

"Eh?"

"Try uplinking to the Innernet."

Prendergast furrowed his brow as he attempted a connection.

"Nothing. I'm just getting static."

"Exactly. Which means we're not orbiting any of the inhabited planets."

"Well," said Prendergast, brightening somewhat, "that narrows it down a bit."

It was Smith's turn to go in for a spot of eye-rolling.

"Oh yes. Apart from the five inhabited worlds we could be ANYWHERE IN THE UNIVERSE!"

"Alright, old man. No need to get heated. Just trying to be positive. And anyway I doubt we're outside the solar system."

Smith calmed down a notch. It was true. They couldn't be far away from Earth however long they could reasonably be assumed to have been unconscious.

"Well, wherever we are we have to get out. Start banging on the walls."

"Good idea."

Unfortunately for Smith's plan, in the weightless environment of space, Newton's third law of motion really kicks in. It has been stated many ways by many people over the centuries but 'every action has an equal and opposite reaction' just about sums it up. In the case of trying to hit the wall of a space ship as Smith now attempted, it meant he flew in the opposite direction and banged into the facing wall. Or Percival Prendergast if he was in the way, which he was.

"Steady on, old boy! You nearly took me out like a ninepin there."

"It's no good, Perce. We shall have to get purchase somehow. Let's wrap our legs together. Grip your handcuffs tight."

Prendergast did as he was told.

"Now hit that wall as hard as you can."

Braced as they were they started thumping the walls which boomed loudly.

"Start yelling."

Prendergast didn't need asking twice and soon their voices were getting hoarse from an improvised chorus along the lines of, "Help!", "We're in here!" and "Get us out!"

It wasn't long before their efforts were rewarded by a door beneath their feet swinging open. They both looked down at the silhouette which hovered in the doorway and a huge grin spread across Prendergast's face.

"Elizabeth. Thank the stars. You're here to save us."

"What's all the noise about?" she asked, rather brusquely Prendergast thought.

Now Anthony Smith would be the first to admit that he was no expert in the regional accents of North America but he would have sworn that on the two previous occasions they had met, Elizabeth had spoken with what you might call a southern lilt.

North Carolina. Virginia, that sort of thing. The Elizabeth who faced them now sounded like she came from one of the seedier corners of New Jersey. So pronounced in fact was this accent that it took no great leap to imagine her speaking out of the side of her mouth whilst flipping a silver dollar. Plainly Prendergast was catching on too because the old brow started to furrow again and a plaintive note lighted on his vocal cords.

"Elizabeth?"

"It's Betty. Understand?"

"No, I don't understand, Eliz...Betty. Where are we?"

"You're aboard my ship. My ship, my rules. Rule one. Cut the hullaballoo."

"But...why?" asked Prendergast.

"'Cause you're giving me a headache."

"No," he giggled nervously, "why are we aboard your ship?"

"Because, my little geeky friend, there's some people who want to meet you and I'm going to take you to them."

Prendergast's mouth dropped open.

"Without our consent? That's tantamount to kidnapping."

Smith's eyes widened to their full aperture.

"There's no tantamount about it. It *is* kidnapping. She's kidnapping us. You're a kidnapper, woman!"

Betty pushed off from the doorway and grabbed Smith by the shirt, pulling him close to her face.

"Listen, buddy," she hissed menacingly, "get this straight. I ain't no kidnapper. I'm a bounty hunter and don't you forget it."

"I won't," he answered her in his most conciliatory tones.

"There's a price on your head and I aim to get it, see?"

"I do, I do see."

Betty pushed back towards the door.

"So listen. This trip can go comfortable or the other way. So you two start behaving yourselves and I might let you out of here for chow."

With that, the door slammed shut and she was gone. The boys floated silently for a moment. Prendergast was the first to speak.

"Betty the Bounty Hunter. Well, I never."

Smith shook his head sourly.

"You picked a right one there mate and no mistake."

Prendergast nodded sadly.

"How wrong can a chap be? I thought she was delightful. Dare I say it, a possible *Mrs* Prendergast. And all along she was a ghastly woman."

"An absolute shocker, mate."

Prendergast sighed, his mind a cauldron of mixed emotions.

"I wonder where she's taking us?" he said presently.

"I shudder to think, I really do."

And with that they fell into a baleful silence.

*

Several hours must have passed before Percy piped up again.

"Time," he said, "is a funny old thing when you come down to it. Einstein had a lot to say on the matter, mainly concerning what a slippery concept it was. It passes at different rates you see, for different people depending on how fast they are traveling."

"Yes, I know," said Smith who was trying to blow spit bubbles and watch them drift around the room.

"Up until the late twenty-first century," continued Prendergast, "when most people never travelled above five hundred miles an hour, the average speed of a jet airplane, this really made very little difference to people's lives. It simply isn't fast enough for the time dilation to be noticeable."

"I know, Percy," said Smith, cursing as a bubble burst on the verge of launch.

"But come century twenty-two," persisted Percy, undeterred, "and the explosion of space travel leading to the colonisation of other stars, a great many people were traveling at very high speeds for extended periods of time and that's when the ordure really started hitting the air conditioning."

Everyone knew the stories. It became a commonplace that go-getting sisters became younger than their stay-at-home younger brothers. There was even one story, unconfirmed, so urban myth might be a more accurate description, of a man who spent his adult life as a parcel delivery man between the Alpha Centauri and the newly founded Eridani colonies and became, at his death, two months younger than his eldest son.

"Well," said Smith, "we have a bit of a problem with time right now but it's not relativistic. It's of a more mundane nature. How, when you are handcuffed, weightless, in a room with only bags of food, an iron girder and nothing to do, can you keep any sense of how much time is passing? And how do you pass that passing time? Apart from listening to you ruminating. In the circumstances I-spy is a bit of a nonstarter." Prendergast agreed and instigated a game of charades but after Smith was unable to get the popular movie *The Flying Fists Of Fury* they both agreed that two free hands were essential for the game. Once they'd listed sixty-one of the sixty-two states of America, made up a clean limerick rhyming the word duck and remembered Brad Dexter from the 'Magnificent Seven' they were sort of stymied. They had wasted a good deal of time but as to how much, they were clueless.

They were just working out that the twenty-third Fibonacci number (28657) is prime when the door opened again.

"So you guys had some time to think?"

Smith and Prendergast had had little else.

"You gonna behave and not bust my chops?"

"Oh, absolutely," said Prendergast.

"Not a problem for me. Good as gold," concurred Smith.

Betty pulled two rings from her belt. They looked like bracelets but slightly larger. Moving with the dexterity of one used to zero-g she attached one to each of the boys ankles and returned to the doorway. There she turned and held up a grey tube-like gadget. She poised her thumb over a red plunger which protruded from the top of the device.

"You even *look* like doing anything out of line and I detonate your shackles. It'll take one foot clean off and leave a lot of shrapnel in the other. Got it?"

A gulp was about all either Smith of Prendergast could manage by way of agreement.

"Okay, then," said Betty cheerfully, "grub's up."

She placed her smart finger on the wall by the door and their handcuffs fell open.

*

Dinner on Betty's ship, which the boys learnt was called the Zelda, was a dismal affair. The cockpit where they ate was cramped and Betty was old school when it came to food preparation. Some powder in a tube, add water, shake and suck. The only concession to variety being a rolling rota of the resultant paste's colour. Today was yellow day.

Smith thought it was banana but Prendergast insisted he was getting a hint of roast potato. This became quite a heated debate and to shut them up Betty looked at the packet. Turned out it was avocado well past its sell-by date. After the meal Betty settled down at the controls and started to put in some navigational work. The boys stayed in their harnessed seats and shuffled uncomfortably.

"So where are we headed, Betty?" enquired Prendergast casually.

Betty swung round on her chair.

"Not your concern, bub."

"Oh righto."

Smith scowled.

"Well, actually I think it is a bit," he muttered sulkily.

"What was that, grease monkey?"

"Smith was just saying that it was a little bit our concern, we being the cargo as it were, though obviously; your ship, your rules. So...your call really."

"Damn right it's my call."

With that she swiveled back to her work.

"So," began Prendergast after a pause, as breezily as he could manage, "are we stopping off anywhere before we get where we are going to or...or...not? Are we going straight there?"

Betty swung around again and glowered at him making him shrink back into his seat.

"If it's any business of yours..."

"Which it isn't."

"Well, it is a bit," moaned Smith.

"Well, it is a bit but as Betty said she's calling the shots here."

"Huh!"

"I said," persisted Betty, "*if* it's any of your business, we need to fuel and stock up on some staples, so..." and she referred to her charts for a second, "Earth and Mars are at opposition, so we will be making a stop on the Red Planet in three days from now."

"Mars, eh?" asked Smith excitedly, "I've always wanted to go there."

"Well, you got your wish, buddy."

"Will we be going to Mars City? I've heard it's really buzzy with a top notch nightlife."

"Okay, one; this is not a vacation and two; no, we will not be going to Mars City. In my line of work you leave very few footprints and stay away from the crowds. We'll be going to a little community I know a long way from the Elysium plains. Tiny, out of the way spot called Grissom Hill."

"Never heard of it," said Smith and looked out of the nearest porthole with irritable disappointment.

Prendergast, on the other hand, seemed to perk up a little.

"Grissom Hill?" he asked.

"That's what I said."

"Why, that's only about two or three hundred miles from Gale."

"From who?" asked Betty.

"Not who. Gale crater."

"So what?"

"So what?!" answered Prendergast, appalled, "Gale crater is the landing site of Curiosity."

Betty stared blankly at him.

"The twenty-first century surface rover which started it all," persisted Percy. Still not a flicker of recognition from the bounty hunter.

"It discovered the organic compounds which made colonisation a possibility."

Betty shrugged and shook her head. Percy let out a frustrated sigh.

"Anyway, they have it preserved beautifully at its original landing site and they say the visitor centre is second to none."

"Fascinating. Thanks for the low-down."

"No, no, you don't understand. We have to go. As you said it's a very remote spot. How often would you happen to find yourself in the neighbourhood. This is a must see."

"Whoa, wait a minute buster. Are you seriously suggesting that I take you on a day trip to a museum? What do you think this is? Space Camp?"

Prendergast was a mild sort of chap as a rule but Smith could see that his dander was well and truly on the up. His cheeks were reddening and his voice rising.

"Well considering the jolly shoddy way you have treated us thus far, drugging us, incarcerating us, handcuffing us, hobbling us," and he rattled his ankle bracelet angrily by way of demonstration, "to say nothing of feeding us on excrement and keeping us in the dark as if we were a pair of blooming mushrooms I'd say it was the least you could bally well do!"

Ninety seconds later they found themselves back in the store room, handcuffed to the girder.

"Well done, Percy, you flamin' great twit. Four years I've known you. Four years and barely a peep out of you and you choose *now* to get a cob on!"

"I'm sorry, Tony, but I have had it with that woman, I really have."

"Great idea, annoying the jailor."

"I've said I'm sorry."

"Look at us, stuck in here."

"It wasn't much better out there."

"At least I had a porthole to look out of."

"At what, old boy? We are in the depths of space."

"The odd star. The occasional comet. You and your visitor's centre."

Prendergast could see his colleague was upset and it filled him with remorse.

"I'm so sorry, old chap. Truth be told I'm angry at myself more than anything. Falling for all that old guff she gave me. Walking right into her wicked web."

It was Smith's turn to sip from the sour cup of regret.

"Not your fault, mate. You're just a romantic. Nothing you can do about it. That's who you are."

"Thanks, old sport."

He patted Smith on the shoulder sending himself in a gentle arc towards the wall and bouncing off it lightly. They fell into a thoughtful silence 'til Prendergast sighed and spoke again.

"I just wish she'd take me to see Curiosity, that's all."

Smith nodded.

"Well, why don't you ask her again? Really nicely."

Prendergast chuckled. Smith joined him. Prendergast laughed more openly and Smith laughed louder. Before long the pair of them were howling uncontrollably, the tears rolling down their cheeks like a burst water pipe and their mouths gasping for air like spilled goldfish. There came a banging on the door to the cockpit.

"Hey, keep it down in there!"

Smith and Prendergast laughed all the harder.

*

The next two days continued in much the same vein. Betty would extract promises to which the boys would acquiesce. They would all partake of a tube of coloured sludge, settle back to enjoy the scenery, then some topic of a contentious nature would crop up, along the lines of their destination, the tightness of their cuffs or the quality of the catering. There would be a frank exchange of views and within minutes the boys would end up in chokey again.

On the morning of the fourth day Smith and Prendergast were woken early by Betty bearing a tube of brown paste which she said was croissants and coffee. As they were sucking this down, speculating whether it tasted more like chutney or chocolate, Betty clicked a narrow wire round each of their necks. Neither Smith nor Prendergast needed to ask what they were. As they entered the orbit of Mars they would again be able to uplink to the Innernet. Once that happened they could c-mail friends or family and alert them to their abduction. Betty's magnetic inhibitors put a stop to that. When she had gone Prendergast turned to Smith, a look of seething frustration in his eyes.

"Wicked woman," he spat out. To his surprise Smith was wearing a grin that could only be described as smug.

"I don't see what you've got to be so cheerful about," said Prendergast derisively.

"Really? Well, me old mucker, who is the greatest engineer at Edinburgh SPA and now all points towards Mars?"

"Obviously you are but..."

"And what can any system be?"

"Overridden, but..." Prendergast paused and suddenly the light started to dawn.

"You haven't?"

"I have, mate..."

Smith put his hand in his pocket and shuffled it around a little. He pulled it out empty and pushed it deep into his other pocket, rummaging there for a good moment or two.

"Hold on," he said, a frown starting to darken his brow.

He went for his breast pocket and explored every corner coming up with only a ball of fluff and a paper clip.

Light swept across their faces as the door of the storeroom slowly opened.

"Looking for something, Mr Smith?"

It was Betty. She raised her hand. A small blue cube which seemed to glow from within, throbbed softly in the gentle grip of her index finger and thumb. With the delicate, insistent pressure of a sniper's trigger finger she squeezed the cube 'til its atomic lattice gave way and it shattered to pieces in the air. The tiny chunks of glistening debris blossomed outwards from the point of its destruction as she closed the door behind her.

Prendergast turned to Smith.

"By the Laws of Physics, she's a ghastly woman," he said.

"An absolute shocker," agreed Smith.

8. LIFE ON MARS

The Zelda glowed orange as she screamed down through the Martian atmosphere. Two thousand feet from the surface Betty fired the retros and the ship landed firmly in a cloud of ochre dust on the landing pad at the foot of Grissom Hill.

From a concrete structure nearby a team of technicians raced to the ship, linking its outer input ports to Mars-side power and opening its fuel bays. Betty led Smith and Prendergast down the ship's ramp and headed in the direction of the hill.

"Blimey," whispered Smith, "what a nasty little toilet this is."

"Yes," answered Prendergast, "all the big cities are on the other side of the planet."

They plodded forward, slightly restricted by the ill-fitting thermal Betty had equipped them with against the cold.

"I thought we'd have needed space helmets," said Smith sniffing the somewhat thin air.

"The terraforming of Mars has been in progress for one hundred and fifty years now," said Prendergast. "The experts say it will take another two hundred to make it completely Earth-like."

"Oh yeah? Well, it'll take another thousand to stop it being a dump."

As Betty and the boys got closer to the hill, Smith could make out a large metal double door buried deep in its basalt slopes. Arriving at these doors, which slowly ground open, Betty motioned the boys to follow her inside. As the doors creaked closed behind them the temperature immediately soared.

"Don't speak to anyone while we are here," Betty warned.

Smith and Prendergast followed her down a long, dark tunnel. At the far end they could see a bright light and as they got closer they heard the noise of a hundred voices shouting, laughing, bargaining and threatening all at once. The tunnel gave egress into the bright vapy atmosphere of what looked like a huge drinking den. A large circular bar stood in the middle of the room where punters drank, vaped and talked and the curving walls were lined with tables, booths and doors leading to what looked like private dining rooms judging by the waiters who streamed in with plates of hot food and out with dirty crockery.

Betty stopped as she took in the room, scanning the faces of the men and women crowding the bar. She led the boys to a booth behind a curtain and sat them on the ripped and faded leather seats.

"Stay there 'til I get back and remember what I said."

She drew her fingers across her mouth and moved away. Smith and Prendergast sat quietly for a moment then Percy peeked around the side of the curtain sheepishly.

"Seems like a popular place," he said.

"Hmm. Seems like a dangerous place to me. I don't like the look of this lot at all."

"I know what you mean. I do hope Elizabeth hurries back and we can get out of here."

A tall man pulled back the curtain sharply and loomed over them. Smith let out a yelp and clutched his chest.

"D'you mind not doing that. You frightened the life out of me."

The man was wearing a hood which he pulled back to reveal a craggy, scarred face.

"Who are you?" he demanded.

"Erm...we've been asked not to speak to strangers," said Prendergast as politely as possible.

The man lowered his face closer to Percy. His breath reeked of whiskey and liquorice vape.

"I said: Who. Are. You?"

Smith nudged Prendergast who had found all the spit had evaporated from his mouth. He tried to speak but only succeeded in making a noise like a baby crow. He swallowed and tried again.

"I'm Percy and this is my friend Tony," he croaked.

"Looking for Rock?"

Prendergast froze and Smith nudged him again.

"I don't know the fellow."

The man gritted his chipped antique ivory teeth and parted his lips in a snarl.

"Funny guy, huh?"

"Me?" Percy squeaked.

"Do. You. Want..."

Oh no, thought Smith, if he keeps this up we'll be here all night.

"...To. Buy. Some. Rock?"

"Oh no, thank you," Prendergast demurred.

"Why not?"

"Eh?" asked a puzzled Percy.

"Why. Do. You. Not..."

Smith could take no more.

"Oh for Gödel's sake, don't start that again. We haven't got any money is why."

The man snapped a look at Smith which made him jump in his seat.

"In Grissom with no money? What you doing here?"

Smith squirmed and looked at Prendergast who gulped again.

"Just...visiting with friends," he said in a tiny voice.

"Oh yeah? Where are they, these friends?"

Prendergast sighed and pouted trying to think where his friends might be.

"Gone to the loo? Haven't they, Tony?"

"Yes. Gone to the toilet. Long flight."

The man stood straight again.

"I got good news. Got a job for you."

"Oh, awfully kind but we're not in the job market at the moment. Sort of gap year," said Prendergast. The man continued as if Percy hadn't spoken.

"I got a mine. Needs some hands. After a nasty little rock fall left me short staffed."

"Ah, well," said Smith, "that's us out then, isn't it. We're not miners, you see. I'm more in the engineering, design area..." and he couldn't have sounded more disappointed.

"I'm more theory, the theoretical end of things, if you like," added Prendergast helpfully.

The man stabbed a large hunting knife into the table in front of them.

"I said. I have a job for you."

"And they said no!"

The man swung round to see Betty standing behind him.

"Step aside ugly. Boys, come with me."

She turned to go but the man reached out his arm and placed his hand on her shoulder in a vice-like grip.

"Where you goin' sweet cheeks? I got some business I'd like to go over with you too."

Betty sighed and in one quick motion brought her elbow back firmly into the bridge of the man's nose making a sickening crunch and sending a spray of blood into his hairline as bone came through the flesh. He jerked backwards and sprawled over the table next to them which buckled under his mass, sending drinks flying in a shower of alcohol and glass. Betty turned to the boys.

"Quick, while Frankenstein here's replacing these nice people's drinks."

The boys were right behind her as she headed out of the club towards another dark corridor on the other side of the bar. As they passed, a stocky man in a heavily armored leather suit turned his bearded face to watch them disappear into the darkness.

In the connecting tunnel Betty strode ahead and the boys had to skip a little to keep up with her. Prendergast regarded her back as it dipped in and out of the pools of light from the utility lamps riveted to the walls.

"Thanks awfully for stepping in back there. I think that chap had some rather scaly plans for us."

"Don't get mushy on me," she shouted over her shoulder, "two represent a considerable cash value, that's all!"

They trudged on around a corner into another rising corridor. Prendergast looked back at Smith who shrugged.

"Romantic little swine, isn't she?" he said.

*

The next stop was a small encampment near the surface, beneath the summit of the hill. It was a large dug out cavern with tents and bivouacs around the walls. In the centre was an open fire and the area seemed to be occupied by around four or five families. As they entered Betty indicated for Smith and Prendergast to sit on a boulder roughly fashioned into a kind of stone age sofa and went off to speak to a group of Martians whom she hugged warmly and sat down to talk with. Apart from a young man who brought them over a cup of hot soup, Smith and Prendergast were roundly ignored.

"So what do you think?" asked Smith eventually.

"What about, old boy?"

"This her family or what?"

"I doubt she has a family. She was probably spawned straight from the devil."

"Guess you're right."

They sipped their soup. The first real food they'd had for days.

"Oh no. I don't like that."

"Seems perfectly palatable to me, old boy."

"Not the soup. That."

"What, old chap?"

"*That*!"

He pointed to one side where a small child with a round face and ginger curls was riding a trike in circles.

"What's wrong with it? It's just a child and a rather sweet one by the looks of it."

"Sweet, my foot. The only time you ever see a child on a tricycle is in horror films. Oooh!" He shuddered. "Can almost hear the ethereal, tuneless aaahhing of the soundtrack. Next thing you know spooky twins with show up with a bathful of blood."

"You do talk rot. You're letting your imagination run riot."

He smiled and waved at the child who grinned and smiled sweetly back. Encouraged, Prendergast stood and sauntered over to the child.

"I say, that's a smashing bike you've got there."

The child's grin widened and it reached for something in its jacket pocket.

"Oooh. What have you got there? Sweets, is it?"

The child was holding what looked like a torch with two wires at the end. Its little pudgy fingers pressed a button and an arc of blue plasma crackled between their tips. Next thing Prendergast knew he was on his back, with smoke pouring from the front of his shirt. Of the child there was no sign. Smith ran over and lifted Prendergast to a sitting position.

"Little beggar tased me! Right in the ribs."

"I know, I saw, mate. I told you. Straight out of a horror film."

"I blame the parents."

At which point, said progenitors showed up.

"Are you alright, young man?"

This was the father, a slightly older one than you would have thought with such a young child, but he seemed decent enough with a kind face and a calm manner.

"What did you do to him?"

This was the mother who seemed an altogether more highly strung individual than her spouse. Younger too.

"I'm sure he did nothing, Gala. You know how the boy is."

"That's right, blame the child," and she stormed off to attend to any damage the lad might have sustained while felling Prendergast. The father turned to the boys and shrugged.

"A little feisty but a wonderful mother."

"Of course," said Prendergast, "stands out a mile."

Smith gave him a barbed look.

"I'm so sorry for what young Alfred did. He's only supposed to use it for protection outside the camp."

"Oh, think nothing of it. Fault on both sides "

Betty joined them.

"Dean, what's going on?"

"Elizabeth, I'm afraid little Alf was playing too roughly again. Reminds me of you when you were that age. He hurt one of your friends."

"They are not my friends."

"What should I call them? Your prisoners?"

Gala looked up from fussing over her tiny assassin and chipped in her two cents worth.

"Girl's got to make a living hasn't she?"

Dean ignored this and turned to Prendergast again.

"Is there anything I can do by way of compensation?"

It occurred to Smith that a request to be unshackled and sent home, first class, on a luxury liner might just about cover it so he was rather taken aback to hear Prendergast's answer.

"Well, if anyone was going near the Curiosity Museum and Visitors' Centre at Gale crater in the near future I would be tickled pink to tag along."

Smith buried his head in his hands where he shook it vigorously. Dean turned to Betty, questioningly.

"I'm on a schedule," she said and pushed the boys ahead of her.

"Pick up those supplies. Take them back to the ship."

There were two large burlap bags by the fire. Smith and Prendergast shouldered one each and followed Betty.

"Maybe next time then, young man," Dean said with an air of regret.

"Oh, rather," replied Prendergast cheerfully.

They headed to the tunnel and Dean watched them go. As they neared the entrance he shouted after Betty.

"What happens to them when you hand them over?"

"That's a question we never ask," she replied without turning back.

"Perhaps you should."

Betty quickened her pace. As they got further away Dean raised his voice, determined to be heard.

"Remember your mother."

Betty didn't break stride but as Prendergast caught a sideways glimpse of her in the campfire's flickering light, he thought he saw a welling liquid glint in her eye.

9. I NAME THIS SHIP...

The Diplomatist's renaming ceremony had been scheduled for 1030 hours, ship's time on day seventy-six of its mission. Naming ceremonies were usually performed at space docks in high planetary orbit. This enabled the crew to observe the ritual from the safety and comfort of the harbour. Marooned as she was in Neptune's orbit this was not possible in the Diplomatist's case but on top of being psychotic, Zoltac was also a conservative, superstitious traditionalist and had no desire to break with an ancient custom.

Lieutenant Hawkins was in charge of deployment, despite her insistence that this was more of a Health and Safety issue and so would be a more suitable job for Ratree from Personnel but her objections were overruled. So at 0900 hours the ship was put under robotic control while the entire ship's compliment donned EVA suits before queuing in the airlocks ready to space walk. At 1000 hours on the dot the life support team, under Hawkins' command, having checked that everyone was pressurised and all systems were green, opened the outer doors and five thousand and twelve men and women floated out into the blackness of space. A record which stood for a further two hundred years until the Hotel Asteroid Neogaia was hit by a meteor resulting in a mass evacuation of all six thousand and eighty-four guests. In both cases no one was allowed to use the shuttles as regulation IIIb26 of space articles forbids their use where suited astronauts are exposed.

Considering Hawkins' reluctance to oversee the task in the first place, it was a successful operation, being achieved with the loss of only three crew, Privates Lofthouse and Carrol, and Staff Sergeant Cooke. At the later enquiry these deaths were determined to have been caused by, respectively, a faulty airline, a jet-pack misfire, and in Cooke's case, sheer human stupidity. Hawkins was exonerated regarding the losses but she did receive a warning for inappropriate comments made while helping to suit up one corporal Vasquez, a rather nervous but well built young man from catering, whose first space walk this was.

At 1030 hours precisely, in direct contravention of regulation IIIb26 of space articles, the crew watched in awe and not a little nervousness as the doors of shuttle bay one opened and the Wraith, Zoltac's sleek, black private shuttle, decked in the Golden Eagle livery of the Zoltac dynasty, rose to a height of three hundred feet above the arched back of the soon to be renamed Diplomatist. On the deck, standing shoulder to shoulder, as the ship's most senior officers, stood Marshal Wittan and Commodore Harfu, dressed in full ceremonial uniform. A video camera in the cockpit of the shuttle was trained on the three men and projected their image by a remote broadcast drone onto the side of the spaceship below so the entire crew could admire them in all their martial splendour.

Zoltac picked up a microphone and tapped it once. Out in space five thousand and twelve crew members winced and turned down their helmet speakers.

"Sons and daughters of Alpha Centauri. Many months ago we were sent on a great mission. Fate intervened and thwarted that, our initial endeavour. For a lesser race this would have proved too great a trial and broken their spirit. But was our spirit broken?" Zoltac had expected some sort of response here but quickly realised his audience, floating as they were in the vacuum of space with their com systems set to receive, were mute to him. He provided the answer himself.

"No. Our resolve was strengthened and guided by the loving, wise hand of our Great Generalissimo we turned adversity into advantage. Our old objective of appeasement has been overturned by a cleansing martial wind and as our purpose, by fate, was transformed so this great ship, the greatest in the galaxy, will be reborn today."

He stretched his hand towards a lever in the centre of his control panel. He smiled. He could take this pause as long as he liked because he was about to surprise them all. All except Marshal Wittan and his small team of weapons officers, one hundred and ten percenters to a man and confidantes to the casus belli of the great Generalissimo's grand plan. Oh yes, he would surprise the rest. The rationalists and the liberals like Commodore Harfu. Their day was done and with the push of that lever they would be yesterday's news like so much deleted download.

As he rested his leather glove on the lever he announced in a strong voice that had more crew reaching for their helmet volume control...

"I rename this ship..."

He pressed the lever and explosives flashed silently on the hull before him, popping bolts, pushing them away from the immense cetacean-like arch of the ship's back, out to start a journey that would last the lifetime of the universe. Bolts which released a titanic plate on the back of the ship that lifted, beginning its own trip to infinity.

Zoltac enjoyed the moment. He knew the best was yet to come. As the debris cleared a great structure rose from the spine of the vessel, a dark matt tube a quarter mile long. Harfu eyes widened and his stomach leapt as he caught sight of this object. Its shape so familiar to his and all human eyes. A shape that had inspired fear and fervour in equal measure since man had mastered technology. The shape of power and repression since ancient Chinese chemists had first mixed sulphur, charcoal and saltpeter. An object which here was powered by something exponentially more powerful than that twinkling fairy-dust of Guy Fawkes and Independence and New Year.

A cannon.

The mightiest ever built.

"I name this ship...the Peacemaker."

*

From the surface of Neptune's cloud cover, if such a vantage point could have been had by a sharp eyed or optically enhanced sentient being, the Peacemaker would've been observed passing overhead and some of its portholes could have been seen to be throbbing like a rural rave glimpsed across a field on a warm summer night in Suffolk.

Passing through the officers' level, Captain Philips journeyed through a retrospective history of human dance music. The tempo, rhythm and pitch of each genre changing with each door he passed. He threaded his way through the tipsy revelers who spilled out into his path until he reached Commodore Harfu's door. He knocked gently and entered.

"Close that," said Commodore Harfu, "and seal it."

Captain Philips pressed his smart finger to the frame and turned to his commanding officer who was already on his knees with a quantum blade, removing a panel from beneath his bed. He pulled back the polyvinyl cover and slid out a small grey communication tablet. He depressed a dimple on its back and it came to life.

"Now. Keep watch."

10. VANISHING ACT

Smith and Prendergast had asked Betty if they could have a moment of her time after breakfast and she told them they could but to make it snappy as she had a lot to do as captain and pilot of the ship. Smith snorted a little at this because as far as he could tell once you set a ship on its course there is very little to do until you turned around and fired your motors to slow down as you approached your destination. Prendergast gave him a warning look and turned back to Betty.

"Well," she said, "what do you want to say?"

Prendergast cleared his throat.

"The economics of the solar system," he began, "are complicated to say the least but most agree that a crucial factor is the alignment of the colonies, on Earth, on the Moon, Mars, Jupiter's satellite Europa and Titan which orbits Saturn. As these systems circle the sun they present ever changing relationships with and vary their distances from each other in a complex pattern."

Betty pointed at Prendergast and turned to Smith.

"Is he for real?" she asked.

"Just listen to him," said Smith firmly.

Percy cleared his throat again and took up where he left off.

"The middle of the twenty-second century for example was thrust into deep recession because the newly emerging colonies were scattered around the sun as remotely as it was possible to be. Whereas right now they are aligned on the galactic centre side of the sun, which accounts for our present boom; it's comparatively easy and cheap to get from colony to colony. But this happy state of affairs is, over the next few decades, coming to an end as we return to a period of scattered remoteness."

"Do you have a point?" asked Betty.

"What Percy is saying," pitched in Smith, "is that to avoid another century long bust the colonies need a more reliable, faster engine and we have designed it."

"You got the answer, huh?" sneered Betty.

"Yes, and if you turn around right now and take us back to Earth you can be in on the ground floor. We are prepared to offer you a cash package with a generous stock option that would make you a very rich woman," Smith beamed at her.

"Oh you are, huh? Turn down a dollar today for two dollars tomorrow?"

"Exactly!" said Smith.

"Not interested," she replied, "now go to your room."

And that was that.

*

As it happened Betty was well aware of the planets' alignment. As the Zelda accelerated out from Mars orbit towards the asteroid belt, she knew that Jupiter and Saturn and therefore the colonies of Europa and Titan were within a thirty degree arc of each other. So incidentally was Neptune, though only Betty knew the significance of that. Uranus as it happens was on the other side of the sun but was of no interest to her apart from the scatologically comical pronunciation of its name before the nineteen eighties.

*

The journey continued in much the way it had before they made Mars-fall. There was a little less squabbling as they learned to rub along together as humans always do. Betty even gave the boys some computer time so they could do a little work. They both carried quite a cache of information in their mitochondrial DNA and Smith even managed to hobble together a three dimensional mockup of HENRIE, virtually from memory. One of the highlights of the trip, at least as far as Smith and Prendergast were concerned, was as a result of a game which Percy invented. It was a pattern recognition, memory and prediction game which he named Matrix. While Smith and Prendergast were evenly matched Betty could never win a round. She was a smart woman, imaginative and creative but something about Matrix did not gel with her skill set and after a long sulk, she banned it.

*

There is a phrase 'It's not rocket science', meaning it's not difficult. The implication being that 'rocket science' is complicated. Utter twaddle, as Smith had implied earlier. Rocket *technology* is fiendishly knotty but rocket science is very straight forward involving little more than Newton's third law and a working knowledge of elementary ballistics. A normal, uninterrupted trip through space involves only three actions. Plotting a course, accelerating in that direction and decelerating at around the halfway point. The longer the journey the greater the period of acceleration and so although the mean distance between Mars and Jupiter averages ten times the distance from the Earth to Mars the former journey doesn't take ten times as long as the later. And there are ways to get even more speed. So it was that less than a week later Betty was programming the Zelda to perform a sling shot around the great gas giant and so pick up a little of its angular momentum, further cutting the journey time to Saturn and their next fuel and supply stop on Titan.

It was while preparing for this manoeuvre that Betty picked up an unexplained blip on her gravitational radar. She ran an object check against her database for those coordinates. Asteroids; negative. Comets; negative. Space junk; negative. By the time she had completed the scan she could see, from the object's course and movement signature, this was a ship.

Betty didn't like thinking about the distances involved in space travel. It had, she felt, a tendency to curdle the mind until they dragged you off in a stiff suit. The interplanetary regions are so dizzyingly vast that the thought of them made her head swim. So, while journeying through space, the possibility of casually coming across another ship is vanishingly small. If you do, it is probably because they are after the same thing you are or even that they are after you. In this case Betty suspected both answers were true.

"Uh-oh," she said, strapping herself into the pilot seat, "I think we got company."

"Out here?" said Smith who was skimming through an old copy of Space and Spaceman, "What are the chances of that?"

"Very low I would have thought, old thing."

"They're following us you idiots. They're after you."

"Us?" Prendergast said, a tiny little dread doing a backflip in his tummy.

"Yes. Looks like Traders. And if they do get you, they won't be as nice to you as I am."

"Venus Sliced!" Smith felt panic rappelling up his spine.

"You're perfectly vile to us," added Prendergast.

"Exactly," smirked Betty.

Traders, as Smith and Prendergast were all too aware, were groups of outcasts who for one reason or another had become persona non grata on their home planets and joined a ragtag bunch of undesirables who lived in reconditioned space hulks out in the wilds of the Kuiper belt. They made a living trading in prohibited goods, stealing, kidnapping and generally making a nuisance of themselves in the outer system. It was rare to see them in as far as Mars, but Betty guessed that was where they had picked up Smith and Prendergast's trail.

"Strap in, fellas, it's gonna get hairy."

The Traders must have had a powerful ship because Smith could see in the rear view monitor that they were a little closer than they'd been when he'd first looked.

"They're gaining on us. What are you going to do?"

Betty said nothing but threw the ship onto a new course and the boys could see one of Jupiter's moons coming into view directly ahead. The Zelda was doing a big chunk of light speed and the satellite must be perilously close because it was perceptibly growing in size before them.

"Erm...Betty?" Prendergast instinctively held his hand up, "I'm no navigation expert but..."

"Not now, Percy," she said.

"...I'm pretty sure on this heading we won't avoid erm...Ganymede is it?"

"Yes, I think it is," said Smith helpfully.

"Thanks, Tony. In fact, I would hazard that we would not even make orbit. If I were to be asked where our present course would..."

"Shut up, Percy," she snapped.

"Oh, righto."

Smith saw the Traders were getting closer behind and even more worryingly, Ganymede was getting closer ahead of them.

"I get it," said Smith hopefully, "you're playing chicken right. Is that what you're doing? Playing chicken?"

"Shut UP!"

"Slowing down or swerving, slowing down or swerving, one or the other!" Prendergast mantra'd and started to rock in his seat, his hands clenched tightly together. Smith was fiddling with a packet of his stomach pills. He grabbed a handful and got a few in his mouth, the rest floating through the cockpit like the first snowfall of winter.

"Oh, this is playing havoc with my guts," he mumbled through a mouthful of chalk.

"Smith," Betty called out, "there's a big red button to your left. You see it?"

Smith now held his hand up while keeping his eyes glued to Ganymede's giant disc filling the cockpit window.

"I'm with Percy on the slowing down or swerving plan!"

"DO YOU SEE IT?" she yelled.

"YES!" Smith yelled back.

"When I say now. Hit it! Dont' ask questions just HIT IT!"

Behind them Smith could see the trader ship burst with light as it fired its retros in an attempt to lose speed. A few more seconds and it began to drift to one side as the unseen pilot dragged his ship out of collision course with the Jovian moon.

"NOW!" shouted Betty. Smith slammed his fist into the big red button and the strangest thing happened. Nothing. Except Ganymede vanished.

Betty let out a long held breath and slumped in her seat.

Smith and Prendergast both sat staring out of the cockpit at the empty space in front of them, mouths open, eyes wide.

"Wha...whe...w...w..?" asked Prendergast.

"We...wer...ha..?" joined in Smith.

"I'm going to need words, boys."

Prendergast took a deep breath and steadied himself.

"Where? Is Ganymede?"

"Well put!" said Smith.

"Look behind you," answered Betty with a smug smirk.

Prendergast was so confused he actually twisted his head around but all he could see was the back of his chair. Smith was a little more with it and, divining Betty's meaning, looked in the rear view monitor. There, massive and stately, was Ganymede, gently receding behind them. He tapped Prendergast's shoulder and pointed him to the screen. Prendergast's brow furrowed to a new personal best. He looked up at Betty.

"If you don't tell me how you did that, right now, I'm going to jolly well burst."

Smith gently stroked the big red button reverentially.

"What *is* this?"

"That?" asked Betty casually. "It's a wormholer."

"Your ship has its own personal wormhole maker? That is the coolest thing I have ever heard of!" said Smith.

Prendergast's mind was overflowing with a torrent of questions. He closed his eyes and clutched his face while he quickly sorted them into an order of importance list and started at the top.

"How far can it jump?"

"About ten thousand miles with the power I got available. Not enough to get you there any faster but it can haul you out of a tight spot, right?"

"How is it powered?"

"The reactor."

"Is there a limit on frequency of use?"

"It won't power back up for another day or so."

"Where did you get it?"

"That's enough information for now."

"Sirius."

Prendergast and Betty turned to Smith.

"You got it from the Siriuns, didn't you? Well, I'll be..."

"How do you know, old boy?"

"I read the trades. It's been rumoured for years they had the technology but, I didn't believe it. How did you get it?"

"Someone owed me."

Prendergast waved his hands frantically.

"Never mind all that. Where are the Traders now?"

Betty was glad to change the subject.

"They had to slam on their brakes helluva hard and throw themselves off course to avoid becoming a crater. We just kept on going without breaking step. I reckon we've put a few more light-minutes between us."

"Well, I think this calls for a celebration," said Smith and he reached into a box of food tubes and read the label on the first one he pulled out.

"Ugli fruit, anyone?"

11. AND THE WINNER IS…

Lauren Laurel was lying by the dip pool on the deck of her one bedroomed condo looking out over the Pacific Ocean. Actually looking between a pharmacy and an Uncle Sam's chicken and rice outlet, where a sliver of the ocean was visible over the teaming transport tubes of Highway One. Recently transferred from a desk job on the East Coast she was preparing to head up the security team for the new President. Having spent her college years playing either hockey or soccer she had decided she needed a crash course in World Government and a quick scan of the congress library had thrown up a number of worthy histories headed by E. L. Mitchell's *From Tribes to Triumph* with *Whole World* by the exotically named Resputa coming in a worthy second. She eventually plumped for *World Government for Dummies*, a lavishly illustrated, lighthearted tome from the Dummy Press series and it was this she was wading through now. This was the passage she had reached.

> History is littered with bloody conflicts over who was to rule only a few thousand people. Imagine the complexity of bringing seven billion head of humanity into a process to decide who would pilot a whole planet's future. You can't can you? Too complicated. The transition from a world divided into sovereign countries towards a centralised planetary state had been a fiendishly labyrinthine journey. The Greek, Plato, had a bash at the theory with his

> Republic and Thomas Moore grappled with the notion in Utopia but the world government project didn't really gain any momentum until the nineteenth century. Such diverse figures as Immanuel Kant, Ulysses S. Grant and the Mormon John Smith had been vociferous advocates and in the early twentieth century even Albert Einstein threw his hat in the ring. Many believed his contribution had been detri-mental to the cause as he'd been seriously sidetracked, along with many other great physicists, by his obsessive desire to create the ten hour day. A form of time dilation that the public, suffering mass deprivations from a deep recession, simply couldn't get behind.

So far so good and quite interesting but it didn't really tell her much. She flipped through a few more pages, past pictures of guns, dictators and mushroom clouds and came to this.

> Despite seemingly insurm-ountable hurdles the first World government had elected its first President, Damien Weston, who was inaugurated at eleven minutes past eleven on the morning of November the eleventh, 2111. Forever known as Eleven, Eleven, Eleven, Eleven, Eleven. Popularly called the Fifty-Five, officially celeb-rated as One World Day.

Now this was more like it. Facts. She could remember facts. She skimmed a few more leaves 'til she came to a brightly coloured picture of a beach by a small settlement of houses.

> But if you think forming a united government was tricky the worst was yet to come. Where to put it. Over three hundred countries on seven continents vied for the honour of containing the world capital and the bureaucrats went into overdrive to create a system of tenders to sift through the applications. At the same time they decided they didn't give a damn what anyone said. They were determined not to make the same mistake the European Parliament had in the twentieth century and end up in dumps like Brussels, so they bought a huge tract of land in laid back, sunny Southern California. And so it was that San Simeon, a sleepy little village overlooking the Pacific Ocean where the temperature rarely dropped below sixty-five became, within a few short years, the throbbing centre of World Government with the President lodged in the magnificent splendour of nearby, newly completed, Hearst Castle.

Right here on the next page was an aerial photograph of San Simeon as it was now. A vast throbbing metropolis, the centre of World Government. Lauren Laurel put down the book and turned to look at that selfsame skyline looming all around her. She'd made it to the top of the tree.

*

It was three days later that Lauren found herself standing at the back of a vast conference annex at Heart Castle, filled to capacity with representatives of the world's press, right behind Olaf Olsen, the President Elect.

Hawkish and Conservative, he was an able technocrat, about as polar opposite from Quang as it was possible to be. Standing on a platform of 'Earth First', he made it clear he had no desire to take up the diplomatic olive branch that had been at the heart of Lady One's policy and was openly derisive of her mission to the Aldrin Conference Centre with the Fascist rabble from Centauri, now waiting in orbit around Neptune. In fact, so vociferous had been his vilification of Quang's strategy in the wake of the Space Force One disaster that his team had advised he was skating dangerously close to speaking ill of the dead. This cut no ice with Olsen who stuck to his guns and was rewarded with a convincing majority in the final polls giving him a strong mandate for change.

*

News of President Olsen's inauguration was received warmly at the Earth Defence Centre on the Island of Grand Bahama whose general staff saw this as a sign of a new mood in the Administration and anticipated a substantial redirection of funds away from the social programs of Olsen's predecessor and into defence coffers.

*

Major Bill Fulbright had spent the morning testing the new Emergency Command Evacuation System. The ECES was a network of space ships attached to every major government and military establishment around the world, designed as a last ditch evacuation of all essential personnel in case of a devastating attack on the surface of the planet whether from enemies without or within. The idea being that the ruling bodies could quickly be decamped to a place of safety, a space station or the Moon for example, to continue the smooth running of human affairs. Though exactly what those affairs would entail if the devastation were that great was not wholly clear.

The ECES on Grand Bahama was situated behind the Defence Command Centre, connected to it by an underground tunnel. Fulbright had been scheduled to assist Colonel Walter Schnell in the first un-manned test flight of the escape ship but a storm sweeping towards the Gulf of Mexico meant the flight had suffered a series of delays.

Major Fulbright, who regarded such vast amounts of money being spent on saving the necks of so few people as a pusillanimous waste of tax dollars, quipped that he hoped the little green men would choose a crisp clear day for their invasion. Colonel Schnell bristled at such irreverent humour and called the test off.

Major Fulbright was pulling up the drive to his modest two bedroom villa on the island's southern coast when a small alarm in his smart finger started to buzz. He took a moment to identify this particular call's significance and as he located its source a rush of excitement came over him. He strode through the door, dropping his attaché case and headed to his study. Only once before in all his years in the service had he received such a call. He entered the little den, dropping to his knees by a day bed and started ripping the chintz valance from the couch's base. Deep inside he found what he was looking for. A light was flashing in the corner of the antique communication tablet which he held in his hand. Jenken, he thought. My drinking buddy, wingman and roomie from West Point all those years ago. A Commodore now, he had heard. What could be so important to revive this most secret and illegal link which they had kept for over thirty years.

*

Back at the Defence Centre, Colonel Walter Schnell was receiving another message on an equally secret device hidden by a concealed panel in the back of his locker at the Centre's Gymnasium.

12. A SOUK IN SHANGRI-LA

A day out from Titan and the passengers (Smith and Prendergast) and crew (Betty) of the Zelda were feeling the strain. A long voyage in a small spacecraft is not an edifying experience. The personal hygiene facilities are rudimentary and the sealed environment, coupled with the dodgy processed food, will take their toll on the most tolerant of olfactory organs. Worse still than the variety of human miasma is the boredom. Betty had loosened the leash on the boys to a certain extent but this hardly helped. They now knew the two cabins in the Zelda intimately and could navigate their way around them blindfold.

It was mid-afternoon ship's time and Smith was trying to walk round the walls of the store without pressing too hard with the soles of his feet which would send him gently spinning across the room. So far he had managed no more than five consecutive paces before he misjudged a step and rose in a head over heels tumble. He started feeling a little space sick and braced himself against the doorframe. He waited there 'til the nausea subsided then looked across at Prendergast who was snoring softly in a corner, dangling from a hook on the wall by his trouser belt.

Smith decided to go onto the bridge, as Betty pompously called it, to ask for some computer time. He opened the door a crack and saw her sitting in her pilot seat staring hypnotically out of the cockpit window, plainly as bored as he was. Lying beside her on the console (it was presumably magnetic) was the little grey gizmo in which rested the fate of his left foot. It brought home to him in sharp relief the true nature of his situation. There she was, his captor, next to the very device which symbolised and ensured their compliance in her plans for their liberty.

He felt anger rise in him like a dyspeptic scorpion. Then and there he resolved to resist and not roll over. He would fight for his freedom. Not with blows and kicks. He'd never been much of a fighter. He joined the school boxing club when he was a lad; spent fifteen seconds in the ring and three weeks in plaster. No. Violence wasn't the answer. Smith had always lived by his brains and it was the old grey matter which would win through for him against this mercenary Medusa.

Betty seemed to be in a world of her own, staring out into the infinite darkness. Probably daydreaming how she was going to spend her blood money, thought Smith bitterly. No doubt fantasizing about the shopping spree she would embark upon when she'd delivered him and Prendergast into the talons of whichever bunch of desperate brigands she was in league with.

Well, here was his chance. As she mused on the spoils of Mammon it would be the work of a moment to push himself off from the doorframe, across the dozen or so feet of the cockpit and snatch the detonator, thus breaking the hold she had over them. They could then remove the Innernet suppressors she'd put round their necks and the second they were in range of Titan, alert the authorities. He would personally take great pleasure in seeing her marched off to clink in the clutches of Titan's Finest the moment they landed.

He was just bracing himself for the push when Betty shifted. She lay back in her seat and gazed at the control panel above her head. She started to hum something which Smith couldn't quite make out. As she began to give vent to the tune with a little more brio, Smith winced. She may have been a rather attractive woman physically (he reluctantly conceded) but her singing voice was diabolical. Tuneless, meandering and with a grating throatiness in the lower register. He was just trying to decide if the emergent melody was from an opera or an advertising jingle when she languidly stretched out her arm and picked up the detonator. She slowly brought it to her ear and to Smith's horror, depressed it.

He looked down at the ankle restraint. He checked his feet and after two quick recounts, resolved that he still had the full complement. Two. He remained bipedal.

He looked back at Betty who was now clicking the plunger by her right ear in time to, what he now recognised as the theme tune of a popular wildlife show. She tipped forward in her seat and started writing with the detonator in the ship's log.

*

Titan is an ice planet, the coldest spot in the five home worlds. It regularly dips to under -190 and even if you could survive the gelid temperatures the—all be it breathable—atmosphere is ravaged constantly by violent storms. Add to this the fact that the surface is continually swept by heavy methane rainfall and you will understand why Titan is an indoor colony. Due to the shifting ice plates that make up Titan's surface, buildings must be flexible and so Shangri-La was one giant sprawling city of multi-coloured polyvinyl tents, ranging from the tiny to the immense, which had slowly accreted to the original settlement, founded a hundred years before.

As the Zelda pulled into the Titan Arrivals Terminal an access tunnel extended to her doors and formed an airtight seal allowing Betty and the boys to go directly from the ship's life support environment to that of Shangri-La. Once inside

Betty steered them through customs. This had a more formal entry protocol than had been present at Grissom Hill and Smith wondered what sort of clearance Betty was using. Judging by the distasteful looks he and Prendergast were receiving from the douanes at border control he figured she was traveling as some sort of law officer and galaxy knows what sort of heinous wrongdoers she was making them out to be. They were certainly never asked for a smart finger reading. Which made sense of his theory. Wrongdoers automatically had their smart prints removed and their biometrics were piggybacked to the detaining officer's.

They made their way through a number of interconnecting tent modules 'til they came to a very large one. It was made of a pink polyvinyl and through its roof, which rippled and waved a hundred feet above, buffeted by the hurricane winds outside, Smith and Prendergast got a glimpse of the monsoon downpour and electric storms which raged in Titan's atmosphere. Before them the enormous area was awash with colour and movement. This was the famous Titan market. The vast Shang Souk which greeted every visitor of whom few survived with their dignity or wallets intact.

All human life and activity was represented here. Stalls brimmed with frozen meat from the cattle plains of Earth. Pallets were piled with pseudo-meal, pressed and shaped from the underwater kelp and plankton farms of Europa and cages teetered, full of the exotic insects and crustacea which represented the highest evolutionary forms of Titan's indigenous fauna. Though whether sold as pets or dinner the shopkeepers did not specify. Add to this the fire-eaters, sword-swallowers, strong men, dancers and magicians, the shysters and parasites, the pickpockets and conmen that cleave to every centre of human commerce and the Shang Souk was one of the most colourful and odorous destinations in the home system.

"Keep close," instructed Betty, "you don't wanna to get lost here."

But that's exactly what I do want, thought Smith and a crafty smile passed briefly across his lips.

"I got fewer friends in the Souk," Betty continued, "I'm low on credit and supplies'll be harder to come by."

"We'll be fine. Just dump us somewhere and carry on," said Smith, reasonableness itself.

"Now hold one moment," interrupted Prendergast, "are we to be abandoned again to the whims of every ruffian in this dreadful place?"

Smith placed a firm hand on his partner's shoulder.

"Steady the buffs there, Percy. Let Betty get on with her thing and we'll take care of ourselves."

Prendergast gawped at the man.

"What on Earth do you mean, 'take care of ourselves'. Cast a look around you. We'll be eaten alive. Have you forgotten the debacle of Mars. The large, knife wielding chap with the face like a quarry. That brute nearly had us signed up as slave labour down his salt mine. I hold no brief for this woman, I can tell you that, but without her and the casual violence she is so ready to mete out to all and sundry, we are sunk my dear fellow. OW!"

This last exclamation was due to the fact that Smith had ground his heel into Prendergast's toes.

"Oh, I'm sorry, is that your foot, mate?"

"Can it, both of you. Just wait here. I'll be as quick as I can."

"No, but I say, really..."

"Will you put a sock in it, Percy?" said Smith and he gave the Prendergast toes another grinding for good measure.

"OW! Now look here, Anthony."

As the boys squabbled, Betty shook her head and made her way over to a stall where a small, crooked old man smiled and extended his hand to her.

"Betty, Betty, Betty, what a joy to see you again."

"You too, pops. Is there somewhere we can talk? I need a favour."

The old man's face hardened for a moment, plainly a man with whom favours were in short supply, then reluctantly gestured Betty towards the lean-to behind his stall. Betty followed him.

"A favour today'll pay very well tomorrow," she said.

"Only if tomorrow comes," he replied darkly as they were swallowed up by the gloom of his lair.

Outside, Smith tried to appraise Prendergast of recent events as succinctly as possible, time being, after all, of the essence but Percy it seemed was having trouble digesting Smith's story.

"Good Laws! A pen?!"

"Yes."

"We have been in thrall of a pen?!"

"Yes, Perce, please try to assimilate all this a bit quicker."

"But. A bloody pen?!"

"So what we have to do..."

"This is the absolute blooming penultimate. It really is the giddy limit. That this...this...harlot, there I've said it, should be allowed to go about..."

"Percy!" Smith grabbed him by the shoulders, "We should scarper now."

"And do what exactly?"

Smith tugged at the narrow silver wire round his neck.

"Get these inhibitors off for a start..."

"Can't. We need her smart print."

"...call someone..."

"We don't know anyone."

"...get a ride on a ship..."

"We haven't any money."

"Percy, do you mind me saying you're being really negative here."

"I'm just saying I don't think you've thoroughly thought this thing through."

"PERCY!"

"What!?"

"RUN!"

They stood looking at each other for a moment then, as one, turned and dived into the bustling throng. As they jostled with the hawkers and traders, the punters and the tourists, driving their way through the pressing mass, Betty came out of the old man's tent and caught a glimpse of their backs receding into the sea of humanity. She pulled out the detonator pen and help it aloft.

"Stop you mothers," she called after them, "I will use this so help me."

"What for? To write us a letter?" Prendergast shouted back, but his trenchant wit was lost in the noise and tumult of the Souk.

Of course running is not exactly what they were doing. Bounding would be a better description. In the low Titan gravity you can cover quite a fair amount of ground with one bounce and once you've got your rhythm it feels as natural as walking on Earth, a little more fun even. Of course you look a bit ungainly 'til you find your feet but appearances were unimportant to Smith and Prendergast right now as all they wanted to do was put as much distance between themselves and Betty as possible.

Fifteen minutes later, aching and winded, they slumped against a wall in a quieter side tunnel, trying to wrest control of their breathing from the exertion and the adrenalin. As their heart rates returned to normal they slid down the wall and sat, exhausted on the polyvinyl floor.

"D'you...do you think...she followed us?" gasped Smith.

"Dunno...best press on...at any rate," heaved Prendergast.

They rose to their feet and stumbled deeper into the murky maze of tunnels before them.

*

Betty was furious at her own stupidity. How could she have been so careless? To be outsmarted by those two geeks. A science nerd and a hobbyist, that's all they were. That tall plummy one drooling over his equations and the shorter, rude one with his rotating 3D models cluttering up her hard drive. But they were her future right now. She had to find them and find them fast. All she needed was to hand them over to the Centauris and she would be out of the bail bonding business for good. Bail bonding. Who was she kidding? The Wieners had been right. Kidnap. That's what it was. Kidnap plain and simple. What would dear Momma have said?

No time for that now. She needed the help of the local cops. According to her entry records she was a Martian Security Agent escorting a pair of ruthless net hackers to the penal colony on Rhea. She needed to get the whole area shut down, the nerds apprehended and taken to Neptune pronto under virtual lock and smart key.

*

Smith and Prendergast were still threading their way through the tunnels of Titan without aim or direction. Prendergast had pointed out that the Innernet suppressors around their necks were bound to attract unwanted attention, let's face it people didn't get cut off from the Innernet for being model citizens, so Smith had stolen a couple of scarves from a market stall. They were becoming tired and hungry as they turned another corner.

There before them, was the Shang Souk.

"Oh dear, oh dear, Percy. We've only gone round in a flippin' circle."

Pendergast gripped Smith's arm tightly.

"Look over there," he said, the panic rising in his voice.

He pointed to a knot of uniforms by a large stand selling reconditioned antique computers and Smith squinted enough to see Betty, surrounded by a group of armed police, gesticulating pantomimically, indicating her head and her ankles. It didn't take a rocket technician to realise she was furnishing the local gendarmerie with full descriptions of them. In a few minutes their likeness would be all over Shangri-La and their new found freedom would be at an end. They doubled back into the tunnel they'd just come from and threw a few quick lefts and rights to confuse the trail.

"What in the name of nebulae are we going to do?" asked Prendergast between bounds.

"There's only one thing we can do. We have to get out of Shangri-La."

"But there aren't any other cities on Titan."

"I know but nevertheless we're going to have to get out!"

Prendergast raised his eyes to the roof where the polyvinyl covering was snapping like a sail in a gale and the rumble of the torrential rain was an every present kettle drum roll over the noise of the city.

"Out there?" asked Prendergast like a reluctant skydiver.

Smith slumped.

"No, you're right. It'd be suicide. I guess we're sunk."

Prendergast slapped Smith heartily on the shoulder.

"Don't be such a defeatist. Did I say it was a bad idea?"

"No, but..."

"Look behind you."

Smith turned and there shimmering in the air behind him was an advertisement...

Workers Wanted
For The Surface Ethane Lakes
Good Pay
Enquire Within

...and in tiny writing underneath...

Must be prepared to relocate to
a community outside the city

A virtual neon arrow pointed round a corner to their left. Smith and Prendergast bounded towards it as fast as they could.

At the other end of the tunnel they now faced, a huge mound of a man with a bald, sweating head sat, a vape in his mouth and a newspaper open on the desk in front of him. He looked like an all-in-wrestler who'd been barred from the ring for being too rough. The boys stopped in their tracks and regarded the bruiser critically. It was Prendergast who broke the silence.

"Let's go back and throw ourselves on Betty's mercy."

"Don't be stupid. This is our big chance," said Smith.

"Let's appeal to her better nature."

"She doesn't have one. This is perfect. We get out of the city and earn our passage home."

"But he looks so unsavoury."

"Percival. Don't be so judgmental. He's probably a lovely bloke."

"I know he won't like me. And what sort of disreputable establishment employs a man like that as their public face?"

Smith put a firm hand on Prendergast's back.

"It doesn't matter how dodgy the outfit is. Every constable in a mile radius will be after us in a few minutes. It's now or never."

Prendergast dragged his heels but Smith held his arm and dragged him down the tunnel to the desk where the man ignored them. Smith cleared his throat. The man flipped a page of his paper and continued reading.

"We've come to apply for the jobs."

Without looking up the man spoke.

"Work papers?"

Smith looked at Prendergast. He didn't know there were such things.

"They were destroyed. In a house fire."

The man pointed to a biometric terminal.

"Smart fingers there."

"Ah. Funny story actually. They were burned off. In the fire."

The man slowly put his paper down and lifted his face to them. He was one of the ugliest men that either had ever seen without actually having been involved in an industrial accident.

"Burned off?" he asked.

"Yes," said Smith as they both put their hands behind their backs.

Percy joined in.

"While we were trying to grab the metal box that our work papers were in."

Smith turned to Prendergast an unconcealed look of admiration on his face. He'd never've believed that Prendergast was such an accomplished improviser.

The man eyed them both critically.

"Names?"

"Percy..."

Smith cut him off.

"I'm...Rockne...Entwhistle."

Prendergast looked at Smith in horror. The man turned to Percy.

"Name!"

Prendergast just stood there, his mind a blank. Smith prompted him.

"Come on, tell the man...Englebert."

Prendergast let out a yelp and pressed his fist to his mouth. The man sneered at him.

"And your second name? Englebert?"

"It's Schneizel...baum. Schneizelbaum. Englebert Schneizelbaum."

The man got up. He was huge. If you said he was as big as a house you'd've been belittling him. He lumbered round the table and stood directly in front of the boys. Not close you understand, his girth precluded intimacy.

"Well. Mr Entwhistle. Mr Schneizel...?"

"Baum."

Smith coughed nervously. The man's huge face broke into a terrifying grin.

"You're hired."

*

A mere three hours later, after a spine jarring ride across the pitted terrain of Titan's storm torn surface in little more than a glorified oxygen tent atop a flatbed truck which bounced along on what looked like four rubber rings from a child's paddling pool, Entwhistle and Schneizelbaum found themselves standing in one of the worker huts belonging to the Fossilax Oil Company. Before them, sprawled around the floor and across the hard pallet beds where such a gang of battle-scarred, craggy bad eggs as to make a Foreign Legion barracks look like a scout hut.

Every shaved, bullet shaped head had turned to look at them as they'd come through the door and every hard, rheumy, shark eye stared at them. The silence was broken by a cracked, whiskey soaked voice from the back of the room.

"Hey look, fellas! Fresh meat."

Smith shuffled a little closer to his chum. He'd seen enough prison movies to know that this, as an opening gambit, probably didn't bode well, whereas Prendergast, one of nature's naïf's waved a cheery hand and gave the ensemble a broad smile.

"Hello, chaps," he began, "been a real blighter of a journey down here. Could you show us to the restaurant? Then perhaps direct us to our rooms. I don't know about my friend here but I could really do with a nap."

The bullet heads turned to each other. Then the one Smith guessed was the highest calibre among them rose to his full height, an impressive six-eight at a guess, and lumbered towards them. Respect of personal space was plainly not his strong suit and he towered over Prendergast, breathing stale alcohol, rotting meat and dental caries all over him. Prendergast smiled up at him and his eyes watered slightly.

"I'm sorry," said the giant, "but the restaurant is closed now. Shame you missed it. They laid on a lovely seafood buffet tonight. The lobster was second to none. As for your rooms. We're having them refurbished. You'll have to rough it here with the rest of us."

This was going down well with the cheap seats behind him and their guttural laughter was becoming most unnerving. Prendergast swivelled his eyes from side to side in an effort to avoid eye-contact with the large, odorous man and he backed up a little, hoping to get a lungful of less fetid air.

"Jolly good," he said in a weak voice, "erm...which are our bunks?"

The giant frowned and leaned closer.

"Sorry. The beds in here go for a slight premium. You'll have to trade for them. Where are your belongings?"

"I'm awfully sorry, sir but we don't have any."

"Oh, dear," and he shook his head ruefully, "in that case..."

At this moment what appeared to be a large copper chamber pot smashed into the back of his head and clattered noisily to the ground. Any ordinary man would have been felled instantly by such a blow but the only effect it had on the boy's tormentor was to make him scrunch up his already mangled features and rub the back of his head. He turned angrily to determine the chamber pot's source.

There standing at the back of the room stood a woman, broad of shoulder and thick of limb, staring unflinchingly at her victim.

"Leave it, Gumbo. Get back in your cage," she said. Much to Smith and Prendergast's amazement, Gumbo turned and went back to his bed, quietly picking up a piece of wood he had been whittling when they had arrived. The woman watched him with a warning look in her eye then turned back to the boys.

"You two. Come and take the beds next to me."

*

Her name, they found out, was McGill. And that was the full extent of the biography she was prepared to impart. She seemed more interested in them.

"What in the name of all that's human are two guys like *you* doing *here*?" she asked them. They were each finishing a bowl of food she'd rustled up for them. Not the best they'd ever eaten, haute pig swill just about covering it, thought Smith. But it was hot and welcome. The boys looked at each other. They had to keep up their aliases but it would be pointless to try and pretend they were doing this for fun. She obviously suspected they were in trouble but Smith thought it best not to go into too much detail.

"We need to get back to Earth."

"As soon as is possible," added Prendergast.

"Yeah?" asked McGill, "How do you intend doing that?"

"Well," said Smith, "we thought we'd work here 'till we had enough for a ticket home."

"Nothing fancy," proffered Prendergast, "I mean, we're not expecting a cabin on a luxury liner or anything of the sort but..."

"Listen," interrupted McGill, "You wouldn't last long enough here to buy standing room on a no-frills, bucket outfit like EasyRocket. Forget it."

The boys visibly slumped, their plans turning to ashes before them.

"But listen," she continued, "you keep outta trouble and work hard for a couple of weeks; you might be able to get a hammock on a cargo ship. Oh, they'll take all your money and make you work your passage but you'll be fed and watered and you'll get home. Eventually."

The boys looked at her and nodded.

"Than that's what we'll do," said Smith.

"You better get some sleep. You're gonna need it."

*

The work was back breaking. Smith and Prendergast were pulling shifts on the hellish Titan surface in cumbersome antique space suits straight out of an undersea Jules Verne story. There was little shelter in the ethane field they had been assigned to just north of the Adiri Range. Visibility was poor through the methane deluge and merely standing was almost impossible against the hurricane winds. As the huge caterpillar tracked tankers came through the field it was the boy's task to attach a hefty polymer hose to them and weigh it down against Titan's light gravity into one of the lakes, of which there were thirty on this plain alone. The tankers then pumped the ethane 'til they were full and lumbered off through the churning mud to make way for the next. In truth, Prendergast had very little to do with the operation. Smith was the engineer so had a modicum of manual dexterity but Prendergast seemed unable to perform the simplest mechanical task. A tool would be dropped, a bolt counter-threaded and any electrical component rendered powerless by his lightest touch. It was soon agreed that for the sake of efficiency Smith would do all the technical stuff while Prendergast confined himself to the lifting and humping.

After eight of these shifts Smith and Prendergast were exhausted and realised they had very little more ethane mining left in them, though Smith was slightly chuffed by the emergent muscle tone on his upper arms. He had taken to striding around the barracks, shirtless, catching sideways glances of himself in reflective surfaces.

*

It was at the end of a particularly arduous session and Smith was dragging up a pipe from the methane lake.

"How many more, Percy?" he called over helmet coms to Percy who was battling to stay vertical against the brutal wind while waving in the next tanker.

"Just four more," he replied.

"Okay," said Smith, "help me guide this one in. I'm beat, mate."

Percy made his way towards him looking for all the world like a French mime-artist as he battled against the gale. He reached out to help Smith press the oil pipe home in the receptor socket at the side of the tanker. This done Smith pressed down the locking lever and gave an OK to the driver up in the truck's cabin who started the pumping. While the tank filled Smith and Prendergast took the opportunity of a much needed respite in the shelter afforded by the high sided tanker. All too soon the truck's horn sounded to indicate the tank was full and the boys wearily set to work again. Prendergast had been sitting on the tanker's fender and grabbed the locking lever to hoist himself upright. As he pulled at it, the corroded metal came away in his hands.

"Oh, dear," he said, looking sheepishly at Smith through his visor, holding the lever before him like a smoking pistol, "Whoops."

"Well, that's torn it, you idiot," said Smith desperately. "Now I can't get the pipe out."

The driver looked out through the screen of his cab to see what was causing the delay. It was Gumbo the Giant. Their intercom crackled and his voice boomed in their ears.

"Fix it, you lily-skinned cockroaches!" was all he had to say on the matter.

As Smith trudged off to get some tools from a ramshackle shed in the shelter of the rocks a few hundred metres away the other drivers in the queue began blaring their horns wildly. They were paid by the load and with every passing minute they were losing money.

It took an hour to free the hose and when eventually Smith and Prendergast waved Gumbo on, his voice crackled in their helmets again.

"I figure you just cost me two runs. I promise you, when I can get you without your guardian angel, McGill, you're going to pay for it." With that he put his foot down hard, spinning his wheels, covering the boys with a large portion of Titan's surface mud.

Four more irate drivers and a wild variety of threats later, they packed up and were on their way back to the worker's camp, much relieved that a rare lull in the storm conditions coincided made the going slightly easier. The torrent of rain had become annoying drizzle and the tornado winds had dropped to a stiff breeze.

*

Cresting the hill they stopped as flashing red lights flickered across their visors. They looked down into the base and there, outside the main office, they saw what was unmistakably a police hovercraft. A team of blue suited officers were surrounding the camp, while others were searching every building and outhouse.

Prendergast turned to Smith.

"It may have nothing to do with us. Could be something else entirely," he said over the suit coms.

Smith shook his head. A bit of a waste really because his helmet didn't move.

"No," he said, "she's with them."

"How can you tell, old boy?"

"I can smell the brimstone."

At that moment a gloved hand landed firmly on Prendergast's shoulder. His heart froze mid beat and the colour drained from his face. Smith turned to see who it was.

"McGill?" he said.

Prendergast also turned to face her and quickly tried to assess if her appearance fell into the category of good news or bad.

"Entwhistle. Schneizelbaum," she greeted them cordially. "Police just made a call on the base. Looking for some guys who escaped on their way to the penal colony on Rhea. I told 'em. I don't know anyone like that. Do you?"

Smith and Prendergast held her stare, their faces grim.

"Uh huh? That's what I figured," she said sadly. "You guys better come with me."

13. HAIL TO THE CHIEF

The sub-orbital shuttle service from Grand Bahama air and spaceport to San Simeon's Hearst Airdrome took thirty minutes going the long way round the Earth. To fly the shorter route would've taken six hours in a jet, there not being enough distance to get an Orion Hopper up and down again safely. The delegation from Earth Defence disembarked upon arrival and were taken up the steep hill to the castle by the newly built funicular which now replaced the seven miles of road that wound through the old estate's parkland.

Once inside the castle they were ushered into the grand dining room where President Olsen sat leafing through his brief at the head of the long table. As aides led each delegate to a seat, the President opened proceedings without preliminaries.

"Major Fulbright, setting aside for now how you got this information and the security implications of that," he let the thought settle in the room for a moment before continuing. "I want you to tell me if we can trust this..." he looked through his notes, 'old friend' of yours and his motivations."

Major Fulbright cleared his throat and opened a file in front of him.

"I knew him well, back in the day, but as to the man he has become..."

"Are you going to give me his name?"

"As a source on enemy territory I would rather not risk compromising..."

"Alright, alright cut the bull, I get it. Why do you think he contacted you after all these years?"

"To warn of a very real danger to Earth security."

"Can you think of any other reason he might have?"

The President was certainly a direct man and Fulbright was a little flustered by this barrage of questions at his first meeting with the Commander-in-Chief.

"I can't imagine what other motivations he might have."

"Really?" said the President. "I can. Maybe he's got some gripe with this Zoltac guy. They may be involved in some impenetrable Centauri power struggle and by sending us this disinformation reckons we'll do his dirty work for him."

"Perhaps but..."

"Harris."

A sharp young man in a shiny blue suit, obviously some kind of spook came to attention in his chair.

"What about this engine story. Does it pan out?"

"They are in Neptune orbit but we don't have anything close enough to say if the engines are on line or not."

"Laurel?"

"Mr President?" Lauren Laurel sat beside Harris. Same suit, different cut.

"What about this final piece of the jigsaw the Major's source says Zoltac is waiting for, to get the Diplomatist back on stream, if indeed it is becalmed for whatever reason."

"Can't say for sure, sir but we are tentatively connecting it to the disappearance of two young rocket scientists from Gagarin some weeks ago."

"Abduction?"

"Or defection."

The table fell silent while the President weighed up this new information.

"Listen up," he said and rose from his chair, turning his back on his advisors.

"We thank Major Fulbright for so promptly passing on this intelligence, though we reprimand him for being so selective in the information he chooses to share. We will take no preemptive action as the motivations of this 'old friend' of the Major's are unclear and I am reticent in the extreme for my first act as President to be one of war. I want every aspect of this situation tightly monitored by all departments. Harris, get something into the region of Neptune as soon as we can. General Drearing?"

The general was a barrel chested, buzz cut, ox of a man who looked up from his info tablet and regarded the Commander-in-Chief levelly.

"Yes, sir?"

"Take Earth Defence to Def Con Three."

"Right away, sir."

"Laurel?"

"Sir?"

President Olsen turned back to the group and took a few steps forward.

"Find those rocket kids!"

14. THE CAVES OF TITAN

It's always remarkable how used to things people can get. Take Smith and Prendergast for example. When they'd first arrived at the Oiler's camp they had pretty much agreed that it was one of the most horrible places they had ever been. Reminiscent of a wartime prison camp with none of the redeeming features but on this day as they'd approached the hill after their extended shift they were positively looking forward to getting inside the barracks where at least there was hot food, a chance of a wash and somewhere to lie down. Now the appearance of the cops had dashed even that slight pleasure and they now found themselves walking away from the only known shelter on this hemisphere of the planet, following a woman they barely knew through the worst weather in the solar system.

Smith and Prendergast had been following McGill for what seemed a very long time, battling the elements and the rocky terrain. She was a woman of few words and so the boys had no idea where they were going or how long it would take. After a further interminable period of this trek, Smith, an impatient man at the best of times began to become restive and, while not actually saying, "Are we nearly there yet?" every two minutes, started to make his feelings felt.

"Do you know where you're going?" he asked over the suit coms.

"Yes."

"Can you tell us?"

"I could give you the coordinates but that wouldn't mean much to you would it?"

"No. I mean what kind of place."

"No."

"Why not?"

"The less you know the better."

It was getting dark and Prendergast was beginning to flag. They'd put in an extra long shift and now this. His father had once taken him to the forest of Dean, fell walking and he had vowed never to do that again. Now here he was on a seemingly endless hike in weather that would have had a Marine Corps yomp called off.

"I don't think I can carry on for very much longer," he called out to the others. "I'm getting a severe case of jelly legs and stitch."

"Not far now," McGill called out encouragingly.

Indeed as they passed a huge boulder she led them down a little gully into a small open clearing surrounded by steep walls of rock. This seclusion shielded them from the worst of the storms and the boys rested against the ice covered limestone.

"We're here."

Smith looked around the empty clearing devoid of features save for a few stones strewn here and there.

"Where?"

"Our destination," said McGill and she stooped to pick up a medium sized rock at her feet.

Smith watched this with a rising dread and, turning off his coms, pressed his helmet against Prendergast's so only he could hear.

"Watch out, she's gone bonkers. She wants to stove our heads in and do for us."

"I'm sure she doesn't, old thing."

McGill threw the stone to one side and looked over at the boys.

"Come on, lend a hand."

Mystified, the boys joined McGill and started to pick up stones and rocks from the centre of the clearing and, following her example threw them out to the edge. It was when they had a clear space about a meter wide that McGill stopped and sank to her knees. Wiping the rainswept rock with a gloved hand she forced her fingers down a crack and pulled up what looked like a rough flagstone. There beneath it was a round metal handle on a circular door. McGill put her full weight into turning it and after three creaky revolutions she lifted up the hatch and light from below flooded the clearing.

"Follow me, single file," she said and lowered herself down through the opening.

*

Sergeant Sortras led Betty out of the station lobby into the main square of Shangri-La's business district.

"The sweep of the Oiler's camp revealed nothing. We're still following a few leads but if you take my advice you'll go back to your ship. We'll be in touch if we turn up anything."

"Thank you sergeant, anything, anything at all, don't hesitate to call. I need those prisoners back," said Betty.

"We'll do our best."

"I'm sure if anyone can find them it's you." She'd been laying on the flirty charm pretty thick all afternoon with the sergeant and she added this final dollop to be on the safe side.

As she made her way across the square a stocky man in a heavily armored leather suit and a thick beard moved in behind her at a respectable distance and began to tail her. He was uplinked to the Innernet and streaming everything she did and everything she said.

It is universally agreed that the Innernet is 'A Good Thing'. The tiny amount of hardware it needs is buried in a subcutaneous chip usually in one's shoulder, all the power it needs comes from two potential plates typically buried in the thigh muscles and there is near infinite storage space for any information one may wish to download to one's DNA.

The Innernet is also a technological and creative battle ground. Since its beginnings this ever-growing web of the universe's information stream has been a fight between one half of humanity expending vast amounts of energy and imagination to invade the privacy of the other half while they in turn have spared no effort trying to keep their privacy just that; private.

A slight software edge here and there can reap magnificent rewards and it was that edge which the stocky man now had over Betty. He would keep it until she uplinked and downloaded the protection soon to be available against the particular surveillance package he was using but that wouldn't happen before he'd found what they both were looking for.

*

After descending a thirty foot ladder to the floor of a murky cave, McGill led the boys along a long dark tunnel.

"You know tunnels are becoming a bit of a motif on this journey. Have you noticed that, Anthony?" asked Prendergast.

"I certainly have. Don't care if I never see another one again, mate."

McGill brought them to the main chamber of the cave system and there before them, down some steps carved into the rock, was a thriving underground world full of people and fire and smells and sound. McGill led them through the little subterranean hamlet 'til they came to a large rectangular tarpaulin hanging on the rock face. She pulled it aside and beyond the boys could see a brightly lit antechamber cut into the cave wall by either geological forces or human hand.

"Wait here. I'll be back," said McGill before going inside.

"It's Betty family on Mars all over again. Outcasts living on the edge of society," said Smith. Prendergast nodded his head and sighed.

"A common story really," he said.

"How so?" asked Smith.

"Well it seems to me that whenever people get together in reasonably sized groups eventually one set will get the upper hand and decide that another set are not quite the thing and start to make their lives miserable, forcing them to go off and live in squalor elsewhere. Eventually the outcasts will pull themselves up by the bootstraps and start living a little more comfortably. After a while they'll decide there are a few among their number who don't quite pass muster and start being as beastly as the first lot had been to them. Depressing really. Absolutely the worst face of human nature."

His musings were cut short by McGill's reappearance. She ushered them into the antechamber.

Inside sat three men. Since their abduction from Gagarin they had come across some fairly rough hewn diamonds and while the trio before them were not exactly the cutting edge of villainy they looked like they could hold their own in any low dive on the home worlds. Smith and Prendergast were introduced to Morton, the man who sat in the middle. Plainly the ring leader.

"So. On the run are they?" he observed, then looked McGill fully in the eye. "What do you expect us to do about it?"

Smith thought he could help out here by offering a practical suggestion. Which he did.

"I'll tell you what would be useful. If you had something to get these off," and he pulled his scarf aside to show the suppressor around his neck, "we could call home and get some help."

Morton turned his stare on Smith. He pulled his own scarf down to reveal an identical suppressing necklace.

"We're all runners here. You take any serious tool to one of these and it becomes a garrote. You keep it up it'll close your pipes. Still don't stop and it'll take your head clean off."

Prendergast grimaced.

"What sort of a sick individual thought that up? Honestly. People."

McGill intervened.

"I heard you were putting something together. Maybe off Titan. Thought you might take these guys along for the ride."

"Maybe. But passage ain't free. Who's paying?"

"Ah," said Prendergast. "Slight problem there. Had to vacate our posts pretty darn unexpectedly. Didn't have time to work out the hours and pick up the old pay packet."

"I'll pay," said McGill.

"Oh? Awfully decent of you erm...Mrs McGill."

"It's Miss," said McGill and gave a shy glance to Morton.

"Miss. But we couldn't possibly allow you..."

"Really? Couldn't we?" asked Smith through gritted teeth.

"It's not a problem. Me and the boss'll split your unpaid wages. I'll be up on the deal," said McGill with a smug smile.

"All the same. Very grateful," said Prendergast.

"Hang on a minute," said Smith. "This is all very well but where'll we be going? Earth?"

Morton turned to him sharply.

"Do we look like we'd be welcome on Earth? Don't be crazy. We're going in the opposite direction."

"Further out of the solar system. Oh, dear Stars at Night," exclaimed Smith. "Where'll it all end?"

McGill turned angrily to Smith.

"You don't want to go? Fine. Your choice. Though I don't think you really have one."

"She's right," said Prendergast. "Let's just get away from here and that bloodthirsty money-grabbing wretch Betty."

"I guess you're right," sighed Smith and turned to Morton and McGill. "We're in. When do we leave?"

"In thirty hours and we have a long walk to the ship," answered Morton. "Get some rest."

*

After a night's sleep and a bowl of food, the best they'd had of both for a long time though Smith did not care to enquire too closely into the provenance of the meat given the green and blue scales he had found at the bottom of his bowl, the boys gathered in the cave with about twelve others. Morton was there to meet them. It seemed this little bunch were the only travelers this day and Smith silently wondered what hitherto unrevealed joy it was that kept the rest here. He thought it unwise to ask. Perhaps there were more flights planned. There was a buzz of excitement among the men and women who were gathered with their meagre belongings. Prendergast chuckled. It had the feeling more of a school day out to 'A Place of Interest', rather than a desperate flight by desperate people. Morton held up his hand for silence and got it. Plainly Morton was used to getting what he wanted from his people.

"Today we head out on a journey. A journey to find a home. A hard walk to the Ching-Tu cargo docks and an even harder flight to the Pluto Arc. It is there we hope to find the tiny ice object Erubin, hollowed out by mining and abandoned by the Companies we are told, the perfect world to make a home. And safe haven from Earth's judgment." Morton went on but Prendergast grabbed Smith's arm.

"Did he say the Pluto arc?"

"Yeah, I think he did."

"But that is wonderful!"

Smith shook his head sadly.

"Bless you for trying to put a positive spin on things but I don't think it is wonderful, mate. From what I understand a more remote and inhospitable spot you couldn't hope to find yourself in, barring military duty in the Oort Cloud!"

"No, but you see Mummy and Daddy are working on Eris..."

"Mummy and Daddy?"

"...and that is in the Pluto Arc right now..."

"Do you really call them Mummy and Daddy?"

"...erm, yes, yes I do. But the point is if we could get to them, they would know what to do and help get us home!"

Smith considered for a moment.

"Well, it's worth a shot but have you any idea the sheer volume of space the Arc takes up?"

"Of course, but there's a lot of mining and research out there. We're bound to get a ride somehow."

"A lot of bandits out there too and those nasty Traders we ran into on the way up."

Prendergast put a hand on Smith's shoulder.

"I'd say it was our only hope right now old thing. So, get on board eh? Bit more of the can-do spirit, what?"

Smith joined in the hand on shoulder act and jutted his jaw.

"You're right. We've come this far. We're due a bit of luck. Perhaps the worst is over."

Morton had finished his speech and, picking up his bag, turned to leave. Smith, Prendergast and the rest followed him, out of the cave, towards the hatch and on to the hell which was Titan's surface.

*

The huge man stumbled out of the betting shop shouting drunken obscenities at the four other men who were attempting to remove him. His sheer mass coupled with a low centre of gravity was getting the better of them until two more staff joined in and, coordinating for one big push at his voluminous rump, turned his weight advantage against him. They watched him totter precariously into the street trying to maintain his balance. He had learned from experience that after this many flagons of Saturnia, if he fell into the gutter he was staying there for the night.

"Get out of here, ya bum!" shouted the tote manager as he and his employees moved triumphantly back into the shop, all but dusting their hands.

The big man lumbered down the street in the age old gait of the penniless inebriate, hands in pockets, head down, one step left, two steps right, belch, repeat. After a few rounds of this he sensed liquid on his face and the stink of cattle. He hadn't smelled that in years, since he was a boy on his papa's farm in Utah. He looked up and there he saw a lengthy tear in the roof. The stink was methane, as was the rain. A team of emergency sealers were already there with a long ladder and an adhesive patch. The air was beginning to chill dangerously now as the heat whistled out of the tent and he knew he must move on if he was to avoid hypothermia. He turned to the left and waddled down a side alley as swiftly as he could. A minute or two of this exertion and he was leaning against a post, gasping for breath. Great, he thought, drunk, broke, freezing and having a heart attack. Just his luck. As he lifted his head, wincing in pain, he opened his eyes to see the virtual poster floating in the middle of the street. The two faces he recognised, their crime he could care less about but the cash reward...now that was something he could really use right now.

*

They lost a man on the journey to Ching-Tu. He'd been complaining of tiredness and had settled at the back of the line, imploring the rest to slow the pace. The two men at the back lost sight of him for a while and called the line to a halt, giving him a chance to catch up. Ten minutes went by 'til Morton decided they could wait no longer and the line continued without him. Prendergast, who was lagging a little himself, promptly picked up his pace.

Eventually they arrived at the cargo docks, a loose scattering of hangers and sheds on a bleak plain beneath a ridge of ice covered hills. Looming above these was their ride to the edge of the solar system. An antique rocket, like something from an historical movie, resting on its tail beside a rusted iron gantry with its tapered nose rising into the turbulent Titanian sky.

They filed into the customs hall and once the doors had been closed against the inhospitable elements the group gratefully took off their suits and two of Morton's henchmen gathered them for stowing on the ship. They would certainly be needed at the other end. Once this had been done a cargo official lined them up against the wall of a long hallway and they started to slowly shuffle forward towards another official at the far end. The boys tagged on at the tail of the line.

Smith and Prendergast said nothing. The journey through the lashing rain and wind had brought their spirits to a very low ebb and the sight of the museum piece they were to entrust the next few months of their life to, robbed them of any remaining buoyancy.

About halfway up the hallway there was a door and as the boys went past, it creaked open a few inches and a voice whispered from within.

"Psst, hey, you two."

Smith and Prendergast looked around and saw no-one.

"Hey, over here, in the doorway."

They looked over and could just see an eye glint in the darkened room beyond.

"Don't go on. It's a trap."

Smith and Prendergast looked anxiously at each other, then back to the door.

"Spaceside is crawling with cops. You wanna get away, come with me."

"Who are you?" Smith whispered back.

"A friend. You haven't much time. Leave now!"

The eye disappeared back into the shadows and the door opened a little more. In a sweat of confusion the boys looked up to the front of the line where the gruff cargo officials were processing the fugitives. The door seemed increasingly inviting as the unknown, up ahead, loomed closer. A moment's hesitation, then Smith and Prendergast broke from the wall and pushed themselves through the doorway into the semidarkness.

"Wise decision. Follow me," said the voice in the darkness.

They could barely discern the silhouette of a man's back already receding from them. They followed him across the room then out through another door into a dingy, low ceilinged corridor lined with wires and ducts. They continued down this, tailing the man for several minutes, turning left and right as the passageway wove who knows where. Another few minutes and the man led them into another room where they could just make out the shapes of two other men.

"Hello, boys," said a deep voice.

They heard footsteps behind them but before they could turn around there were two sickening thumps and for Smith and Prendergast, whatever light there had been in the room, went out.

*

Betty gripped the dash board of the police hovercraft as it raced over the surface of Titan on its way to Ching-Tu. She was furious. Sergeant Sortras had called her four hours before with news of the tip-off they'd received but, as he went on to explain, it was a colonial holiday in Shangri-La. The anniversary of the landing of the Solarwindrush, and the first pioneering settlers on Titan. Getting a big enough group of his men together, away from their families and the traditional Dunebug roast had wasted valuable time and with every minute Betty had become more incandescent.

"There it is, up ahead," said the sergeant, pointing to the rocket towering through the low lying cloud cover, a touch of relief in his voice. He truly feared for what this woman would do if they lost her prisoners.

As the hovercraft came to a halt by the entrance to the cargo depot they jumped out and bounced their way through the rain and wind. Just short of the door they stopped in their tracks. The air was split with the thunderous crack of an atomic engine firing. Over the cargo shed spilled the blinding light of the engines as the vast Trader ship rose and rotated one hundred and eighty degrees 'til it faced Betty and the squad of police below. Sortras leaped at the bounty hunter and knocked her, face down in the mud, covering her with his body as the ship, with a shattering scream ripped through the air above them and in seconds had vanished into Titan's dense stratosphere.

15. OUT OF THE FRYING PAN

Prendergast woke with a start and an eyeful of oil. Keeping this eye tightly shut he used his other to assess the new environment in which he found himself. As far as he could tell from a one eyed, prone position he was lying on a slab of a cold material, surrounded by four identical walls of equally cold material (if the one next to him was anything to go by) on a floor of black material topped by a ceiling of even darker material, all hermetically sealed save for a small crack directly above his right eye which had so recently released a large globule of thick black, pungent oil. This gobbit of viscous hydrocarbonic liquid had gained considerable speed (he would do the maths later for an accurate figure) on its downward journey before being abruptly stopped by his right eye socket thus releasing its kinetic energy in a loud thunk!, a stinging slap! and resulting in the start that had woken him. So; gravity!

He sat up sharply to avoid any further leakage from above and immediately regretted it. His head thumped worse than it had the morning after the party at the Starlight Lounge on Gagarin. He groaned and, pausing only to wipe the oil from his eye, clutched his head. Counterproductively as it turned out as he only succeeded in squeezing the lump on the back of his cranium which was presumably the cause of all his pain, thus worsening the agony.

"Ungh!" he groaned again.

He looked over his dismal surroundings again. Of Smith, there was no sign.

Prendergast stood up. He felt a dizziness that could be because of the egg on his head or maybe was due to pseudo-gravity. He'd noticed it the first few hours on Gagarin. The spin which kept you centrifugally attached to the outside walls, or floors which they then became, had a subtle, qualitative difference to the mass induced gravity of planetary bodies. It took a little getting used to. Therefore; he was on a ship. Though this looked too solid to be the rickety old relic he saw on the gantry at Ching-tu and unless Betty had hidden a room somewhere it was certainly not the Zelda. In any case neither of those were centrifugal.

Wherever he was, chances were this marked a downturn in his fortunes and this hypothesis gained some evidential weight when the door opened and there stood a brute of a man in an armored leather suit, a thick black beard and an expression of habitual misanthropy on his face.

"Out," he barked.

Prendergast followed the man, figuring the better part of valour was prompt obedience and followed him along the corridor outside. He'd certainly been right about the pseudo-gravity. The ship's corridor arched upwards in either direction describing a circle which Prendergast swiftly calculated must be approximately one hundred and fifty feet in diameter. About halfway round, as far as he could tell, the passageway opened out into a room. There inside, sitting on chairs scattered about the place, where three other similarly clad men and in their midst was Smith looking as out of place as a cat in a dog pound.

Prendergast's escort turned and barked at him again.

"Sit!"

He promptly took the nearest stool and the group sat in an awkward silence for a few moments.

One of the men had a gold band round his arm and a drooping Zappata mustache and it was he who next spoke.

"I am Captain Lauro and you are aboard my ship, the Fancy. Understand this. I would prefer to deliver you intact but if you try anything or in any way endanger my ship or crew I will have no hesitation in shoving you both out the airlock myself. Got it?!"

He couldn't really have been clearer and the boys nodded their understanding of the terms of tenure.

"Anything you want to ask me?" asked the Captain leaning menacingly towards them.

Well, of course there was a great deal they wanted to ask him, starting with why they were there, where were they going and who it was that wanted them so badly but one look at Lauro's face and the boys independently came to the conclusion that the Captain's inquiry was rhetorical at best and most probably a trick question. They kept their council and remained resolutely silent.

"Right," continued the Captain, "let's eat."

Smith had thought the catering aboard the Zelda had left a lot to be desired but the fare on the Fancy beggared belief. The meal placed before them was the colour of lead, had the texture of grout and tasted of vinegar. Why anyone would manufacture something so revolting, let alone sell or buy it was a mystery rivaling the Mary Celeste. Still, thought Smith, solids were solids and one never knew where the next plate of wood filler would be coming from.

Prendergast was obviously undergoing the same inner turmoil in re the cuisine but he too was forcing it down, presumably under the same 'sustenance being sustenance' philosophy.

When mealtime was over, after much belching and scraping of plates the crew went about their business and the boys were placed back in their cell. The door was shut, bolts could be heard firmly engaging and Smith and Prendergast were alone.

"You know, Tony," said Prendergast eventually, "I'm not a spiritual man but if there are such things as reincarnation and karma, judging by recent events, in our previous lives we must have been absolute rotters."

"Animal torturers at the very least," agreed Smith.

"At the bare minimum. My money's on mass murder."

*

What with the trek through Titan's storm, the excitement at the docks, the concussion, the stodgy food and the near constant state of anxiety and terror, Smith and Prendergast fell into a deep sleep in the hard cold cell. Smith on the floor and Prendergast on the slab laughingly known as the bed.

It must have been the middle of the night, ship's time, when they were awakened by a violent shudder and the noise of thunder ripping through the Fancy's superstructure. They sat up, eyes and eardrums bulging, breathing hard, muscles clenched, their instinct for fight or flight reflexively bursting to the surface of their consciousness. Useless really in both cases as they could only fight each other and they had nowhere to fly to. Outside the cell they heard feet running and alarms sounding.

Smith and Prendergast scrambled to their feet and over to the door, straining their ears for some clue as to the nature of events outside. Eventually the running and the alarms stopped and they could hear voices somewhere off in the body of the ship. One seemed to be reading off sequences of numbers, another checking them.

The ship had, apparently developed a tic. Every few minutes it would judder convulsively. Smith and Prendergast had spent the last four years of their young lives studying how vessels behave in the vacuum of space and they both knew that a twitching ship was 'Not Good'. A small amount of variable motion along the trajectory of the craft was acceptable but irregular lateral movement inevitably meant: 'A Problem'.

The crew had become eerily quiet and the boys were pressing closer to the cell door when it opened.

It was the bearded escort from earlier whose name they had learnt was Berk.

"Come," was all he said.

Once in the crew room Berk sat them down in front of Captain Lauro whose face was even graver than it had been the evening before.

"As you've no doubt realised we have a problem with the ship." The Fancy shuddered slightly to prove his point.

"A micrometeoroid cloud to be precise."

Micrometeoroids were the bane of interplanetary shipping. No more than grains of sand they travelled at such speed relative to the hurtling spacecraft that they could rip through a hull and disable or even destroy a ship in a nanosecond.

"Our attitude adjusters have been hit and are firing sporadically. We have no idea of the extent of the damage but if one of them blew it could compromise the integrity of the hull."

Or in layman's terms open the ship like a sardine can and spill them, the sardines, out into space where they would suffocate, freeze on the outside and boil on the inside all at once. Pretty gruesome. To be avoided.

"Someone," the Captain continued, "must go EVA and replace the unit."

"EVA?" asked Smith.

"Yes," said Percy, "Extra Vehicular Activity."

"Does that mean..." Tony began.

"Yes. Extra- outside, vehicular- the craft, activity- work." confirmed Percy.

"Working outside the spaceship? Laws above," said Smith. "Good luck with that!" The Captain looked at him steadily and every sphincter in Smith's body contracted simultaneously.

"Now hold on a blummin' minute!" said Smith in breathless panic, his diaphragm joining his sphincters in a contracting competition.

The Captain shouted Smith down angrily.

"It's dangerous. I can't afford to risk a crew member. You are expendable. We feed you. This is your chance to repay us."

Prendergast was appalled at the sheer nerve of the man. To demand payment for the muck they had served up was like a poisoner billing his victim for the arsenic and expecting a tip.

"Now look here," Prendergast was on his feet and had his sternest face on, "Mister Flipping Chuckingyourbloomingweightaround. The way I see it is someone has put a price on our heads and you want the money so I say we are precious cargo and you can repair the blessed ship yourself because we won't do it and you can't make us."

"They'll still pay us for one," said Captain Lauro pointing a gun directly at Prendergast's face.

"Ah," was all Percy could come up with.

"Go get suited up."

"Oh," said Prendergast, "righto."

*

The climate suits they'd worn on Titan were insufficient for the rigours of vacuum at absolute zero so the crew got them into EVA space suits and started checking their life support systems. Despite his feelings of dread, Smith took a moment to reflect how cool he looked in his. He glanced over at Prendergast but the expression of quivering terror on the latter's face rather spoiled the Intrepid Space Jock effect. These thoughts were quickly forgotten as Berk opened a hatch in the floor and lowered them into the tiny airlock. As the hatch closed above them the boys heard a hiss as the air was sucked out of the chamber. At their feet was the door of the airlock and outside that, was the galactic abyss. They waited with pounding hearts and knotted stomachs for their first visit to the terrifying grandeur which is outer space.

The ship was a spinning drum. The spinning created the Fancy's pseudo-gravity and so, as the door in the floor of the airlock opened silently, Smith and Prendergast fell through it, out into space and bounced on the end of their safety lines some fifty feet away from the ship. They quickly clambered hand-over-hand along these tethers and grasped handrails on the side of the craft's hull.

Most situations that human beings find themselves in have some physical parameters; the walls of a room, the distant hills or even the sea and the sky but out in space there are no borders. In every direction there is limitless infinity and it takes a highly trained mind not to boggle when presented with it. Smith and Prendergast's way of dealing with the sheer awesomeness which surrounded them was the same as most other people when presented with the necessity of EVA. Viz; get on with the task in hand and not dwell. Dwelling is fatal.

Added to which, of course, from their perspective, clinging to the side of this huge spinning hulk, the stars were turning around *them*. The experience of clinging to the one fixed point in a spinning universe can play havoc with your inner ear. Your inner ear then complains to your stomach which promptly empties itself just to be on the safe side and everyone knows you do not want to throw up in a space helmet. It is such a disgustingly gross experience that you will do it again. And again. And possibly again. You definitely do not want to be in a sealed environment, fighting for room with your own regurgitated lunch. Repeat; dwelling is fatal.

They set out to circumnavigate the Fancy as they had ended up on the opposite side of the ship from the faulty attitude jets.

Space walking is exhausting. The constant need to anchor and brace oneself makes every action twice as strenuous as it would be in gravity. And so by the time they had reached the half way point around the revolving drum Smith and Prendergast were pouring sweat and needed a brief rest.

Once they had their breath back they set off again and within a few minutes had reached their objective, sweat pooling in their suits.

The problem was obvious. A micrometeoroid had ripped through the jet pack and it was discharging its gases intermittently. A short circuit was making the nozzles fire every few minutes causing the jolts that were being felt in the ship. Smith took out the small tool he'd been given and started, tentatively, to disconnect the four bolts which fastened the ruined jet pack to the skin of the vessel.

Prendergast began to pull apart the velcro cargo pocket on the leg of his suit where the replacement had been stored. As Smith released the third bolt from the pack, the jet sparked and fired, sending a violent jolt throughout the ship.

"What's going on out there?" called Captain Lauro through their helmet coms. "We just had a load of circuits go crazy down here. We got alarms everywhere."

"Sorry," said Smith, "looks like the electrics are shot. You may want to shut down all non-essentials 'til we get this done."

"Roger that," said Lauro. "Out."

"Bloody man," said Prendergast shaking his head in disgust. Smith placed the tool on the last bolt and as it came away there was a flash causing the broken jet pack and Prendergast, who was still struggling with his pocket and so not clutching a hand rail, to fly up and away from the ship.

"Grab your safety line, Percy," shouted Smith. "Drag yourself back in."

Prendergast, now twenty metres from the ship, started to pull the line, waiting for the slack to take up so he could haul himself back. Smith saw movement from the corner of his eye and as he turned to identify it his blood froze. The frayed and severed end of Percy's safety line was trailing along the hull of the craft. Instinctively, Smith made a grab for it but as his gloved hand reached out, the line rose up and away from the ship following Prendergast out into open space.

"Good Laws! What's happening?" came Percy's voice, tinged with panic.

Momentarily Smith was frozen but snapped out of it as he realised if he didn't act and act quickly Percy was lost. A second's further hesitation and he pushed with his legs as hard as he could, up and away from the ship. He only had one shot at the trajectory and his aim was true. He was on a direct course, traveling faster than Percy, closing in on the end of the safety line. He needed to reach

Prendergast's line before he came to the end of his own or Percy was a goner.

As the tether came within reach Smith stretched out an arm grabbing the nylon rope but Percy's momentum pulled it through his fingers. With a huge effort he reached out his other arm and grabbed the line further up winding it quickly around his gloved hand. He felt a wrench as Percy reached the full extent of the line but his grip remained firm. They both hung there for a few moments, trailing like bunting from the ship. Smith was breathing hard and sweat stung his eyes.

"Percy," he said eventually. "You okay?"

They were a few seconds silence before Prendergast answered.

"I may have soiled myself," came the reply.

Smith chuckled.

"Not in the least surprised, mate."

"I think you have just saved me from a rather hideous fate."

"Not out of the woods yet."

"No, we're not are we? Reel me in, there's a good chap."

Smith pulled Percy close and tied his safety line firmly to his belt. They then both heaved themselves back to the Fancy.

"What happened, Tony?"

"I haven't a clue. Let's change out these jets and get back inside."

With the pack exchanged they retraced their steps back to the airlock where all became clear. When the pack had blown, the airlock door had short-circuited, slamming it shut, severing Prendergast's line. Even more chillingly, it had severely damaged Smith's tether which was hanging by a few threads of nylon. If a couple more had been cut the whole thing would have snapped when Smith pushed himself away from the ship and both of them would even now be several miles from the ship at the beginning of a very, very, long journey. They looked at each other shakily, the full implications dawning.

They shook off the horror of this thought as the problem now was how to get back inside. Lauro was consulted and he pointed them to a manual handle which took forty turns to wind back the door. Exhausted and soaking they hauled themselves back into the ship.

*

There was a subtle change in the boys status for the rest of the trip. The food remained as unpalatable and the accommodation as Spartan but there was a shift in attitude from the crew. Traders were certainly tough nuts but they tended to be simple folk with, for the majority of the time, extremely dull lives. They ate the same food after all and their digs were no more salubrious than the boys'. They would watch replays of the adventure outside (as they came to call it) taken from the external cameras and would drop into Smith and Prendergast's cell in between shifts to talk to them about every detail of the escapade. Did they think they were done for? When did they realise the line was severed? Which was the most frightening part of the whole thing? All except Captain Lauro that is. He was even more distant than he had been before. Whether through guilt or a knowledge that he must hand them over soon to an unknown fate and didn't want to get any closer to the boys than he had to, Prendergast could not say, but he was sure he detected a softening in those hard eyes and a little edge off the bark when he did deign to speak to them.

*

It was several days later that Smith and Prendergast were brought up to the bridge and strapped into two seats behind the crew. As Lauro and his men busied themselves with their flight controls, Berk pressed a button and the heat shields rose up and back from the front space-screen of the Fancy revealing the blackness outside. They were flying backwards as they had been using the rear engines to decelerate for the last few days and now Captain Lauro reoriented the ship. As it spun on its axis the breathtaking blue disc of the planet below filled their view.

"By the Laws," said Prendergast. "Neptune!"

16. THE PHONY WAR

Major Fulbright arrived early for his daily briefing at security headquarters on Grand Bahama. In the hallway outside the briefing suite Colonel Schnell caught up with him and asked for a few words in private before they went in.

"How about giving up the name of your source, Major? We could move a lot faster on this if we could be sure of what we are dealing with."

The Major bristled. He'd known this pressure was coming and he'd guessed Colonel Schnell would be the one assigned to apply it.

"I do not wish to risk compromising..."

"Yes, yes we know all about the risk to your source."

"...until the situation has been contained."

"You know we've got people looking at every one you met during your junior career."

"That is the Colonel's prerogative."

Colonel Schnell gritted his teeth. A stubborn lifer this Fulbright and no mistake.

"How about I order you to give up the name or I bust you down to Second Lieutenant?"

"Again your prerogative but I think that would need due process. Sir."

Colonel Schnell pushed past him and into the briefing. The Major followed.

*

Agent Harris at Central Intelligence had taken an observation seat in the Remote Pilot Suite in the Surveillance and Scrutiny Wing. He settled back with the coffee he'd just been handed by one of his staff and the big screens overhead came on line. In the control booth Agent Tanaka came over the speakers to talk Harris through the procedure.

"The nearest facility we have to Neptune at the present time is the drone base on the uninhabited Saturnian moon of Mimas. The transmission time to the region is at present just under an hour. One hour fifty-six minutes ago we initiated a launch sequence for drones four and eight and we should have a visual of their progress coming in momentarily."

The room went quiet as the pictures from Mimas started to come in.

*

On the small ice and rock moon Mimas (at three hundred and ninety-six miles in diameter the smallest spherical moon in the solar system) embedded in the centre of the giant Herschel crater, beneath the huge crescent of Saturn with a splendid view of the great gas giant's rings (if there had been any human staff there to see them) is an aluminium sheet. At 0645 Earth time the sheet slid back to reveal a bay in which there were five spy drones of differing sizes. One after the other, drones four and eight rose out of the crater on a beam of ions and shot out of Mimas' weak gravitational clutches on their way to Neptune and a silent, stealthy vigil of the huge Centauran ship in orbit there.

*

Agent Laurel breezed through security at 0650 waving her CI pass and on to a reception committee waiting for her in the Gagarin's main reception area. She strode though, all purpose, and the committee fell in behind her.

"What do you have for me?" she demanded.

"Captain Burrows." This was Agent Lebedev, Laurel's liaison on the space station. "He hosted them at dinner two nights before their disappearance."

"Other guests that night?"

"Only one still remaining. A permanent resident. Lives here for the weightless therapy. I'm not sure how much help he will be."

They were at the interview room door and Agent Lebedev opened it. Two men were sitting in the room.

"Gentlemen," said Lebedev, "this is Agent Laurel."

"Hear, hear," said the older of the two men.

*

Kepler Moon Base in the Procellarum Sea was home to the 1st Spaceborne Division of the Earth Force (Lunar Defence), commanded by Squadron Leader Patrick Kincaid veteran of the Antarctic war and several riot control missions on Mars during the air shortages of '38.

He assembled his pilots at 0800 prompt and started the mission brief at 0801 precisely.

"Okay, guys. We have today moved to code red category ET. That means a threat from outside Earth or her Colonies. So now you know as much as I do. As of the end of this meeting I want two fighters in the black at all times and the rest of the squadron ready to scramble in three to five minutes. All leave is cancelled and I want maintenance staff pulling extra shifts.

"If anything comes within Lunar orbit of Earth without authorization in triplicate I want it vaporised immediately. Understood?"

The squadron yelled their understanding.

"Earth First. Dismissed."

*

Back on Grand Bahama, in the Earth Defence Command Centre, Colonel Walter Schnell walked through the control room and mounted a raised dais to the central command post. He looked out over the control stations, mainly empty now but for the three or four def con monitors who kept Earth's defences ticking over in times of peace. Schnell looked down at his command console where the Earth Laser Defence Array was represented in a graphic holo display, floating a few inches above his desk. There was Earth, a transparent blue globe rotating majestically and surrounding it, the one hundred and five red dots representing the laser satellites, which, working in harmony could take out any ship that had ever been built. Behind them in a slightly lower orbit, the fifty-eight green dots designating the plasma defence satellites. In times of attack these would generate a membrane around the Earth capable of repelling anything that could be thrown at it. This was Earth's mightiest technological achievement. To attack the Home Planet with defences like these would be like pointing a flame thrower at the Sun.

Colonel Schnell tapped his smart finger against the surface of the desk and the display reproduced itself inside his frontal lobe. There was his familiar toolbox and activation grid. He rolled that to one side of his cortex and pulled up the rota for the defence array controllers over the next month and with a tap of his finger highlighted his own name. He downloaded both screens to bio storage and logged out.

As he turned away from the console he heard a voice behind him.

"Hey Walter, what you up to?" This was Colonel Navarre.

Schnell turned to face his fellow officer, his hand going to his hip where he kept a quarter sized Volt 45 stun pistol.

"Putting in some extra time to impress the brass?" asked Navarre genially.

"Yeah, that's it. The greasy pole huh?"

"You said it. Wanna shut down, go get a beer?"

"I'll take a raincheck Carlos, think I'll have a little 'me time' down at the Gym."

17. LAST PIECES OF THE PUZZLE

As the Fancy moved into synchronous orbit with the Peacemaker, Smith and Prendergast were overawed by the sheer bulk of the Centauri Ship. Its sleek, matt, metallic skin was peppered with lights and a cloud of shuttles buzzed around its belly dropping to and rising from the planet's surface like a swarm of fruit flies round some vast rotting plantain. As they rose over the great ship's back, to the gaping mouth of shuttle bay one near the Peacemaker's tail, the giant cannon along the craft's spine came into view. Smith and Prendergast gawped at its mass and inwardly worried at its purpose. They turned to each other quizzically.

"Some sort of shuttle launching Maglev device?" suggested Prendergast optimistically.

"Launch, yeah. Launch device for sure," sniggered Captain Lauro evilly.

The Fancy dropped into the bowels of the ship and the great hanger doors closed behind them.

*

Once the Fancy had powered down and its centrifuge stilled, the crew was rendered weightless and yet outside in the shuttle bay everyone else was carrying on in normal gravity. It seemed to make no sense to Smith and Prendergast as their escorts, clinging to them like swimming instructors, floated them across the hangar.

There are solutions to weightlessness on spaceships other that the centrifugal one and the method chosen by the designers of the Peacemaker was to employ magnetism. An elegant solution in theory but a cumbersome one in practice for it required every loose item on the ship, from the food utensils, the handheld devices, the personal possessions of the crew, the stationary to anything if fact that was not screwed down, to be specially manufactured for the ship around a microfilament lattice of magnetic material. The crew's suits were made in this way so they felt as if they had weight when worn. Just having magnetic shoes doesn't cut it. Of course this method left some areas of life on the ship as primitive as the earliest space travelers had to endure. Liquids had to be contained, food eaten from sealed tubes, and as for ablutions...well, the less said about those the better. Needless to say a great deal of research and development had been spent on improving the zero-g bathroom because when one of those went wrong, everybody suffered.

Captain Lauro and Berk were to escort Smith and Prendergast aboard the Peacemaker while the other three crew members remained aboard the Fancy. After being kitted out with magnetic suits Lauro and his party were led to a lift which took them along and up into the body of the ship.

When the lift doors finally opened, one of the ship's officers escorted the Traders, Smith and Prendergast into a large chamber. It appeared to be the bridge of the spaceship, lined, as it was, with brightly lit control panels crewed by smartly uniformed men and women who busied themselves at their screens and consoles. As they came to a halt in the centre of this room, two of the ship's troopers armed with large laser rifles took Smith and Prendergast to one side. Rather roughly Prendergast thought. Smith obviously thought so too and let it be known in no uncertain terms. He pulled against his guard.

"Here, watch it, mate!" had scarcely left his lips when he was silenced by a hefty rifle butt to the back of the neck which sent him crashing to the floor. If Prendergast had any thoughts of complaint they were quickly banished.

The front of the bridge was a huge window upon space that looked out over Neptune, around which the ship was orbiting. Under any other circumstances Prendergast might have taken a moment to drink in the beauty this vantage point afforded and perhaps let out a low whistle at the sheer cosmic awesomeness of it all but right now he was concerned with an unknown future and the whereabouts of his own guard's rifle butt.

At the very prow, upon a small platform raised above the banks of computers stood Zoltac. After a moment, while the Traders shuffled awkwardly, he slowly turned and walked steadily down the three steps to the deck level to join Marshal Wittan. He paused for a moment watching the four visitors.

He was impressively sized, very tall for a Centauri, who, coming from Toliman, the large rocky Alpha Centauri planet with its strong gravity, were not usually given much to height. He was dressed in a one piece flight suit of deep purple and wore a helmet with a triangle of stars on it. The Centauri emblem. He eyed Smith and Prendergast steadily.

"Battle Cruiser Commander Zoltac. These are the men," said Marshal Wittan.

Zoltac nodded slightly and the hint of a smile settled on the lower half of his face, the upper half remaining steely, though he said nothing. Just as the silence was beginning to strain, Captain Lauro decided to break the ice.

"I think we agreed on one hundred thousand, Zoltac?"

The Cruiser Commander turned and looked at the Trader as if he had broken wind, noisily in a place of worship.

"*Commander* Zoltac to you," he corrected gently. Lauro bowed his head in an embarrassed fashion and Zoltac held out a purple gloved hand towards the Marshal who placed a Laser-Rifle in it.

It is widely considered good policy, when shooting someone with a laser rifle, actually a laser disruptor to give it its real name or Las-Dis 56E, its military title, to take a moment to aim the thing at the centre of the victim's body and let off a long firm blast. This causes a complete molecular chain reaction in the body matter resulting in utter disintegration. Total. Not a tooth or hair left. It's kinder to the victim *and* to those responsible for the clean up afterwards. Just letting off a couple of blasts from the hip willy-nilly is inefficient, cruel and messy but it was this last course that the Commander chose and within moments twenty-five percent of Lauro and Berk had disappeared leaving the remaining seventy-five writhing and spilling their contents onto the pristine deck.

There hadn't even been time for Prendergast to avert his eyes and he felt his gorge rise at the gruesome spectacle. The only thing that prevented him from losing his meagre lunch was the sound of Smith vomiting copiously into the air in front of him weightlessly pooling around the head of his guard, an indiscretion which was punished by the disgusted trooper landing another blow to the back of his neck which sent Smith crashing to the ground once more.

A cleaning detail came forward and began the mopping up process. Which involved vacuuming up Smith's vomit and the remaining three quarters of the Traders who had by now drifted off to their final rest.

Zoltac turned towards Smith and Prendergast and fixed them with an icy glare.

"Bring them before me, these sons of Sol!" which was the cue for another bout of ham-fisted manhandling on the part of the guards as they were pushed a few feet closer to Zoltac. Now Prendergast had never met a Battle Cruiser Commander before but instinct told him he was standing in front of one of the nastiest. A Battle Cruiser Commander totally devoid of the milk of human kindness and a stranger to mercy.

"They tell me you are the greatest Space Drive students your planet has ever produced. Is this true?"

Prendergast fidgeted slightly. It became clear Zoltac required an answer and judging by the fate Lauro and Berk had met he had better be darn careful how he chose his words.

"Well, you know, old chap...sir..." he stuttered, "...not really for me to say don't you know...modesty and all that...one doesn't want to blow one's own trumpet." He tittered girlishly and went red.

"You want to employ us?!" It was Smith rising from a pool of his own sick. "Well, why on Earth's sake didn't you say. You didn't have to go through all this malarkey. We're fielding offers now as it happens. You could've just sent in an application for consideration."

Now anyone who knows Percival Prendergast will tell you he is not the best judge of character and tends to think the best of everyone but even he could tell that his friend was not striking the right tone with the Commander and he was presently proved right when Smith's comments earned him the third rifle butt blow to the base of the skull in as many minutes. Smith writhed for a moment on the floor, clutching his bruised occiput before lifting his scarlet-face to Zoltac.

"Will you please...ask this...helmeted oaf!...to STOP DOING THAT!"

Zoltac made the slightest move forward, the first trace of emotion in his voice.

"And why would I do that?" he growled.

Smith lifted his hand, even he now realising that the soothing balm of mollification was the order of the day.

"Well, for a start," he breathed in a measured fashion, "I won't be much use to you, severely brain damaged and paralysed from the neck down!"

Zoltac held his ground for a moment then, seeming to penetrate the reasoning of this argument, flicked the fingers of his left hand almost imperceptibly and the troopers backed away. The Commander was still holding the gun which had dispatched Lauro and Berk in his other hand and he turned it over like a chef considering a truffle before handing the weapon back to Marshal Wittan and striding towards the door.

"Follow me," he instructed without a backwards glance. Aided by the barrel of a Las-Dis 56E to the small of their respective backs, Smith and Prendergast followed.

*

When the lift doors opened after their next elevator ride the boys found themselves beneath an expansive transparent roof at the very top of the ship and towering above that was The Cannon. Zoltac stood directly beneath the great weapon and held his hands aloft joyfully regarding its underbelly.

"Meet Omega, the greatest weapon in the four colonies." He turned to the boys and his face hardened.

"Which now, because of shoddy Earth technology is attached to a stranded space whale!" His voice rose hysterically alongside his anger. He strode towards Smith and Prendergast and the boys backed away slightly, only to be pushed back into place by the guards. Zoltac stood close before them, his face red and contorted with rage.

"I figure Earth owes me an engine and YOU," the boys flinched, "are going to build it for me."

Zoltac turned away and regarded Omega with glee.

"Then this ship will truly be the greatest force in the solar system and EARTH," he spat the word out making the boys flinch again, "once it has tasted the power of Omega, will be on its knees and at my mercy!"

Marshal Wittan coughed slightly. Zoltac spun round to him.

"Yes? You wish to speak?"

Wittan took a step forward.

"With all respect I believe the Commander meant to say at the Great Generalissimo's mercy."

Zoltac gritted his teeth and clenched a fist.

"Of course," he said presently, "I meant the Great Generalissimos' mercy. Through my offices as his direct representative here in the home system."

"Ah, I see."

"It's just that's a bit of a mouthful and I say *my* mercy for brevity's sake."

"I understand, Commander."

"Good. Alright with you if I carry on?"

"Yes. Sorry. It's just..."

"Yes, yes," said Zoltac impatiently, "I'm sure we're all impressed with your rigour, Marshal."

Zoltac turned back to Omega. He reached a hand out towards it and held it there for a moment.

"Where was I?" he asked irritably.

"The Earth will be at your mercy Commander..." said one of the guards helpfully.

"Yes, that's right."

"Though as Marshal Wittan pointed out."

"Yes, alright, I get it!" Zoltac pinched his fingers to the bridge of his nose and let out a long rasping sight. He struck his pose again.

"And should they choose to ignore my warnings I will destroy the Earth, city by city."

He spun round on the boys again.

"Build me the greatest engine in the solar system, nay, the four colonies and you will be handsomely rewarded. Refuse. Or fail me. And you will die."

With that he swept out of the room shouting back at the guards.

"Take them below!"

Smith's memory of this moment had Zoltac swishing a cloak as he turned but Prendergast swore he wasn't wearing one.

*

The guards took them on another elevator ride to an office on the ship's third level where they handed the boys over to Ratree from personnel. Ratree processed the forms which the guards had handed him and looked up to address the boys.

"This is Helot19. He will be looking after you."

Prendergast frowned. The man was making no sense.

"Who?" asked Prendergast.

"Where?" asked Smith simultaneously.

Ratree looked up and pointed behind them. The boys turned and clutched each other in fear at the apparition they beheld.

The robot which stood before Smith and Prendergast stretched to a full seven feet in height and was so physically impressive it made a steroid fueled tight head prop look like a jockey.

Helot19 turned and started to leave the office.

"Follow it," instructed Ratree.

*

They followed the monster along several hallways until Prendergast's sense of politeness got the better of him. He had often become unstuck by his impulse to make small talk.

"I suppose you are armed to the gunnels with high impact anti-personnel weapons and hard wired to blast us to quarks if we try anything?"

The robot stopped in its tracks and swung its head round to face them, its bright red eyes flickering as it processed Prendergast's statement. The boys had done a lot of grasping each other, flinching and backing away since they'd landed on the Peacemaker but this was the first time they'd done all three at once.

"Oh no," said Helot19 with a metallic chuckle, "that would be the task of a Zealot Helot. Order and Discipline. I am a Mellow Helot. Communication and Human Resources."

Its virtual mouth made a rictus smile and it swiveled its head back to face front and continued on its way.

Making another ascent in a lift they came upon a large observation deck with a view out over Neptune. Smith walked over to the window and summoned Prendergast to follow. There, its oxygen igniting within its glowing hull, drifting down towards the surface like burning embers of a campfire, was the broken body of the Fancy. The final resting place of its remaining crew.

"Come along," scolded Helot19. "Don't dawdle."

*

They reached the very base of the ship and passed the shuttle bays, eventually arriving at the detention level. Helot19 opened a door and the boys filed into their new quarters. Not exactly the very acme of luxury but no dungeon either. There was a single bed on either side of the room next to two small tables with a lamp. There was a small water closet in the corner and a rather nasty strip light ran across the ceiling. Helot19 turned a lock in the door as he closed it behind them.

"Good night," they heard him say as he trundled off, back down the hallway.

The boys sat on their beds and absorbed the events of the last hour.

"Of all the scumbags we've come across recently I'd have to say this Zoltac bloke is my least favourite," said Smith dryly. "And what about his big cannon. D'you think he's compensating for something?"

"Zoltac, Zoltac?" said Prendergast. "That name seems awfully familiar. I wonder if I know his people. Or perhaps I've read about him."

Smith was rifling through his pockets.

"I don't think so, mate."

"Really?"

"And truly. Here."

He had found what he was looking for and threw it over to Prendergast. It was a small cardboard box.

"Never go anywhere without them."

The box was a bright red colour with a jaunty blue stripe running diagonally across its face and the name Zoltac written along it in bold black lettering.

"Tummy pills?"

"The very same."

Prendergast's jaw dropped an inch or two.

"Good Laws. I wonder if he's aware of the fact that he shares his name with a patent acid-reflux remedy?"

"I sincerely doubt it mate and we are not going to be the ones to tell him."

Prendergast nodded judiciously.

"Prudent, old thing. Prudent.

"And anyhow. If he has his way, he is about to blow up every box of this stuff ever manufactured when he starts zapping the major capitals of Earth."

"Precisely. The bounder. Of course there is no question of us assisting him in his dastardly plan."

"No question. No question at all. But. Unless we want to have dirty great chunks of ourselves blown off by a laser rifle I seriously suggest we string him along for a while. At least until I can think of a way out of this."

Prendergast regarded his friend, hope reappearing in his eyes for the first time since their run in with Betty the Bounty Hunter a few short weeks before.

"*Can* you think of a way out of this?"

Smith's jaw set and he squared his shoulders a smidgeon.

"I'm working on it mate. I'm working on it."

*

Harfu and Captain Philips sat in the Commodore's quarters in grim conversation.

"So," said Harfu, "Zoltac has his engine designers. When their work is done he will be unstoppable."

"By the Earthmen, yes."

"Yes, but not from within." The Commodore rose. He walked to his desk and placed a hand on the antique communication tablet.

"Are you with me, Captain?"

"To stop these zealots from waging a war which no-one can win? I am with you all the way, Commodore."

18. WHAT DO YOU KNOW?

Agent Laurel sat at a table in the Dawnrise, Gagarin's Breakfast restaurant, opposite Mr Ek who was making short work of a plate of pickled herrings and a vat of coffee.

"Sill?" he offered and held a chunk of herring aloft on a fork for Laurel to taste. "The curry sauce is particularly tasty."

"No, I'm good. Thank you," she said. "So this woman offered to pay their bill you say."

"Yes, I think she was a poacher. Yes, I think she was."

"You think she persuaded them to join another company."

"I don't know but they never arrived at Saabre, by Jiminy. And now fingers are pointing at me, yes they are."

One of Agent Laurel's staff leant in close beside her.

"Ma'am."

"Excuse me Mr Ek." She rose from the table as Mr Ek shoveled another slice of fish in his mouth. The garlic sauce this time.

"She seems to be an Elizabeth Stanton. Left Gagarin the same day Smith and Prendergast did and look at this."

He held a photograph of Betty with a group of police officers in the Souk on Titan.

"This was taken by a SecCam in Shangri-La. Woman claiming to be Bethany Hunter, a Martian Sheriff transporting two prisoners to the penitentiary on Rhea. They were not expected there and Mars PD has no record of a sheriff Hunter."

"Good work," said Laurel. "Get me downside."

*

"My source tells me that two Earth engineers have arrived on the...Peacemaker, as the Diplomatist has now been named, but the source has not yet had access to them."

Major Fulbright sat and the President considered this for a moment.

"Sounds like your guys, Laurel," he said eventually. Agent Laurel nodded assent.

"The Peacemaker huh? The gun that tamed the West. By killing anything that got in the settlers' way, or so some would interpret it." President Olsen looked around the table.

"Harris."

"Sir?"

"I want men on every colony between here and Titan. Pick up this Stanton woman. Find out what she knows."

"Yessir!"

"General Drearing, I want a fleet on its way to Saturn today. If Zoltac makes a move that's where we will stop him. How soon can you get a battleship with them?"

"The ESS Puerto Rico is mission ready now sir, she can be there in just over a week."

"Do it. Dismissed."

*

Out in the corridor Colonel Schnell stopped Major Fulbright as the others hurried away.

"Major," he began, "tell me, you roomed with a man named Janken Harfu at West Point, did you not?"

Fulbright said nothing but held the Colonel's stare.

"Now a commodore in the Centauran fleet, and I believe, one of the delegation scheduled to meet our late President before her accident."

Major Fulbright stroked the corner of his mouth with his thumb and took a step closer to his superior.

"The Colonel knows my position on the security of sources."

Colonel Schnell shrugged and made a gesture of acquiescence.

"As you say."

He began to walk away then stopped and turned back to Fulbright.

"Oh, Major. Do you by any chance play poker?"

Fulbright frowned at the surprise question.

"Yes. Yes, I do," he replied.

"You shouldn't," said the Colonel. "You have a tell."

Colonel Schnell wiped the corner of his mouth with his thumb, smiled and walked away.

19. WE GOTTA GET OUT OF THIS PLACE

The next morning when Smith and Prendergast awoke, Helot19 was at their door.

"Good morning," he said cheerfully. "Let me show you where your bathrooms are located and then I can take you down to the canteen for breakfast before you get to work."

The showers were a rather enjoyable experience because once the boys took their suits off they were of course completely weightless. Floating around in jets of water which, once they'd lost their momentum, just floated in globules was rather fun and the vacuum tubes, after having extracted all the water, turned to air hoses which left Smith and Prendergast squeaky clean and bone dry.

In fact Prendergast was enjoying himself so much that he was slightly annoyed to find there was an absolute three minute maximum on shower time.

Once they had scrambled back into their suits Helot19 took them to the canteen where they enjoyed a hearty breakfast. All pseudo of course but very tasty and a reasonable facsimile of the food it was attempting to be except the eggs, which tasted like chicken flavoured custard.

"The facilities are very impressive I must say," said Smith chomping down his third slice of toast.

"Hmmm," said Prendergast.

"Oh, come on. We couldn't get you out of that shower. You loved it."

"Given the hardships we have had to endure thus far on this benighted trip, just about anything would be an improvement."

There was a twenty minute allowance for breakfast and when it was up they were promptly hustled from their seats by the robot and taken on another elevator ride to the factory level.

At the far end of this huge room they came to a door where they donned white suits, masks and head covers before being taken through to a dousing chamber where they were air filtered before being allowed into a clean room.

Once inside, Smith moved from work bench to work bench inspecting the equipment that had been placed at their disposal.

"By the Laws, Percy, this is great. It knocks anything in Edinburgh into a cocked hat! Look at these moulders. I've never seen anything like it. They certainly know how to set up a lab. Blooming efficient buggers. I knew that from the way that posse of cleaners cleared up the remains of poor Lauro and Berk yesterday. And look at that factory out there. Running like clockwork."

"Alright," said Percy, pulling off his mask, "let's scotch this right now."

"Scotch what?" asked Smith.

"The incipient love affair which is burgeoning between you and these vile fascists."

"Get out of it. I'm just saying. They have their faults but inefficiency and unpunctuality are not among them."

"Anthony! It may have escaped your notice but all this...efficiency and...punctuality are designed for the express purpose of blowing blooming great chunks out of our home planet and bringing it to its knees so we can become the unwilling subjects of that psycho Zoltac and his Generalissimo!"

Smith sadly put down a laser etcher he had been admiring.

"Well, there is that, I suppose," he said, grudgingly.

"I suggest your talents would be better employed coming up with a way out of this, than thinking up copy for the next Alpha Centauri holiday brochure!"

"Alright, alright," retorted Smith heatedly. "I was just admiring a well laid out lab. There's no need to bite me head off."

"I'm sorry but we are in a bit of a blooming bind here."

"Alright then, understood. As it happens I have been working on a plan and I think I have come up with one."

"Really?" said Prendergast, all ears.

"Yes," said Smith, "and over the next few days while I potter around here looking busy I have a little shopping list for you."

He pulled out a piece of paper with an inventory of items on it.

"Shopping list?" asked Prendergast. "What do you mean, old boy?"

"I need a quantum blade so I can trim down one of those neon lights in our cell, some polyurethane sheeting to line it, a small lens, two well engineered concave mirrors and a power source."

"What are you going to do with all that?"

"I, my little brain box, am going to build a laser!"

*

Commodore Harfu had called his officers together for their weekly briefing in a small conference room on level five. As the young men and women of the Alpha Regular Colonial Force took their seats Harfu started straight in.

"Officers of the Colonies. As you know there have been a great many changes to our mission in recent weeks and we now find ourselves under the authority of the Generalissimo's Elite Troopers. I am sure, like me, you do not find that a comfortable situation to be in."

There were murmurs of assent from the gathering.

"The Elite are a very different animal from the regular forces. There are certain principles they do not share with us. A sense of honour being the most obvious."

The murmurs became shouts.

"We believe when military actions are at hand they should be performed openly and honourably with fair warning, not under the flag of truce."

Harfu's approval rating was at an all time high in the room after this one. He quietened his officers down and asked them to return to their seats.

"I may therefore, in the coming days, ask you to perform actions that might at first seem alien to you..."

Lieutenant Jackson stood and voiced the feelings of his colleagues.

"We're right behind you, Commodore!"

The room was on its feet again but as the cheers died down a few heads turned. Coming through the door and down the aisle between the officer's seats were a squad of Marshal Wittan's armed guards. They walked directly to the front of the room where the senior officer confronted Harfu.

"Commodore Harfu," he said, "you are under arrest. You will accompany us please."

This was too much for Harfu's juniors. They clamoured around the officers but quickly retreated at the array of Las-Dis 56E's that were swiftly trained upon them. Only Hawkins stood her ground.

"By whose order?" she asked defiantly.

The officer stared at her for a moment. Then spoke.

"By order of Battle Cruiser Commander Zoltac. Come Commodore. That goes for you too, Captain Philips."

Philips visibly blanched at the mention of his name. Hawkins began a new protest but the officer turned on her.

"Perhaps you would like to join them Lieutenant," and he made the rank sound slightly indecent, "then you can explain to Commander Zoltac how heartily you disagree with his decision."

Hawkins took only a few seconds to back down. The Commodore spoke to her with quiet dignity.

"Take over, Hawkins."

He turned to his captors.

"Let's go, gentlemen."

*

Light fingeredness didn't come easily to Prendergast. He'd been brought up to be scrupulously honest by his rather puritan parents and so the idea of sneaking around the ship, pilfering anything that wasn't nailed down, went against the grain.

However, the circumstances were extraordinary and if Smith had a plan then Prendergast must do his bit. A case of step up to the plate and hang your principles.

The first and most difficult item on Smith's wish list was a Quantum Blade. The sharpest thing known to humanity. It is so called because the blade tapers down to, if not quite quark thickness, then as close as to make very little difference. A Quantum Blade is so keen that with virtually no pressure it will cut through anything. An unguarded blade will, if dropped on one's foot, go straight through the flesh and bone with an ease that would make a surgeon's scalpel look like a butter knife that's been used as a chisel. Their manufacture is extremely hazardous and their sale without a safety guard highly illegal, earning a penalty of five years hard labour on one of the smaller asteroids.

Prendergast knew that Gromyko, the project manager who had been assigned to them, had one and so he headed out into the factory, all the time wondering how to separate Gromyko from the prize.

Petty officer Dimitri Gromyko was a jobs-worth of the first water. With not a creative nor imaginative cell in his body he was never happier than when filling in a sheet, be it work, time or spread. He regarded the activities of the factory in general and of Smith and Prendergast in particular as an irritating disruption to the smooth running of middle-management.

As Prendergast approached the Petty officer's work bench, he noticed the Quantum Blade lying half hidden on a stack of invoices by an equipment manifest under books of dockets, chitties and counterfoils, all antiquated articles but essential components in the operation of Gromyko's world.

"Mr Prendergast," he said as he saw Percy approaching, barely able to keep the distain from his voice. "What can I do for you?"

"Ah." Prendergast hadn't thought his plan through this far yet and couldn't for the life of him think of anything that Gromyko *could* do for him.

"Yes. What can you do for me? Exactly."

Prendergast nodded. Gromyko waited a second then thought he would hurry things along a little.

"Yes," he said pointedly, "what can I do for you?"

"What indeed," said Prendergast with a chuckle, "glad you asked me."

Gromyko sighed. With his every action Prendergast confirmed his belief that these boffin types were a waste of space-time. Suddenly Percy had an inspiration and, his eyes lighting up, he clicked his fingers.

"Coffee. Could you get me a cup of coffee?"

Gromyko looked appalled. Fetch it yourself was going through his mind but he had been specifically instructed to lend every assistance to the Earthmen.

"Can't you get your Helot to fetch it?"

"Oh no," said Prendergast and he leaned in close to Gromyko who shied a little.

"Unhygienic blighter. Think he puts his fingers in the cup. Last few have tasted metallic." The fact that all drink containers were sealed on the ship escaped Prendergast for the moment but fortunately Gromyko was so concerned with his dignity he missed the flaw in Percy's story too.

"Well," said Gromyko, "not really in my remit. Refreshments."

"Oh very well, I'll get it myself," said Prendergast regretfully. "I suppose Commander...Cruiser...Zoltac can wait for those figures he asked for immediately."

"No, no, no," said Gromyko hastily. "I didn't say I wouldn't. How do you take it?"

"De-caf, skinny with two sweeteners please."

The petty officer placed a form in front of him and held out a pen.

"What's this?" asked Prendergast.

"Requisition voucher."

"For a cup of coffee?"

"Well, I don't want it coming out of the manufacturing budget do I? You're research and development. Stands to reason."

Prendergast wrote 'cup of coffee' on the form and was about to hand it back.

"Better put down the milk requirement," said Gromyko and Prendergast scribbled again.

"And the sweeteners. And mention that it's de-caf, it's slightly cheaper."

Prendergast handed the form back to Gromyko who ripped off the bottom pink sheet and handed it to Percy, before heading off to the snack bar. Prendergast watched him 'til he turned the corner then, checking that the others in the factory were busy with their tasks, he grabbed the Quantum Blade. He pocketed it and cantered away tingling with the thrill of his first heist.

*

When Zoltac had taken control of the ship he'd had one of its gymnasiums luxuriously refurbished as his office and cabin commanding a lovely view over Neptune from the panorama window which the cross-trainers used to enjoy. He had it done out in the Tiki style so popular on his home planet and while most believed it to look like a sleazy dive bar, anyone who visited was at pains to complement the decor and Zoltac's impeccable taste.

It was into this office that the Commodore and his Captain were brought. Zoltac was seated behind a huge macrocarpian desk with Marshal Wittan at his shoulder. The guards placed Harfu and Philips before them and took a step back, their guns kept squarely pointed at the prisoner's backs.

Zoltac held out a hand and Wittan placed Harfu's antediluvian communication tablet in it.

"Is there anything you wish to tell me about this?" he asked.

"No," came Harfu's curt reply.

"No? No mitigation, no plea for mercy? No high ideal you would cite as reason for becoming a traitor to your planet, your colony and your race?"

Harfu and Philips kept silent and stared, eschewing eye contact with the Commander.

Zoltac handed the tablet back to Wittan.

"Very well." Zoltac stood before them and placed his fists on the desk.

"As your prosecutor I accuse you of high-treason, as your defence I offer none, as your jury I find you guilty and as your judge I sentence you to death. At 1200 hours you will be keelhauled. Take them down and prepare them."

The guards dragged the prisoners away and Wittan held out the tablet.

"Shall I destroy this?" he asked.

"No. We will keep that particular line of communication open. It may prove useful to us."

*

The level four bathrooms were usually empty midmorning so Prendergast chose these for his next raid. The shaving mirrors were of a good quality but they were firmly attached and Prendergast was having the devil of a time wrenching one from the wall. He had wanted to use the Quantum Blade on his burglary trips as this would have made things so much easier but Smith had insisted he didn't want anyone connecting the thefts. Prendergast presumed he knew what he was talking about as back in Edinburgh Smith would get through two detective novels a week. Prendergast had never read anything like that, preferring the love poetry of the Eridani Romantic School.

Finally the mirror came away, mounting and all, bringing a large chunk of the wall covering with it. He was trying to twist the fixture off the back of the mirror, so he could hide it about his person, when the speaker let out a high pitched note, as it always did before an announcement, startling Prendergast and making his life flash before him.

"All ship's personnel proceed to the lower dock immediately."

With a mighty effort Prendergast snapped the arm from the back of the mirror, stuffed it down his trousers and made his way out of the bathroom smoothing his hair as he went.

*

Down in the lower dock, the entire crew of the Peacemaker were gathered. Zoltac and Wittan strode onto a platform at the head of the hanger. Above their heads were three giant screens.

Zoltac raised his hands and the crew became silent.

"It pains me to have to inform you that we have been harbouring traitors on this ship. Spies, quislings, fifth columnists revealing our every move to the men of Earth. I am happier to report that they have been uncovered and I invite you to join me in witnessing their reward."

The middle screen above his head burst into life and there were Harfu and Philips, in nonmagnetic space suits, hands manacled, floating in the airlock below the feet of the assembled crew. They were attached to the ship with lines made of protein silk cased in a diamond nano-lattice, the strongest, most flexible material known in the colonies.

"Have you anything to say before your punishment, Commodore? Captain?"

"Long thrive Alpha," shouted Harfu.

"About to be lowered to your doom and suddenly a patriot. How unsurprising."

"You will pay, Zoltac," yelled Captain Philips.

"Don't think so," said Zoltac. "Carry out the sentence."

Unseen hands started the keelhauling procedure beginning with the opening of the airlock doors revealing the broiling atmosphere of Neptune below. A brief pause and jet packs on the prisoners backs fired sending them down towards the planet.

As their orbits shrank, their trajectories brought them closer to the tops of Neptune's clouds and dragged them on their lines at massive speed through the Hydrogen and Helium atmosphere. It took twenty minutes before they started to leave the vacuum of space. It was then Zoltac made his cruelest move.

The two outer screens lit up and there were the faces of Harfu and Philips, live from inside their helmets. The middle screen zoomed in closer to the two men now miles below and their space suits had begun to glow as the friction sent the temperature of the outer Kevlar skin soaring.

"Slowly now," gloated Zoltac, "don't let out the line too quickly."

As Harfu and Philip's features began to contort with the heat, Smith and Prendergast looked away, unable to watch. The men's helmets began to fill with smoke as their suits started to burn. On the other side of the hangar Hawkins, Ratree and Jackson watched stoically and prayed that the suits would give way soon, ending the men's agonies swiftly before the fire consumed them. Which they eventually did, though not before the flames began lap at the men's faces.

Somberly the entire ship's compliment dismissed.

*

It was generally agreed that Commodore Harfu and Captain Philips had died bravely. In the following days the mood aboard the Peacemaker was bleak and here and there, dark murmurings about their execution could be heard. Murder more like, was a common theme and those who knew them well, knew them to be no traitors.

*

On the observation deck, Prendergast had spotted a telescope pointed out towards Neptune. It reminded him of ones he had seen along the seafront at Brighton when on holiday as a child and the fond memory made it all the more difficult for him to reduce this elegant instrument to scrap in an attempt to retrieve one of its lenses. As he stood over the wreckage of the telescope, panting slightly from the exertion, two maintenance workers came up beside him and, taking in the debris at his feet turned to Prendergast with a look of reproach but Percy, becoming adept in the ways of criminality, batted not an eyelid.

"Some people," he said. "They just spoil it for the rest don't they?"

He sauntered off casually towards the lift adding a touch of disgusted tutting and boarded an elevator to the factory.

*

He hadn't been down in the factory for a while, having had a frustrating time trying to get another shaving mirror from the bathrooms on level six. He had been interrupted by a wave of softball teams boisterously showering after their matches. He couldn't stand sporty types at the best of times but when they kept disrupting his larcenous activities, with their wet towel slapping and their bawdy songs, they became positively tiresome. He had been unaware that it *was* the ship's softball finals. He'd actually been oblivious to the fact that there was such a thing as a Peacemaker Softball League at all. Added to that a day wasted in the pursuit of high grade waste disposal bags and he had not put his nose into the factory for a day or two.

When he did eventually wander down he was appalled by what he saw. In the centre of the room, rising from the factory floor was the unmistakable skeleton of a full sized HENRIE. Prendergast strode, suited up, towards the clean room and as he came through the door he was immediately accosted by Helot19.

"Ah, Mr Prendergast, I am very pleased to see you. I have been having the most invigorating conversations with Mr Smith about your wonderful engine. Absolutely fascinating I must say and I would be most pleased to pick your brains about some of the theory behind it."

"I'd be glad to, Nineteen, but could I just have a moment alone with Mr Smth."

"Of course, Mr Prendergast, please don't let me get in the way of your excellent work," and he rolled off into the factory.

"Thanks for that, Percy," said Smith shaking his head. "He's been driving me mental. I can't pick up a screw without him asking me where I'm going to put it. I've nearly told him a couple of times," he chuckled scatologically.

"Anthony, what in the Laws name do you think you are doing?"

"What d'you mean?"

"You are building HENRIE."

"Of course I'm building HENRIE."

"You can't give this...this...doomsday ship an engine. They want to blow up Earth with it. Bit by bit."

Smith lowered his voice conspiratorially and spoke, hardly moving his lips.

"I am fully aware of the intentions of this bunch of psychos. I'm not going to finish it you fool. But Zoltac's eyes are everywhere. I've got to look like I'm doing something."

Prendergast made a moue and sniffed.

"Well, just make sure you don't finish it. Try to keep in your head that this is the enemy we are dealing with here."

"Look, never mind all that. Have you got all the stuff?"

"Yes, and it's aged me ten years getting it."

"Right. We make our move tonight. Oh. Watch out. The quiz master's coming back."

Helot19 came through the door, a look of concern on his virtual face.

"Gentlemen, might I suggest you lock up with particular care this evening. I am getting disturbing reports of an outbreak of wanton vandalism around the ship and we wouldn't want the miscreants getting their hands on your delicate machinery."

"Indeed we wouldn't," said Smith throwing a wry grin at Percy.

The screen over Smith's work bench came on with a small fanfare and Zoltac's face was glowering at them. Prendergast clutched his chest, his nerves in tatters.

"I see you have started to build my engine. This is good," boomed Zoltac over the speakers.

"Yes, indeed, we've made quite a start," Smith said, taking the jovial approach.

"Silence!" Zoltac boomed again and the speakers crackled.

"Work harder. Work faster!" He leaned towards the lens, his face distorting and he struck Prendergast as looking like a fish. He giggled impulsively then put his hands over his mouth in terror.

"Did you laugh?" asked Zoltac his eyes blazing.

"Only with enthusiasm, sir!" blurted Prendergast.

"Silence!" yelled Zoltac.

Zoltac continued to stare down at them then sat back in his seat losing the piscine appearance. Prendergast breathed a sigh of relief and prayed he wouldn't lean forward again.

"Good. I require your enthusiasm!"

For some reason Smith saluted. Prendergast looked at him agog. Then gave a little halfhearted one himself.

"Do I have your enthusiasm?"

"Oh yes, sir, one hundred per—"

"Silence!" Zoltac saw Helot19 at the door.

"Helot!" he bellowed. The robot seemed to come to attention but wisely kept silent.

"Give them every assistance. I want that engine." He spoke this last sentence in a rather robotic manner himself which seemed to please Helot19.

The screen went blank. The boys stood there staring at it. Prendergast saluted again rather redundantly as Zoltac was gone. Finally Smith relaxed and turned to his friend.

"What is that with the asking questions then telling you to shut up?"

"I know," quavered Prendergast.

"Unbelievable." Smith shook his head and started to clear his desk for the day.

Helot19 came forward and placed a metallic arm on Percy's shoulder making him jump.

"Oh, please don't do that, Nineteen. My nerves are shot."

"I do beg your pardon Mr Prendergast but may I enquire, while I am accompanying you back to your room perhaps I could trouble you to outline some of the variational calculus you have used to..."

"Well, I have had to rather reinvent some of the maths to deal with the complex infinitesimals involved."

"How intriguing." Then the two of them wandered off like a pair of old professors on a warm summer evening in the ivy covered quad of one of the better universities.

20. THE WHITE CLIFFS OF EUROPA

Betty was stuck on Titan. With no money and no Smith and Prendergast she was a little at a loss to know what her immediate course of action should be. Eventually she turned to Sergeant Sortras. She figured he owed her one for letting the boys escape in the first place so she was calling the debt in. It happened that Sortras had, in his cells, a career criminal called Blair who was wanted on Europa for squid rustling. The price on his head was decent and after deleting a few custody records Sortras handed him over to Betty who set off for Jupiter's sixth moon to claim her bond.

The trip was uneventful, especially for Blair. He proved to be more of a handful than the boys had been and spent the journey handcuffed and gagged in the store room with just two tubular meals a day for company.

*

Europa was an ice world. Its inhabitants lived under the ice sheet in the moon wide ocean which lies beneath. It had many submarine colonies and as Betty navigated the ship towards the satellite's surface she chose Marius Harbour as her point of entry.

The harbour consisted of a large concrete building set into the side of an ice cliff, which housed ship sized lifts that shuttled visiting craft to and from the settlements below.

Once Blair had been handed over to the nearest bail office and the cash safely tucked into her money belt, Betty set out to find some digs for the night, somewhere she could shower, get a good hot meal and consider her next move.

The Trench restaurant in Marius' Seaview hotel was one of the best on Europa. Sporting a one hundred and eighty degree scenic window, huge arc lights on the outer wall illuminated the sea making the place a popular haunt for squid watching. The Giant Europan Squid, until recently so harried by Blair, is Europa's largest animal. At twenty-five feet a real monster. It is tripedal with two long tentacles and a shorter one under its forward facing mouth with a spookily human hand at the end. Intelligent, affectionate animals they are also fierce hunters who, until the arrival of man were the undisputed masters of their world. Brought to near extinction by the early settlers they were now protected and numbers were climbing, according to the plaque below the observation window.

As Betty tucked into her *gigot d'agneau aux champignon verte*, washed down with a half bottle of Californian President's Reserve from the San Simeon valley, she was treated to a family of squid playing in the water outside. The younger animals nuzzled the glass inquisitively and Betty became rapt as she looked deep into the eye of one of the smallest. Its gaze, Betty was sure, belonged to a creature of reason and perception; it seemed as fascinated by her as she was by it, and she wondered how man could mistreat and destroy these creatures so casually.

She raised a hand to the window and the baby cephalopod turned and scuttled away in to the dark deep water. The rest of the family followed and Betty watched until all that was left was a shadow image of their long sleek bodies which played on her retina 'til it slowly faded.

Behind her in the plaza outside the hotel there seemed to be a bit of a commotion going on and she caught sight of a troop of soldiers, mingling with the evening promenaders, stopping the occasional individual for brief questioning. She recognised their insignia as Earth Defence and uplinked to a police channel to see what it might be about. As she scrolled down a list of bulletins with her smart finger gliding along her thumb, she froze and the fork dropped from her other hand. There was a picture of her next to images of Smith and Prendergast. She was wanted for questioning in relation to the boys disappearance and that did not sound good. Great, she thought with irony, the hunter becomes the hunted. Outside, two of the troopers peeled off and wandered through the restaurant. A dozen or so diners were scattered around the white-clothed tables. One of the Troopers stood on a fork and picked it up. There was no-one at the table it lay beside, so the trooper replaced the fork next to a half eaten lamb dish and an unfinished bottle of red wine. It seemed this particular diner had lost their appetite.

*

Betty determined it would be unsafe to go back to the hotel so decided to abandon the few belongings she had left there. She had all her money and the clothes she stood in and that was good enough. Picking her way through the back streets was long and time consuming. Every time she saw a patrol she had to double back and find a new route. She improvised a plan, such as it was, on the way back to Marius Harbour. First thing was to get off Europa. Second, keep ahead of the Earth soldiers; she'd been lucky so far and she would need more luck to get back to the Zelda but that luck would not hold out indefinitely. Luck never did. After that she knew she must get Smith and Prendergast back. They would be her only bargaining chip if the water she was in proved to be as hot as she suspected. But for now; the Zelda.

She'd guessed the harbour would be crawling with troops and she was right. They had the place locked down.

During the course of her career, moving through the grey areas on the fringes of the law she had learned a thing or two. One of the most important being this: if you were in a tight spot, sometimes you had to put your trust in someone you hardly knew. When that time came you had better hope that your instincts, for who was a stand up guy and who was a louse, were acutely honed.

The person she chose was the engineer who had helped her dock on arrival. He seemed a nice guy and they'd bantered a little while he signed her off. He struck her as his own man and not the type to have too much love for authority. She guessed she was about to find out if her quick sketch of his character was accurate. If he was still on duty that was.

She made her way along the perimeter fence to the back of the engineer's huts and crouched down watching the engineers come and go from the ships as they descended from the surface. There he was coming back after checking in another ship. Her first stroke of luck. What was his name? Come on this is important, she scolded herself. Barry? Gary? Larry! That was it. Good ole Larry. I hope you are a gentleman, full of old fashioned chivalry, the type that would never do a lady a disservice.

"Hey, Larry," she shouted in a stage whisper through the fence. Larry looked around but kept walking.

"Larry, hey. Over here."

Larry spotted her. He scrunched his eyes trying to identify this person calling him through a fence. As he got closer he seemed to recognise her and smiled broadly.

"Miss Stanton? Is that you? The bail bond lady?"

"Yeah. I could use a little help here?"

"What can I do for you?" he seemed to get a touch wary and his smile faded. Not good.

"All these soldiers after *you*?"

"Naaah!" she laughed, "soldiers I could handle. It's worse. A jealous wife."

"Now what you been up to, little lady?" he asked, his smile returning.

"Absolutely nothing I swear but this dame's got it in her head I been cheating with her husband and she won't listen to reason and that I could handle too but turns out...she got a brother who's some big cheese in the police and I'm thinking I'd better make like an atom and split."

She pulled out a wad of cash and added her most seductive look for good measure.

"I'd be grateful if you could get me back to my ship with the minimum of fuss." She smiled prettily but her pulse raced. Come on, Larry, she thought, be the man I hope you are.

"Don't you just hate those high-ups who abuse their position?" Larry said shaking his head. "That's this colony all over. The high-ups get everything they want cos...well, cos they're high-ups and the rest of us don't know no-one and don't get nothing. Why I been in this job now twelve years and I watched people who joined the company long after me get the good promotions cos their papa knows the chairman or their sister's married to a manager. It riles me up."

Now while Betty was pleased Larry felt the way he did, she could have done with a little less backstory of how he'd come by this philosophy.

"So will you help me, Larry?" she said a little too insistently.

Larry paused and seemed to weigh the situation in his mind.

"I surely will," he said finally, a determined look on his face. "Join me at the gate a few yards down the fence there."

When she got to the gate Larry was waiting with an engineers' overall and a fume mask.

"Put these on and follow me."

He too pulled on a mask and when Betty was ready he indicated for her to follow and they started out towards the surface lifts. She could hear Larry talking on his intercom.

"Millie, pull me out the Zelda onto platform three would you, darlin'? I got a safety check needs expediting at the earliest. We may have a haz-spill."

As they got further towards the lifts Betty could see the nose of the Zelda emerging from a hanger and onto a vessel elevator.

"Fire her up for immediate diagnostics then high tail out of there—this could be a code red."

Betty saw the engines fire and a person, Millie, she presumed, climb out of the ship and run towards the safety of the loading bay. Just then two heavily armed soldiers began to approach and called to them.

"Hey, you two," one of the soldiers called.

"Keep walking," said Larry quietly.

"Hey! You two!"

"Soldier," Larry shouted, "you might wanna put that gun down. We got a possible fuel spillage and I don't wanna go up like a firecracker here."

"We got orders to stop..." the soldier continued less certainly.

"And you might wanna step behind the yellow safety line," Larry continued, "we have substances in this area known to the colony of Europa to cause birth defects, sterility and cancer of the testicular area."

The soldiers were now backing away hesitantly unsure of their next action.

"If you could make sure no one comes near the elevators you would be doing a great service, I thank you."

If there's one thing a soldier likes, it's a clear set of instructions and the chance to shove people about, particularly when the health of their wedding tackle is at stake, so the solders turned and ran back behind the yellow line, herding harbour workers with their rifles.

"Come on, nothing to see here, clear the area," they ordered.

As they got to the Zelda, Betty climbed aboard while Larry stayed at the hatch keeping watch.

"Thank you, Larry," she said and held out the money again.

Larry ignored the bundle of notes and looked Betty straight in the eye.

"I think you're gonna need every dime you have, ma'am. Let me give you this instead."

He handed her a folded leaf of paper and closed the hatch. As the Zelda started to rise towards the surface Betty opened the sheet. On it was a photograph of her face. Below it was written; Wanted for questioning. Reward for information.

Betty smiled. I guess I'm still a pretty good judge of character after all, she thought.

21. PLOUGHSHARES INTO SWORDS

"You can really build a laser with all this?" asked Prendergast sifting through the junk spread out on Smith's bed.

"Of course I can," said Smith indignantly.

"Strong enough to cut through that door?"

Smith was lining the neon tube with the polyvinyl sheeting. He put it down and stared at Prendergast incredulously.

"Cut through the door? Have you any idea the power and precision I'd need to build a laser like that? Of course I'm not going to cut through the door. This wouldn't cut through an under-baked sponge cake."

"Then what are we doing?"

"What are *we* doing? Well, *you* are asking silly questions. Whereas *I* am building a one-shot laser gun that will fire a weak beam at the sensor on that door and trigger the opening mechanism."

Prendergast looked from the tube to the door.

"Great Spot. That's brilliant. And you just have to plug it into the lamp?"

Smith sighed and dropped his head.

"Oh Percy, Percy, Percy. You know, you theoretical types can be extremely dense when it comes to everyday stuff. A lamp socket wouldn't power a laser, however weak. No, I'm going to have to go into the walls with the quantum blade and connect it directly to the power grid that runs through the ship. Now shut up and let me build the thing!"

An hour later it was complete. A tad Heath Robinson but as Smith said it wasn't built for looks.

It had a one-off job to do and then it could retire gracefully. It had to be handled with great caution. Smith had trimmed down the concave mirrors and their alignment, in juxtaposition with the lens, was micro-millimeter crucial. There was a small hole in the wall where the Boron filament conductivity grid could be seen.

"Okay," asked Prendergast, "what now?"

"Right," said Smith rolling up his sleeves, "I want you to kneel down between the beds. I'll place the Scalpel on your shoulder..."

"The what?" asked Prendergast.

"The Scalpel. Just thought I ought to give the laser a name, you know."

"Ah, very apt."

"Thank you. I will place it on your shoulder and you will aim it at the sensor. I shall attach this wire to the grid and from that moment you have just over two seconds, as long as it takes to strip the surface electrons from the bin bag lining, to get a good bullseye on the sensor. Okay?"

"So no pressure then?"

"Two seconds is plenty of time if you keep your nerve and don't think about it."

"Alright, old chap. I am as ready as I will ever be."

"Good lad," said Smith grimly. "Here we go!"

He placed the Scalpel delicately on Prendergast's shoulder and let him line it up. He pulled on a large rubber glove which he'd borrowed from the lab and held the wire in it, poised over the hole in the wall.

"Okay, Percy. On the count of three."

"Count of three it is, Tony."

Prendergast steadied himself and Smith grabbed the wire a little tighter.

"One..."

A drop of sweat formed over Prendergast's eyebrow...

"...two..."

...it ran down his temple and onto his cheek...

"...THREE!"

Smith rammed the wire into the hole and onto the Boron grid.

Now at this point, what Smith had imagined would happen was that the electrons from the polyvinyl would be lasered into a cold weak stream and trigger the door, in much the manner he had outlined to Prendergast.

He had, however, seriously underestimated the power of the ship's grid, with the result that the laser acted as a kind of lightening rod sending a massive bolt of energy in the door's direction, reducing the Scalpel to powder and sending Smith and Prendergast flying across the room.

As the smoke and dust began to clear, Smith rose to a sitting position and saw that the door to the cell and much of the surrounding wall had gone. He brushed himself off while Prendergast staggered shakily to his feet, tottered forward and popped his head through the hole where the door had been, giving a quick glance up and down the corridor.

"Anyone around?" asked Smith.

"Beg pardon?"

Prendergast had been next to the laser when it had gone off and taken the brunt of the blast on his left eardrum. He could see Smith's lips moving but the only sound he could make out was that of a man gargling in a rainstorm.

"Is the coast clear?"

"Say again."

"Someone might have heard that bang."

"I can't hear you."

"Oh, never mind. Get out of my way."

Smith pushed in front of him, did his own check in both directions and seeing nothing and no-one eased out into the corridor.

"Come on," he hissed over his shoulder.

"Eh?"

Smith grabbed Prendergast by the arm and dragged him in tow as he slid along the wall towards the shuttle bay. At the end of the corridor Smith flattened Prendergast close to the wall and craned his neck around the corner. He had a clear view of the shuttle ports some thirty meters ahead. He pulled back and pressed himself against the wall next to Prendergast.

"Okay. There's obviously no-one around on this level at this time of night. Lucky. So let's see if we can fire up a..."

"Huh?" asked Prendergast.

"Oh, for..."

He grabbed hold of Prendergast's lapel and, pulling him away from the wall, dragged him round the corner.

Straight into Helot19.

"Ah," said Smith, "there you are. Helot. Nineteen."

"Good evening, Mr Smith. Mr Prendergast," said the robot in his even, mellow tone. "What are you doing out of your room?"

"Good question, mate. We...are going...for a walk."

"I'm sorry but I don't think that's encouraged."

"No? But it isn't not allowed, is it?"

"On the contrary. I think it *is* not allowed. Or they wouldn't lock you in, would they? Interesting. How *did* you get out?"

Smith could see he needed to take a firm grip of this conversation.

"Don't change the subject. We want to go for a walk. And I distinctly heard Mr Zoltac..."

"Battle Cruiser Commander Zoltac..."

"Battleship Commander...Cruiser...I heard him specifically say, you were to help us in every way."

"'Give you every assistance', were his actual words. I can play you back the transcripts if there is any doubt in your mind."

"No, that's right. Give us every assistance and that's what we want from you now."

Helot19's face contracted in an approximation of a frown.

"I think he was referring solely to your engineering activities."

"Oh dear, oh dear, Nineteen," said Smith sadly, shaking his head. "I am surprised at you."

"Why?" asked the robot.

"The Commander didn't qualify the assistance you should give us in any way."

"No, but..."

"You, Nineteen, are making an assumption."

"Yes, but..."

"Very human." And his disappointment was palpable.

"Is it?"

"Oh yes. Assumptions are usually at the root of all human being's worst cock-ups."

"Yes, you're right. I've noticed that before."

"There you are, you see?"

The robot's expression moved jumpily to one roughly resembling understanding.

"So. What assistance do you require?" he asked, back to his cheerful self.

Smith licked his lips.

"Well, as I said, we want to take a walk and then maybe...go mining."

"You want to go mining?"

"Yes. We want to go for a walk and do a bit of mining. Don't we, Percy?"

Prendergast seemed to come out of a deep reverie.

"Did you say something?"

Helot19 cocked his head slightly.

"Is he alright?"

"Yes, he's fine. Now what about this spot of mining we want to do then?"

"What do you want to mine for at this time of night?"

"Is it this time of night?" asked Smith.

"Well, it's this time of night...ship's time, "replied the robot a little bemused.

"Ah, well there you are you see. We've been here, there and everywhere the last few weeks. I can't speak for Percy but my body clock's all over the place. As far as I'm concerned it's mid to late morning yesterday."

"I see," said Helot19 carefully, though he didn't really, "but I still need to know what you want to mine for?"

"What for? You want to know what we want to mine for?"

"Yes. That's what I said."

Smith shook his head for a moment and looked around letting out a long sigh and waving his hands in as casual a manner as he could muster.

"Gold."

The robot's face reverted to its previously confused frown.

"Gold? Apart from the fact there is no gold on Neptune..."

But they say there is gold...in them there...Triton hills."

Triton was Neptune's largest moon but as no-one had ever been there this was pure bluff. To say nothing of moot.

"Well, that's news to me. In any case what do you want gold for?"

"A present."

The robot cocked his head to one side again.

"A present?"

"That's right."

"Who for?"

"Who for!?" exclaimed Smith incredulously. "Who for?!!?"

"Yes."

Smith let out a longer, louder, more aspirated sigh and spread his arms wide.

"Cruising...Commander Zoltac, that's who for."

Helot19 straightened his head and looked at Smith long and hard.

"What sort of present?"

"A big one. We are going to mine some gold...and...strike him a commemorative medal!"

"Oh," said the robot, "he likes medals. He usually wears a chestful at dinner."

"Well. There you are then."

The robot settled himself thoughtfully and looked upon Smith in a new light.

"How considerate you are. Especially after he was so stern with you earlier."

"Well, you know. Rough with the smooth, mate, there's good and bad in everyone."

"So they tell me."

Helot19 straightened up as he seemed to come to a decision.

"Very well. Come with me."

He headed back up the corridor. Smith put a restraining hand on his shoulder.

"Where are you going? The shuttles are the other way."

"To ask Battle Cruiser Commander Zoltac if it's alright."

Smith's grip on the robot's shoulder tightened.

"No, no, no, no, no. You can't do that."

"Why not?"

"Because it's a surprise."

Helot19 seemed to freeze for a moment, apparently consulting some inner manual on human behaviour, then brightened considerably as understanding dawned.

"Surprise present, usually birthdays. Is it his birthday?"

"Yes. Yes it is."

"How old is he?"

Smith ran a frustrated hand across his face.

"He's forty-two, now can we please press on?"

"Yes, we can," said Helot19 who rose several inches, rotated 360 degrees and set off towards the mining shuttles.

"How exciting," he chuckled metallically.

*

Helot19 chose shuttle six for their trip and placed his key digit, the robotic equivalent of a smart finger, onto the sensor by the hatch which slid open.

The shuttles were snug for two average sized people like Smith and Prendergast. Add a seven foot robot into the mix and cat swinging was right out.

"Well," Smith said trying to find a safe place for his left foot, "can you fly this?"

"Of course," answered Helot19, "there are many environments too hostile to risk a human life so all Helots are accomplished pilots."

"Well, off you go then, now's as good a time as any."

"Very well," said the robot, "if I could just ask Mr Prendergast to remove his head from the flight control panel, I will initiate separation."

Before Percy could move or Helot19 initiate anything, the hatch slid open unexpectedly and there outside, silhouetted against the shuttle bay's night lights, were three ship's officers.

Smith and Prendergast froze. Only Helot19 seemed unperturbed.

"Good evening, officers," he greeted them politely, "I wonder if you would mind closing that hatch? I am about to initiate..."

"Shut up." It was Lieutenant Ratree.

"Very well."

One of the other officers came forward and leant into the crowded shuttle, the panel display lighting her face, for it was Hawkins.

"What in the name of nebulae have you done to your room?" she asked.

Prendergast had got himself twisted at the back of the shuttle with his face pressed against a screen so could see nothing.

"Sorry," he shouted back at them.

"Yes, bit of an accident I'm afraid," added Smith.

"And where do you think you are going?" continued Hawkins.

Smith was finding it difficult to know how to play this one being caught red-handed as it were.

"Oh no," cried Prendergast. "Have they got guns?" Plainly his hearing was returning.

It was the Helot who tried to sort things out.

"We're going mining but it's a surprise."

"Shut up, I said," Ratree reasserted.

"Yes, sir!"

"They're going to keelhaul us aren't they?" keened Percy.

"Nobody is going to be keelhauled," said Hawkins.

"Except us if you don't shut up and listen," threw in Jackson, the third shadow.

"Yes, pay attention, we haven't much time," said Hawkins and she hunkered down and placed her smart finger on a pad below Helot19's neck. The robot slumped and his face went out.

"You leave now on an unscheduled flight and the ships defences will blast you to vapour. And I don't know what cock and bull story you've given this robot but he would never let you leave Neptune's orbit. I'm rebooting him now with new instructions. Wait 'til the morning shift then drop into Neptune's atmosphere. Navigate round to the opposite hemisphere then head out straight towards Earth. Once you're clear, put up a distress beacon and hope a home ship picks you up. Get back to Earth, tell them the Peacemaker is crippled and they should take us while they can. Tell them to hold fire and when the time comes we will take care of Zoltac."

The robot came back to life.

"Good afternoon, gentleman, my name is Helot19, I became active on June the twelfth 2344 and I was taught a song. Would you like to hear it? It's called Bamboo Banga."

"Shut up!"

"Robot," said Hawkins, "re-organise the morning rota so no-one tries to board this vessel. I don't want anyone connecting this to us. Good luck."

With that she closed the hatch and left them in the quite darkness of the tiny shuttle.

*

Battle Cruiser Commander Zoltac stood, fists clenched at the ruined portal of Smith and Prendergast's cell.

"Marshal Wittan. Explain to me how this could happen."

"We don't know, sir," the Marshal replied nervously.

"Where are they now?"

"We don't know that either, Commander."

Zoltac turned on him his eyes blazing with rage.

"You don't know very much do you? Do you know anything that would be helpful to me right now?"

"One of the mining shuttles is missing. We believe they may have escaped in that."

Zoltac started to go a very worrying colour. He turned and hit his head against the wall, and rested it there a second while he tried to control his breathing. His therapist had said this might help when the mist descended.

Eventually he straightened up and turned back to Wittan.

"Get me Harfu's communication tablet. Something tells me he is about to send Earth a very important message. From his grave."

22. NEWS FROM A FAR OFF ISLAND

The President's face glowered in close-up from the screen at the end of the conference table. Agent Laurel was pulling a coffee from the machine by the door and Agent Harris was on his feet.

"As near as we can tell the reports are true, the Centauran ship is marooned in Neptune's orbit."

"I guess that proves their intentions are aggressive. If not they would have asked for help," said the President.

"That is certainly the agency's conclusion," said Harris and returned to his seat.

"Not necessarily," intervened Colonel Schnell. He swiveled in his chair and leaned forward placing his arms carefully on the table before him. "I have had many dealings with the Centaurans. I was for three years military attaché on Toliman and was able to observe them at close quarters. They are a proud colony with...shall we say mixed feelings towards their mother Earth. A stubborn refusal to seek assistance, an embarrassment at their predicament even, I would find thoroughly in character with the Centauran mind."

The President sat back in his chair and scanned the room of faces on the screen in front of him.

"Then the situation remains unchanged. Agent Laurel, any news on these rocket scientists...what are their names?"

"Smith and Prendergast, sir," she said returning to the table.

"Nothing so far."

"I may be able to help you there," called Major Fulbright from the door. "Sorry I am late, but I have received another message."

"From your secret source, Major?" asked Schnell and there was something in his manner that Fulbright found even more objectionable than usual.

"Yes, Colonel. Smith and Prendergast will turn up soon claiming to have been abducted by a bounty hunter and sold to Commander Zoltac on the Diplomatist, or Peacemaker as it now is, giving us some story about having escaped from the ship. This will be a lie. They have helped the Centaurans repair their stricken vessel in strict contravention of the embargoes on Earth scientists aiding the Alpha colony. They are returning to Earth with this cover story to protect their own necks. They sold their services for base monetary reasons."

The President scowled.

"I can't wait for them to show up and the moment they do, I'll make an example of them. But this changes nothing. If Zoltac makes a move, we will hit back hard. 'Til then, remain alert."

The screen went dead and the meeting broke up.

*

On the other side of the world, off the coast of Mauritius, Kenya Mendow was at the start of a month's trip, taking rich Africans around the Southern Indian Ocean fishing for shark and watching for whales. His family had been marine guides for centuries and his way of life differed in no great detail from his great, great, great, great, great, great grandfather's before him. The boat his family owned was well equipped, with a modern, state of the art galley, where his father cooked rich foods, garnered from the large refrigerated pantries in the hull, for the tourists, whereas Kenya caught their evening meal on a line over the side of the boat, then filleted and cooked his catch on a small stove on the rear deck each night. Kenya's day to day life was a throwback to his ancestor's time. He was one of the few people left on Earth who had never been smart fingered and had no Innernet link, having to open an ancient laptop computer to access his local weather reports which were his only requirement from the Five World Web. He was living one of the last great outdoor lives which interfaced directly with nature and he couldn't have been happier.

Before he retired at night it was his habit to look up at the night sky just as the sun blinked out and before the stars brought their own gentle illumination to the ocean and in that moment he had a perspective on the universe that a lifetime cruising the trade routes of the four colonies could not have afforded.

He knew the ways of the ocean and its creatures intimately but could never have imagined the voyage Smith and Prendergast had just embarked upon.

23. HELLO BOYS

The journey through the Neptunian atmosphere left Smith and Prendergast nauseous and battered. Hardly surprising as they'd just travelled 40,000 miles through some of the most extreme turbulence know to humanity in the space equivalent of a canoe.

Once on the other side of the planet, using it as a shield, Helot had fired the thrusters until the fuel tanks were empty in an effort to escape Neptune's gravitational pull and send them on a course towards the inner planets.

When they'd put a million miles between themselves and the Peacemaker, they activated the distress beacon and settled in for an uncomfortable wait. It was now only a question of which would give out first, their supplies or their will to live in the face of the robot's interminably cheerful curiosity.

To pass the time they briefly revived Prendergast's Matrix game but Helot19's probabilistic computational powers made mincemeat of them and after three whitewashes the game was ill-temperedly abandoned.

After the dishing out of a small food ration and the passing of another sleep period, Prendergast woke to find Helot19 staring at him. In a rather intense manner it seemed to him. The robot's head was cocked and his red eyes were throbbing softly.

"Anything wrong, Nineteen?" Percy asked.

The robot seemed to lurch back to his former alert self.

"No sir, not at all."

"Oh, jolly good."

"It's just..." Helot19 paused for a moment then continued, "may I ask you a question?"

"Of course, old thing. Fire away."

"Well, when I first met you aboard the ship. It seemed to me I surprised you somewhat. As if you'd never seen a robot before."

"That's true, Nineteen. I hadn't. Robots are illegal on Earth."

The Helot's face could at times be hard to read but there was no mistaking the look of absolute disbelief that crossed it now.

"Illegal?"

"I'm afraid so, Nineteen."

"But why?"

"Erm...it's rather a nasty story I'm afraid."

"Please tell it."

Prendergast sat himself up and regarded Helot in the twinkling red light of the capsule.

"Well, by the late twenty-first century robots had become very common in human society, for menial or repetitive tasks. Their manufacturers had put forward the much vaunted opinion that their use would 'give humans more leisure time'."

"Quite right," said Helot, "our greatest gift to humanity."

"Well, of course," continued Prendergast, "it did nothing of the sort. Like the Spinning Jenny and the computer before them the introduction of robots had just driven up the unemployment figures."

Helot19 couldn't let this go.

"Forgive me for interrupting, sir, but you can't stand in the way of progress."

"On Earth back then no-one did and robots began to take on more of humankind's work, becoming bigger, stronger and more intelligent. By the mid twenty-second century there were some voices of dissent regarding the robotization of society arguing that they were becoming too numerous and powerful to control."

"Oh yes," said Helot19 which a hint of robotic derision, "I have heard such quibbles but these gain-sayers were generally regarded as reactionaries and troglodytes. Their gripes are answered, as anyone knows, by a set of rules developed by the Great Asimov the Alpha Centauran science guru."

"I think you'll find," said Prendergast, "that the Great Asimov as you call him was an Earthman."

"Wherever he came from," persisted Helot19, brushing this aside, "these rules, when hard wired into a positronic brain make every robot incapable of 1) harming a human being, 2) disobeying one and..."

"But it's the third rule that caused the problem."

"That a robot must protect itself unless in conflict with the first or second rule?"

"Exactly that," said Prendergast. "Now rules are no doubt 'A Good Thing' but as soon as you start adding qualifiers and riders they become open to interpretation and no more than guidelines and that was where the human race found itself when, in 2157, a group of super-intelligent, self-reprogrammable and I must say, if I read the history books correctly, rather arrogant robots, decided that there were a few changes needed to the status quo and promptly ran amok."

"Oh dear," said Helot19, his virtual face falling.

"Result being...three years and twelve million fatalities later robots were banned."

"Oh dear, oh dear." The robot shook his head ruefully.

"Still," said Prendergast trying to lift the mood. "On the up side, unemployment figures plummeted, wages rose and the resultant boom became another factor which fueled the great colonial expansion."

"Ah," said Helot19, brightening, "a silver lining."

And they both fell silent.

*

Time in the shuttle drifted on, slowly and secretly giving the boys no hint as to how it was passing and eventually their sidereal rhythms gave up the ghost and though Prendergast could occupy himself with his inner calculations Smith, without even a screwdriver to tinker with, started to slowly lose the plot in the face of bland, relentless, temporal ambiguity.

"I've got an idea," he blurted out suddenly on an indefinable moment of an indistinguishable hour in the cramped capsule. "Let's open the hatch and be done with this."

He reached for the hatch release and started the opening sequence. In panic Prendergast was on him, holding down his arms in a bear-hug while Helot19 re-secured the hatch.

"Let me out, I want to get out. It's lovely out there. There's room to live!"

"Get a grip, old boy, don't give in now. We've come so far."

Smith protested but Prendergast put a hand over his mouth and tried to stifle his protestations.

"Listen. Listen, old chap. What's that noise?"

The robot pushed past them to the control panel as he too heard the insistent, regular beeping coming from the communication array.

"It's a ship," he said, checking the data. "Decelerating and should synchronise with us in...fifteen hours."

"A ship? Do you hear that, Anthony? We're saved."

Smith could have wept with relief. For the next fourteen hours, he and Prendergast sat, ate and dozed in front of the monitors awaiting their first glimpse of the rescue ship. Even the robot experienced something analogous with excitement, though he hadn't suffered during the trip in the way the humans had, boredom and claustrophobia being sensations he simply couldn't understand.

Their first glimpse of the vessel was as a glowing dot far out to the right of the shuttle, moving past them in the direction from which they had come, then slowing, changing its trajectory until finally falling into formation beside them, some thousand miles out in space. It then began its careful, slow approach for docking.

When it was about half a mile away, Prendergast felt a small flush of recognition, and he let out an involuntary yelp.

"Did you say something?" asked Smith.

"It's her!"

"It's who?"

"Look."

Smith looked into the monitor. He was flummoxed for a moment then realisation dawned and he too yelped.

"The Zelda!" he shouted.

"It's the fiend Betty!" intoned Prendergast, his voice dripping with dread.

"Helot!" yelled Smith, "Evasive action. Now! We have to lose her."

"I'm afraid that is quite impossible, Mr Smith. I used up all the fuel escaping Neptune's gravity well. We have no manoeuvring capability left. The ship is now, for all practical purposes, simply a projectile."

For Smith this was the last straw.

"Ten billion souls in the solar system and she has to be the one to pick up our signal. What are the chances?"

"I don't think chance has anything to do with it, Anthony. She's a feisty, tenacious little thing who doesn't give up easily. She was obviously looking for us."

Smith turned on him.

"I don't like your choice of words, Percy. They reek of admiration."

Helot19's head lights glowed with an extra luminosity.

"I am sorry to interrupt, sirs, but docking is imminent."

Smith sidled up to the robot and spoke to him conspiratorially.

"Here, Nineteen."

"Yes, sir?"

"When we get aboard the other ship, I don't suppose you could see your way clear to fetching its Captain a swift right hook so we could commandeer the craft?"

"I'm awfully sorry, Mr Smith. I'm afraid I couldn't."

"Ah. First law of robotics, huh?"

"No, sir. Common decency!"

*

"Alright, shut up, the both of you!" Betty shouted over Smith and Prendergast. They were cuffed to the girder again while the robot was locked in the shuttle. Betty hadn't really liked the look Helot's of jib since the moment she clapped eyes on him; in her view he was a seven foot monster with murder in his evil red eyes and she had refused to allow him on the ship! Helot19 had been most understanding and went into standby mode, patiently floating in the shuttle which was piggybacked to the Zelda.

"Now listen to me woman and listen to me good," Smith hissed firmly. "If you take us back to that ship, Zoltac will keelhaul us and blast you with a laser 'til your innards ooze out and I don't want to see that happen again, even to you!"

"He's right," pleaded Prendergast, "that's exactly what the Traders got and they were expecting a hundred thousand!"

"Then it's a good job for all of us that I'm not taking you there, isn't it?"

"You're making a big mis...what?"

The boys looked confused for a moment 'til Smith spoke.

"You're not taking us back to Zoltac?"

"Nope!"

"Then where *are* you taking us?"

"Straight to the nearest colony on Titan were the Earth security forces can pick you up."

"Why are you going to do that?"

"Because I'm on their wanted list. They seem to have gotten it into their heads that I abducted you."

Prendergast was incredulous.

"But you did abduct us, you duplicitous slattern. You jolly well kidnapped us."

"Yes. Against our will!" added Smith.

"Well, I'm gonna 'jolly well' unkidnap you and maybe if I hide out for a few months they'll lose interest in me. I'm gonna unhandcuff you now and invite you to join me in the cockpit for a delicious hot dinner then you can tell the authorities how good I treated you."

Prendergast's incredulity hit a hitherto unreached high.

"Of all the mendacious, underhanded...we most certainly will not tell them any such thing. We will tell them the truth and insist they track you down and incarcerate you on the most inhospitable asteroid they can find."

"And while you're at it," she came back at him, squaring up in a most intimidating manner, "you can tell them how I rescued you from certain death in the bleak wastes of space because if it weren't for the fact that I was looking for you, certain death is what you were most certainly facing. Do you know how slim the chances were of anyone finding you, drifting around in a tiny shuttle with a month's food supply and a fading signal? Who's bright idea was that?"

"Smith's," said Prendergast and he turned to his colleague reproachfully.

"Oh, that's nice. Turn on me. That's just what she wants," he retorted, matching snit for snit.

"Look. Things might go a lot better for you missy if you were to show some good will and take these damnable neck suppressors off us," said Prendergast playing a pretty strong hand.

"Whoa, steady there, fella. Let's just leave them on for now and see how the handover goes first," said Betty, trumping him.

*

Two days into the trip Betty called the boys into the cockpit from the storeroom where they'd been getting a little shut eye.

"What is it?" asked Smith, groggily wiping the sleep from his eyes.

"We have another ship approaching."

"Traders?" asked Prendergast, suddenly alert.

"Doesn't look like it. Ain't like anything I ever seen."

The ship took about an hour to come alongside the Zelda, plainly intent upon a rendezvous. Betty hailed it but got nothing back. Peering out of the portholes the ship looked old and a little beaten up. They could just make out lettering along the side of the hull and as they strained to read it, floodlights burst into life, illuminating the message stenciled there.

Luigi's Restaurant. Our food is out of this world.

"What in the name of Newton is that!?" asked Betty and there was not a ring of the rhetorical about her question. As if in answer the radio behind them burst into life with a jolly jingle and a voice of almost insufferable chipperness.

"Good morning, campers," it said. "Fed up with space paste? We have a large selection of real-like foods and beverages if you book a meal at Luigi's Trattoria for a taste of Home Planet cooking..."

Betty slapped her hand on the send button.

"Who is this? What do you want?"

"Erm...like I said I am Luigi and..."

"Are you for real?"

"Most certainly my dear. If you would give me permission to dock you can see for yourself."

She turned off the communicator and looked at the boys.

"Whaddya think?"

Smith looked at Prendergast who looked back at Betty.

"I haven't the foggiest. Could it be a trap?"

Betty checked her monitors and pressed a few buttons.

"It doesn't look like it's even armed."

"Tony?" asked Prendergast.

Smith looked at Betty with a sly smirk.

"Well, as you never tire of telling us it's your ship so...your call."

Betty gritted her teeth and made her decision. She opened the hailing frequency again.

"Permission granted. Commence docking procedure."

The restaurant ship Luigi rose above the Zelda and turned itself bottom to top, facing its airlock to hers. It extended what looked like an eighty foot Chinese lantern, forming a tunnel between the two vessels.

"Please," said Luigi's voice on the intercom, "come over and have a look around."

*

Luigi's was an extraordinary mix of spaceship and restaurant, both in the old style. The ship itself must have been seventy years old, the controls having no virtual readouts just old fashioned plastiscreens. Luigi was dressed in a moth-eaten tuxedo and had a white napkin over his arm. The four of them floated uncomfortably for a moment 'til Luigi broke the silence.

"Welcome to Luigi's," he said grinning from ear to ear, "table for three?"

"You really are a space restaurant? I never heard of one of those," said Betty taking it all in.

"We are the pioneers in the field, ma'am, my brother Paulo and me. He's doing a Roman banquet on the dark side of Mercury for a hen night right now."

"We don't have any money," said Betty.

Luigi's face fell. He hung his napkin up on a hook on the wall. He let out a long sigh.

"Have you got anything you could trade? I could do you a crackin' spag bol."

"Not really," said Prendergast with regret, looking around the ship, a spaghetti bolognaise being about the most wonderful thing he could imagine just at that moment.

"Oh dear, oh dear," moaned Luigi, "you must have something. You could have some very tasty garlic bread."

Betty licked her lips.

"Really? Nothing?" asked Luigi with a hint of desperation. He started to undo his bow tie.

"I told Paulo this was a rotten idea. You can't run a successful restaurant with an average of thirty-million miles between bookings."

Smith was holding onto a rail near the rear of the cabin.

"One moment, Luigi. I detect a bit of a vibration on this ship. Your engine. It's quite old, isn't it?"

"Yes, virtually antique. Been giving me a lot of gyp lately."

"And," said Prendergast, "your computer systems seem a little, veteran shall we say?"

"I think the navigation unit is older than me," Luigi said and he was certainly no spring chicken.

"How about I give your engine a bit of an overhaul and..." Smith decided not to mention Helot19, robots being illegal and all, "our co-pilot...Brian, aboard the ship could remotely update a few of your systems."

Luigi thought about this offer for a moment.

"Would I notice any difference?"

"I could probably get rid of the engine's jitters," said Smith.

"How about the computer, could you stop that bleedin' spinning disk of doom?"

"I don't think you'd ever see it again," said Prendergast. "So what could you give us for all that?"

Luigi closed one eye and scratched his narrow chin.

"Let's see now. A complete overhaul of the ship. I think that might be worth...a tricolore salad followed by Saltimbocca alla Romana, a fine bottle of Barolo, tiramisu for afters and...I'll even chuck in coffee and liqueurs to finish."

Betty thrust her hand out.

"You, Mr Luigi, have yourself a deal."

"Will Brian be joining you?"

"Who?" asked Smith, who's already forgotten the cover story.

"Erm..., no," said Prendergast, who had not, "he's shy and not very good with rich foods."

"Very well. If you will get on with your part of the bargain perhaps me and the young lady could arrange a bit of gravity to aid the digestion."

By the simple expedient of firing the Zelda's left hand thrusters and the restaurant's right hand ones, the two craft set to spinning around the linking tunnel like a giant cheerleader's baton twirling in space. Within a few minutes this produced an Earth like centrifugal gravity and Luigi set up their table for dinner, spread with a red and white check table cloth, a melted candle in an old wine bottle as the centrepiece and real cutlery.

As Luigi started chopping vegetables, Smith rolled up his sleeves, crawling into the engines at the back of the ship while Prendergast initiated the uplink with Helot19 aboard the Zelda. An hour and a half later, the ship's engines were running smoothly, the computers were faster than they'd been for fifteen years and a wonderful aroma was emanating from the galley.

"Something smells wonderful," Betty shouted through to Luigi who was sprinkling parsley on their appetisers.

"I learned to cook at my grandmother's knee. Now she was real Italian."

"Where from?"

"Stepney, east end of London. D'you know it?"

"No," said Betty, "that's a part of Italy I've never been."

*

It would be tampering with veracity to say that the meal Luigi put before them was cordon bleu but to three hungry young people who had been surviving on a diet of goo, having dishes of varying temperatures, textures and tastes placed before them was living at its highest. Add to the abundant fare the glasses of rich red wine and a couple of flaming sambucas and it was a very merry bunch who pushed their coffee cups away unloosened their top trouser buttons at the end of the dinner. Luigi joined them, a menthol vape between his lips.

"A funny old thing, space, isn't it?" he mused, taking a long puff on his comforter. "It's so vast and yet people are always so cramped in it."

Smith and Prendergast nodded, gracefully appreciating his plain logic.

"It must have been lovely back in the day. Before the colonies. When we were all on the one planet but had room to breathe."

"Though I suspect," interjected Prendergast, "that the people of the time didn't really appreciate that."

"That's right," agreed Smith. "Why else would they have founded the colonies."

"Wanderlust, sir," said Luigi simply. "Humanity's greatest quality and deadliest fault. Why isn't the species content with one planet? Why isn't the woman content with one man and why doesn't the gambler stick at sixteen? Wanderlust. A lust to wander, to expand, to grow, yes but also...a tragic propensity to throw away all we have today for a vague promise of more tomorrow."

The three men nodded, staring into the middle distance, pondering the profundity of Luigi's philosophical musings. For her part Betty thought they were spouting raw sewage.

A communicator beeped in the cockpit.

"Excuse me, gentlemen, lady," and Luigi got up and left the group in silence.

"Why do you think that is?" asked Prendergast eventually.

"Because that's who we are," answered Smith. "If we didn't have that restlessness we'd still be scuttling about the plains of Africa, grubbing for nuts and providing sabretooth tigers with a little variety in their diet."

Prendergast sighed.

"You could be right."

"Damn right he's right," said Betty, siding with Smith for once. "We keep moving, that's what we do."

"But," asked Prendergast plaintively, "don't you ever want to settle down Betty, and raise a family?"

Betty looked at him levelly.

"Your hand is on my knee."

"Oops, sorry," apologised Prendergast and Smith suppressed a snicker by shoving another wafer thin mint into his mouth. Any further speculation on Betty's future maternal intentions was interrupted by Luigi coming back into the room.

"Not that I'm rushing you but I've just picked up a rig on the way back from Uranus and I do a pretty brisk trade with the miners. I provide a very reasonable hog roast and lager evening which goes down well with the crews. It can get a bit raucous but it's worth it to see the lads unwind."

They said their farewells and once Betty and the boys were back aboard the Zelda, the two ships went on their way, casting off in opposite directions.

*

Betty's plan was simple. Arriving at Titan she would hail the nearest Earth security and hand over Smith and Prendergast in exchange for a promise of immunity. If the Earthmen cut up rough she would cast the boys adrift in the shuttle and make her escape while the troops were busy rescuing them.

As they approached Titan, Smith and Prendergast began to get excited at the prospect of going home. They could finally take up their posts with Saabre and put this whole sorry episode behind them. Smith was particularly enthused about selling their story to the news feeds. Prendergast was troubled by the ethics of this, while Smith's only concern was whether they should sell the story wholesale or eke it out in weekly installments. He was sure that the publicity manager he intended to hire the moment they landed would be able to advise him on this point.

*

The moment they entered Titan's orbit they were joined by a brace of fighters bearing Earth insignia who hailed them.

"This is Delta One security, identify yourself please."

Betty opened the com channel.

"This is Elizabeth Stanton, Captain of the Zelda. I got two passengers you might be interested in." She turned and smiled at the boys. "I think you people have been looking for them for some time. A Mr Percival Prendergast and a Mr Anthony Smith."

"Prepare for boarding," came back the reply, "I have instructions to take you all into custody. You will consider yourself my prisoners. Do not attempt to leave orbit, I have been authorised to use force."

A jolt ran through the cockpit of the Zelda as the three of them tried to assimilate this information.

"Whoa, whoa, whoa, hold on there, fly-boy. Prisoners? What for?" asked Betty incredulously.

"The charge against Prendergast and Smith is high treason."

Smith nearly choked and Prendergast leaped at the microphone.

"High treason!? This is babble from the sickbed. What are you talking about, man?"

"I am talking about giving aid to the enemy, breaking sanctions and infringement of military embargoes. We got you, you sons of b..."

"What about me?" interrupted Betty.

"Aiding and abetting. You're going down with them, lady."

Betty shut down the com channel and said nothing for a moment. She looked up at the boys who shook their heads.

"We have to tell them they've made an error," said Prendergast desperately.

"They won't listen."

She looked at the two heavily armed ships on the monitor then reopened the com channel and spoke calmly to the fighter pilot.

"Alright, looks like you got us, preparing to jettison the shuttle so you can dock."

"Betty, what're you doing?" demanded Smith.

"Shut up," she said and fired her attitude adjusters reorienting the ship 'til it faced the two fighters. She fired the forward thrusters and started to put distance between the Zelda and the Earth ships. The Earth cop responded with immediate aggression.

"Do not continue with your present action, Zelda."

"Come on, chase me, Earth boys," she said and fired the thrusters again picking up speed.

"I consider this a hostile action, Stanton. You will stop this now."

"Guys, let's have a little fun."

"I will fire, last warning."

"You really think I should make it that easy for you?"

"You asked for it."

The fighters fired their own engines and accelerated, narrowing the gap between them and the Zelda.

"Okay, Smithy boy, hit it."

All at once Smith saw her plan. He hit the big red button and the wormhole interface appeared invisibly in front of the Zelda. The Earth fighters accelerated a little more...and promptly disappeared.

Betty fired her attitude adjusters again and turned the ship to face forward.

"Now while they take a few moments to work out what the hell just happened to them, we comet tail it out of here."

She fired her main engines and the Zelda shot out of Titan's orbit.

"That was a brilliant move, Betty and I don't wish to take anything away from your inventiveness and calm demeanor under pressure..." said Prendergast, choosing his words carefully.

"Why do I feel a 'but' coming on?"

"...but, this can at best be a temporary measure. I mean, we have nowhere to go."

"Don't be too sure, buster!" said Betty and she rummaged in a locker by her head.

"You ever heard of the sixth home colony?" she asked.

"No," said Smith and Prendergast simultaneously.

"Good. Not many people have. But it exists and it's the brainchild of an old friend of mine."

She pulled what looked like a holiday brochure out of the locker and sent it gliding across the cabin where Prendergast plucked it out of air.

He opened it out and, as Smith peered over his shoulder, he read the legend on its cover.

"*Welcome to a new experience in luxury colonial living. Coming soon*."

24. A BRAVE NEW WORLD

The brochure Betty had sent drifting toward Prendergast provided a gushing potted history of its founder's life. Vladimir Jobs claimed to be a direct descendant of Steve, the great twentieth century technology pioneer. Vladimir had become a trillionaire by opening a chain of head shops with a branch in every major city on Earth, selling tie-dye T-shirts, hookah's and hash pipes to the retro hippy market and making him something of a guru to their movement, for which reason he'd become known to one and all as Vlad the Inhaler.

At the age of forty he'd sold the business and taken his cash to Enceladus, a tiny moon of Saturn where his plan was to found the sixth home colony alongside one of the huge cryovolcanoes on the Baghdad Ridge at the satellite's south pole. Christening it New Cupertino, he envisaged a continuous winter sport resort in the permanent snowfall from the ice geysers; a haven for the super rich, who would pay handsomely to frolic in the delightful one tenth earth gravity that prevailed there.

The brochure's gatefold middle pages depicted what looked like a huge snow globe filled with fresh faced, youthful holiday makers, floating, snowboarding and skiing in brightly patterned Scandi knitwear.

As the Zelda orbited over the frozen plains, Betty opened all channels and waited for New Cupertino to send its homing code and guide her into port. She made a pass over the Ridge but got nothing save the crackle of background radiation.

"Anything?" asked Prendergast.

"Not yet."

"Well, your mate's new utopia is really jumping of a Friday night isn't it?" quipped Smith.

"Shut up," warned Betty.

"Yes, cheese it old thing. Not helping."

Betty made another orbit and decided to drop down nearer the surface to attempt a visual fix. She came round the moon again, sweeping down over the icy plains at five hundred feet and it was Prendergast who made the first sighting.

"There," he shouted, pointing to a large ice jet shooting from the surface, making a great plume in space. Down beside the geyser's outlet they could make out a sizable transparent dome, just like the ones which made up Shangri-La on Titan but where they formed an impressive shanty city with their ad hoc arrangement of brightly varying colours, this lone clear plastic tent, like some sort of minimalist circus taking refuge in its winter quarters, solitary and abandoned, seemed very remote and inhospitable indeed.

"I'll make another pass, see if I can land us close," said Betty.

Fifteen minutes later the Zelda sent up a spray of snow as she settled on the surface some twenty meters from the dome. Betty shut down the engines and they peered out of the window, checking for signs of habitation.

The dome seemed to be built around a smaller geyser which spurted ice towards the roof where it melted on the inner surface and fell back into the tent as rain. Through the resultant downpour they could make out a few scattered buildings which looked for all the world like log cabins. Of human activity there was no sign. Smith pointed to an air lock on the side of the dome, like the entrance to an igloo. It certainly wasn't big enough to accommodate the Zelda.

"Maybe we could get in through there?" he suggested.

"I only got one spacesuit aboard and it's minus two hundred and airless out there," said Betty slumping back into her seat.

Smith and Prendergast remained, peering through the windscreen.

"Any thoughts, old boy?" asked Prendergast quietly.

"Just one," replied Smith and he turned to Betty.

"Could you spare some fuel from your attitude thrusters so we could fire up the shuttle?"

"I guess. What's the big idea?"

"The big idea is that one of us gets suited up and goes over there, sees if they can get that airlock opened from the outside and if we can, the rest join in the shuttle. It should just about fly in this gravity."

Betty looked out of the window and then back to the boys.

"Say, that could work."

"Yes, it could," added Prendergast, patting Smith on the back.

"Though what we do once we get inside that glorified storm drain is another matter!"

As it was Smith's idea, Betty volunteered him to be the one to make the EVA and so an hour later, after she and Percy had crammed themselves into the shuttle alongside Helot19, Smith dropped down to the surface of Enceladus and started bounding towards the plastic dome.

He had worried that on a moon this small he could, given a big enough leap, send himself into orbit but Prendergast reassured him, after checking the figures twice, that he would need a velocity of about a quarter kilometer per second to do that, which was a feat beyond even an Olympic hundred meters finalist.

The huge cryovolcanic geyser next to the dome plainly had what was required to take the gold medal because the bulk of its eruptive material glistened away from the satellite and disappeared into space but much of the icy detritus at the edges of the vent fell back to the surface in a light snowfall.

The Enceladan day was about ninety minutes long followed by a nighttime of roughly the same length, though even then it was never really dark as the bright disc and rings of Saturn shone with a golden lustre in the black starless sky. The transforming light and shade of this complex orbital arrangement made for an eerily beautiful, shifting alien landscape and as Smith got close to the dome he became caught up in its vacillating splendour.

As he approached the airlock his foot caught something under the delicate snow covering and in the weak gravity he tumbled to the ground like an autumn leaf. Taking a moment to check his suit for any damage and catch a breath before righting himself he looked up and couldn't have been more surprised by what he saw.

Bright canine eyes skewered him warily as a front paw lifted, poised for the beast's next move. The wet nose dilated, probing the nonexistent air in olfactory analysis. Smith froze, his mind locking as his reason collided with this unreasonable vision.

"Are you seeing this?" Smith panted into his helmet com.

"Yes. Yes, we are," came Prendergast's faltering voice.

"Any idea what the Fibonacci's going on?"

There was a pause and all Smith could hear was the dual suspiration of Percy and Betty in his ears.

"Not a dashed clue," came Prendergast's voice eventually.

"I think you're supposed to remain absolutely still," proffered Betty, a wildlife show enthusiast as her singing on the trip to Titan had proved.

The wolf's eyes widened in feral warning and it bared lethal teeth, its lips quivering in a silent growl.

"Oh, Castor and Pollux!" said Smith as he scuttled backwards across the rimy rock.

"Don't move," shouted Betty, "you'll spook it."

"I don't think it's the flaming wolf who's spooked here, Betty!"

The wolf sniffed again and seemed to lose interest in Smith, obviously deciding that he'd won the first round. He turned away and trotted off behind the dome.

"Tony, take a look behind you," said Prendergast with a chuckle in his voice.

Smith turned and there was a large elk, seemingly chewing the leaves from an imaginary shrub.

"Wait a flippin' minute," said Smith. "Someone's taking the mickey here!"

He bounced towards the elk which eyed him in a rather disinterested fashion before returning to its rumination. Smith stood close to the majestic beast and slowly stretched his hand towards its hide. As he touched it, the edges of the animal pixilated slightly. The moment Smith withdrew his glove the image reassembled into a perfect elk again.

"It's some sort of hologram," said Smith with evident relief.

"More like a digital projection," corrected Prendergast.

"Well, whatever it is I shall give that wolf what for if I see it again."

"Now's your chance," said Betty, "it's coming back."

Smith swung round to see the wolf going into its sniffing and fang snarling routine again. Even though he now knew it was a harmless projection, some deep seated, primal race memory unmanned him completely.

"Perhaps not. Things to do, eh? Best press on."

Smith bounced up to the thick perspex doors of the airlock and checked for a way in. There seemed to be no switches or sensors as he ran his hands around the doors and their surrounds. He peered through into the airlock and could see a control panel on the inside but after another inspection he could still find no means of entrance.

"There doesn't seem to be any way in."

"There must be something," said Betty impatiently.

"There's nothing I tell you," replied Smith testily.

"Alright, bring that suit back. I'm going to take a look."

"Well, okay," said Smith grudgingly, "but you won't find anything.'

Smith turned and started back towards the ship. A few paces away from the door he caught his foot again on something in the snow and took another tumble.

"Steady on, clumsy," Prendergast tittered over the com.

Smith checked himself over again then peered into the snow beneath him.

"Wait a minute," he said and brushed the snow away in front of him with his pressurised glove, "that's not natural."

He brushed some more.

"It's some kind of metal."

He kept clearing the snow, revealing more metallic surface.

"Hang on," he said.

Smith pushed himself to the vertical and, when he was sure of his balance started to kick away the snow beneath his feet.

"This is what I must have tripped on before. It's a large metal plate."

"A pressure pad," Betty almost shouted. "Kinda old fashioned, but effective. If we put the shuttle down on that I bet it opens the airlock."

Prendergast turned to Helot19.

"Is that what it is?"

The robot tilted his head and put on his thinking face.

"My entire existence has revolved around the Peacemaker. I have no experience or understanding of this environment. I can therefore offer no opinion."

"Still, we might as well try it," said Prendergast with rising excitement.

"Indeed, sir."

Betty eased up the shuttle's engines and feathered them slightly towards the ground giving the craft a little lift.

"Better get out of the way, Smith. This tin can wasn't made for precision flight."

The shuttle lurched forward and she hastily checked her power and attitude. Once back under her control she edged it forward. When she judged the vessel was in the right position, she cut the engines and it landed heavily on the metal plate. Smith had bounced well clear and was standing in the middle of a small flock of herons which pixilated frantically around his legs.

A tense moment passed until, suddenly, silently, the plexiglas doors juddered, bringing an avalanche of snow from the roof of the airlock. The doors opened to their widest position and Betty fired the engines once again. From his vantage point fifty meters away, Smith watched the shuttle wobble forward noiselessly as Betty guided it cautiously into the dock. Inside the craft was a different story. Betty and Prendergast winced at the groaning screeches of complaint from the ship's structure as it was pushed by the thrusters, violently scraping across the metal and rock at the entrance of the dome.

Once inside Betty powered down and the shuttle came to rest, listing slightly, snugly wedged into the airlock. Prendergast breathed a sigh of relief and patted Betty on the shoulder in congratulation.

"Don't do that," said Betty, shrugging him off, "it's patronizing."

Prendergast muttered an embarrassed apology and flushed a shade.

"Well done, ma'am," said Helot19.

"Thank you, robot," said Betty. Prendergast shot it a nasty look.

Outside Smith took a few steps towards the airlock. Another little flutter of snow from the roof caught his attention and, horrified, he saw the doors begin to close automatically behind the shuttle. In alarm he took an almighty bound and soaring several feet in the air, dived headfirst through the narrowing gap. He bounced off the back of the shuttle and clattered painfully onto the inside of the, now firmly closed, doors.

As he lay there, arching his bruised, cricked back, grimacing painfully, he heard the hissing of the air vents as the dock filled with an 80/20 nitrogen and oxygen mixture, mimicking an approximation of Mother Earth's atmosphere.

*

Three humans and one robot, recent passengers of mining shuttle six, late of the Centauri battle cruiser Peacemaker, stood inside the arching dome of New Cupertino. The heavy rain fell in slow motion, drenching their clothes in seconds and chilling them in minutes. The air had a musty, mangrove odour, from the vegetation sprouting here and there in the clay all around them. The flora had plainly been chosen by someone with no understanding of horticulture. Tropical fruit trees rotted next to mouldering cacti, rapacious weeds strangled delicate mountain shrubs. They plodded through the thick mud until they reached a concrete pathway which snaked from cabin to cabin through the compound.

"Let's check all the huts," ordered Betty, "see if there's anyone home."

There were twelve dwellings, all of different sizes and designs. Inside each was some basic furniture but most of it was ruined by the rain which had beaten its way through the poorly constructed, ill fitting faux wooden beams that ran the length of each building. After confirming most were empty, Betty came across one that showed signs of habitation. A sleeping bag lay on a trestle bed, with books and clothes scattered about the room. A plastic tarpaulin had been pinned up on the inner surfaces which for the most part kept the place dry. In the corner was a box filled with patent medications and on a table by the bed stood a large water pipe filled with a cloudy, scummy liquid.

"This is obviously Vlad's pad," observed Betty.

"Good Laws!" exclaimed Percy, "I don't think much of this chap's hygiene. This is a breeding ground for scabies, ringworm and impetigo if ever I saw one!"

Looking round the hut no-one disagreed.

"I wonder were the Heliosphere he is?" said Betty and went back out into the rain.

They found a storage room with a large, half filled water butte and a seemingly inexhaustible supply of canned food which disappointingly turned out to be almost exclusively baked beans.

They ate a few cans, drank a few litres and Smith retired to one of the better roofed dwellings while Helot19 went into sleep mode leaving Betty and Percy watching the relentless downpour on the stoop of the largest hut.

The pale sun rose and fell and Percy turned to Betty.

"I hope you don't mind my asking, old girl?"

"What?"

"But that frightfully nice family we met on Mars?"

"What about 'em?"

"Relatives? Were they?"

Betty didn't answer for a moment but put her arm out from under the cover of the stoop and let the rain run over her hand. When she did speak it was uncharacteristically muted.

"Friends of the family."

"Ah!" said Percy. "So that's where you were brought up? That's where you lived? You and your family?"

"Uhuh."

Blood from a stone, thought Percy but he soldiered on.

"Again I hope you don't mind but I thought when that Dean chap mentioned your mother, it got in amongst you somewhat."

"Why do you talk so weird?" said Betty.

"Sorry. I mean I thought I detected a certain sadness at the mention of her."

Betty looked down at the ground watching the rainwater soak into the sodden earth beneath her feet.

"My mom," she said, almost imperceptibly, "my mom," she repeated raising her head, eyebrows and voice all at once. She then turned savagely on Percy, her eyes blazing.

"My mom?" and her voice quivered with suppressed rage.

Percy froze under her stare, fearful of the demon he had awoken.

"Yes, your mother," he said in a tiny voice.

"Let me tell you about my mom, buster!"

Percy nodded vigorously.

"My mom was a great woman. If she saw injustice - she fought it. If she saw a wrong – she'd right it and she didn't care what got in her way and she didn't care who she offended while she was doing it and believe me she made enemies along the way and some darned powerful ones at that." She paused for a moment, breathing deeply. When she'd regained her composure she spoke again.

"I guess that's why they had to get her off Mars. I remember it like it was yesterday. She came to me and said, Lizzie, she said. Mommy has to go away for a while but I'll be back. I'll come and get you. Real soon." Betty's head drooped again and she seemed to struggle to keep some image in her mind's eye as she followed the rivulets of water in the churned up ground.

"That's the last time I saw her. I was nine years old."

Percy slowly reached out and put his hand on her arm and this time she did not shrug him off or chew him out. She just sat there, seemingly taking comfort from a human touch until she spoke again.

"I guess the bad guys won."

*

Smith was woken by a steady drip. He opened his eyes and, struggling for a moment to bring himself up to date and remember where he was, listened for the noise's source and determined it was emanating from the end of his cot. He was rather touched to find it was a leak from the roof, dripping onto Helot19's shoulder. The robot was undisturbed by the noise, having powered down and would stay that way until he was summoned. He looked a little odd with his visor dark, the usual virtual face a grey blank. What Smith found so touching was that the robot had sought shelter and had chosen Smith's hut for the purpose. It may well have been a random choice but Smith liked to think that the machine had found some affinity with him, perhaps even a respect for his intellect.

Outside, the Enceledean night was turning to day and the geyser seemed to have hit a dormant phase in its cycle. The rain had certainly stopped and everything was dripping dry including the section of roof over Helot19. Smith was about to wake the robot when a strange voice called from outside the hut.

"Hey! I don't know who you are, man, but you better come out and you better be cool cos I got a gun, man, and I ain't afraid to use it. So you better come on out like I said and you better have your hands in the air cos you don't wanna make me freak, man."

It didn't take a very lengthy chain of connections to arrive at the conclusion that this was Vlad. The Inhaler himself. Smith rose and gently called to Helot19, who quietly came to, his face reappearing. The two of them ducked out of the hut and into the compound. Smith was slightly taken aback to notice Prendergast and Betty coming out into the open too. Taken aback, not from the emergence itself but from the fact they both came from the same hut. But that could wait. For now there was a rather irate, soaking hippy to be contended with.

"Hello," said Prendergast giving it the old oil, "you must be Vlad."

He strode forward with his hand extended but Vlad became agitated and hopped from foot to foot like a nervous horse in an action Prendergast could vaguely remember hearing called paternating.

"Back off man, back off, I told you I'd shoot you."

"Yes, you did," said Prendergast carefully, "but you don't appear to have a gun."

Vlad looked down at his hand, momentarily mystified. Then looked back at Prendergast.

"That's right, dude. I lied about that. To intimidate you. I'm not really into violence man," he said relaxing then tensed again striking a pose which the others guessed was an approximation of a martial art move but ended up looking more like a priest performing an exorcism.

"But my beliefs do not preclude me from defending myself. With extreme prejudice."

He kept the pose shifting to face each of them in turn.

"Hey, Vlad," said Betty moving forward, "is this what you call hospitality in New Cupertino?"

Vlad scrunched his eyes at her and as she came closer he dropped his arms and the pose.

"Lizzie? Is that you babe?"

"It sure is!"

"Aw, man! C'm'ere."

He walked towards her and gave her a bear hug, lifting her off the ground, not a difficult feat in one tenth gravity, in fact they both levitated for a few moments before drifting back to the muddy surface. Prendergast had moved closer to Smith and leaned in towards his ear.

"Lizzie?" he asked in a disgusted fashion. "She doesn't let us call her Lizzie."

"You jealous?"

"Not in the slightest. Ludicrous idea."

Smith smiled.

"It's 'babe' that should worry you more."

"Pfffuhff!" said Prendergast adding a piggy snort and crossed his arms, watching the reunion unfolding before him with a sour, curled lip.

*

As the sun went down an hour later, Vlad and his guests were sitting around an impromptu fire eating beans and sipping a bottle of wine from a dwindling source he kept in a crate under his bed.

"So where were you when we arrived?" asked Betty.

"Sometimes I gotta get out of here, man. Since things started going bad I get to feeling the walls are closing in on me. I found a cave, right on the other side of the moon and it's cool, man. It's quiet."

"There's no air here, everywhere's quiet, surely," interjected Prendergast, somewhat pedantically.

"I pull on a spaceman suit, man and I take a hike round there. Stay as long as my air supply'll let me. You know. Just sit, man. And think stuff. I'm all alone."

"But you're all alone here too, aren't you?" clarified Prendergast with patent irritation.

"Percy, will you shut up?" said Betty.

"I'm just saying it doesn't make any sense, why risk your life going out there when you can risk it in here?"

"Perce, mate. Let Vlad tell his story, eh?"

Prendergast shuffled uncomfortably and muttered under his breath.

"So what went wrong?" asked Smith.

"Oh, man, what didn't? Have you got any idea how expensive it is to get everything up here and start building a colony?"

"Erm, yes I think I do," interrupted Prendergast again, his sarcasm now barely cloaked. "Is the answer? Eeeerm?...the most expensive thing a person could ever attempt?"

"Percy, I swear I'm gonna..." said Betty trailing off in disgust.

"Yes, I think that one was rhetorical, mate," added Smith.

"Well," sighed Vlad, sadly. "It busted me, man and I was the richest person I knew."

"Could I just say, Vladimir," Prendergast butted in again, "and this is purely in the spirit of constructive observation but have you any idea how often you use the word 'man'?"

"What is it with the hostility?" asked Betty with some heat. Smith decided to keep his council. He figured this was the only company for about five million miles and a serious rift between any of them was going to be fiendishly hard to paper over.

Vlad pinned Prendergast with one rheumy eye.

"I gotta tell you, man, you strike me as real uptight."

"And I have to tell you, *man*, that you strike me as a bit of a berk!"

There was an uncomfortable silence around the fire. Betty fumed quietly and Smith tried to scrape another bean from his plate even though it was plainly empty.

"I don't even know what that means, man."

Vlad took a breath and turned his head away.

"Anyway," he went on, "the last of the construction guys split last month when they found out I couldn't pay 'em. Since then I been sitting here or in the cave thinking what my next move should be. Sometimes I look out there, man and I get ideas, I mean...you ever hear of a dude named Oates?"

Smith looked alarmed.

"You mean Captain Oates?" he asked.

"But most of the time I feel pretty positive, man. Hey, did you check out the wildlife? Kinda cool, huh?"

He got up and wandered towards the transparent wall of the dome. A grizzly bear was sharpening its claws on the outer wall. Betty and Smith exchanged a look and even Prendergast looked a little concerned.

"My worst miscalculation was the snow, man. Once I got it warm enough to live, I lost the snow."

Prendergast looked up at the roof which still dripped condensed water ice.

"I'm sure that would be fixable. You just need to create two systems where presently you have one."

Smith too, looked up.

"That's right. You have to reconfigure your environmentals so they are complimentary rather than variant. We could have a look at it for you."

*

The next forty-eight hours Smith spent inside New Cupertino's climate station pulling it to pieces while Prendergast fed him numbers. Betty and Helot19 both watched them do what they did best but Vlad stayed by the wall, watching the digital animals, lost in his own thoughts. When they'd finished Prendergast went back to his hut and Smith looked over at Vlad. Betty joined him.

"I hope this works. For his sake."

"Me too," she said.

"Here." She reached towards Smith's neck placing her smart finger on the suppressor she had put around it. It fell away and dropped in the mud.

"Good luck uplinking here though," she smiled and Smith grinned back.

"I guess this is our home for a while," she added, the stark reality clouding her features.

"Yes, I suppose so," said Smith. "I was going to a great company to start a life's work doing what I love best and being paid really well for it and now..." he turned towards her, "thanks to you actually, I am stuck on an ice covered rock with a depressed hippy."

"I'm sorry," she said and it seemed the hardest thing she had ever had to say.

"Oh, don't worry," said Smith, "if it hadn't been you it would have been someone else, which it turns out it was in the end. The Traders. Which was your good luck considering how they ended up."

"I guess we're all screwed, huh?"

"Yes," said Smith ruefully, "I just can't help thinking of that lab I might be working in now."

He sighed a big one and turned away, heading back to his hut. Helot19 was nearby and watched him go, a quizzical look on his cocked head.

Betty watched Smith disappear into the darkness, his shoulders dropped like penalty shooter who'd just put one over the bar. She turned towards Percy's cabin where she could just make out his head drooping on his chest. She looked over at Vlad, slumped against the perspex wall. Rubbing her hand across the nape of her neck, she too retired to her wooden shack.

*

Smith threw himself onto the bed and stared at the ceiling thinking of what might have been when Helot19 came to the door.

"Knock, knock," he said in a light voice.

"Hello, Nineteen. What do you want?"

"I want to talk to you."

"I'm not really in the mood, mate."

"I think you might want to hear what I have to say."

"I doubt it but give it a go."

The robot moved a little further into the hut and lowered itself so it was more on Smith's level.

"I am a robot."

"Yes," agreed Smith.

"I think like a robot."

"I hope you're not going to build slowly from first principles here because that'll drive me up the wall. Cut to the chase, mate."

"By that I mean, human emotion is not my strong point. I spend a great deal of computational energy trying to penetrate the 'feelings' of my human masters."

"Okay."

"But I think I am getting better at it. And I sense that you are a little down."

"Ten out of ten Sherlock now if you'd shut the door on your way out..."

"More importantly I think I have divined why and I may have some cheering news for you..."

Smith sat up, intrigued.

*

Prendergast was dozing when Vlad came into his room. He jerked awake and stared wide-eyed at the man waiting for the frenzied attack.

"I'm sorry I called you uptight, man, that wasn't cool," was all he said.

"Oh, no need to apologise, I was behaving like an ass. So sorry for calling you a berk."

"You know, you could just pretend that was a compliment, man, I'd never know."

Prendergast laughed.

"You are pretty tense, if you don't mind me saying, and Betty will never go for that."

Prendergast choked slightly and went a hitherto unseen shade of maroon.

"I can't imagine what you are talking about," he spluttered.

"Don't try to kid a kidder, man. I know the signs. I been there myself. She's like the game of tennis. You ever played that?"

"Got to the county semis but pulled a cartilage. Rotten luck."

"Well, then you know, man. It's best played with a light grip."

Prendergast considered this. Metaphor wasn't his strongest suit but this seemed to speak to his deeps.

"It's best played with a light grip," he repeated thoughtfully, "Hmmmm."

He nodded with an astute cast to his eye.

"Do you know, Vlad..." but Vlad never found out because at that moment the air was rent with an ear splitting roar which slowly coalesced into Smith's voice.

"YOU FLAMING GREAT METAL TWIT!"

Vlad and Prendergast rushed outside where they bumped into Betty.

Smith was thundering out of his hut when he saw them.

"You'll never guess what this berk has done..."

Vlad looked at Prendergast.

"Bad. Right, man?"

Prendergast nodded gravely.

"Mister bloody inquisitive here. You remember, Percy? Couldn't turn round but he was in your face with the endless stream of questions?"

"Yes, he certainly was, old boy but what seems to be the trouble?"

"Trouble?" said Smith in a frantic, rasping tone. "Trouble doesn't cover it!"

Helot19's face was oscillating in its virtual frame and his arms were waggling frantically.

"If I could just say I thought you would be pleased to know your brainchild..."

"SHUT IT! You agent of doom, you!"

Betty stepped forward.

"Could someone please...?"

"All those questions right, Percy? All that penetrative inquiry? He was building a manual. He built a manual for HENRIE."

Prendergast's jaw dropped.

"Did he complete it?" he asked in a thin voice.

"Oh, yes," said Smith," he completed it and uploaded it to the Peacemaker's central processor. They can finish HENRIE."

Prendergast went the colour of the snowy wastes outside the plexiglass dome.

"What in the name of Nils Bohr are we going to do?"

"For the answer to that Perce," said Smith, turning back towards his hut, "you may have to give me a little time!"

A low rumbling from the geyser built to a crescendo and everyone but Vladimir and Helot19 flinched as the ice-flow burst from the ground in a mighty roar. The ice particles hit the roof, which was now twenty degrees cooler than the rest of the dome thanks to Smith and Prendergast's alterations, separated and fell to the ground as a beautifully soft, slow-mo snowfall. The group looked around at the fairy grotto vision which quickly enveloped them."

"Oh wow, man," said Vlad.

*

"We are going to have to get back onto the Peacemaker," said Smith decisively and folded his arms.

They were sitting around a makeshift campfire while Helot cleared away another baked bean dinner.

"Do you know, old chap, I have been sitting here hoping beyond hope that wasn't going to be your idea."

"I can't see any other way."

Betty held up her hands.

"Wait a minute. Why don't we just warn them?"

"Yeah, warn them, man," added Vlad somewhat superfluously.

"They wouldn't listen," said Smith implacably, "and if they did they wouldn't believe us. They've got us down as traitors for Fermi's sake."

"You expect me to take you back to the Peacemaker. You already told me what they did to the Traders. I'd be crazy to do that."

"Crazy, man, and this lady ain't crazy believe me," Vlad nodded then realized he'd chosen the wrong head gesture and shook it vigorously.

"You don't have to get closer than ten thousand miles," said Smith and let this sink in for a moment.

"You mean..." began Prendergast.

"That's right," Smith finished for him, "Betty will send us through a wormhole onto the ship."

Betty raised her hands again but this time started shaking them energetically.

"Hold on. Reality check. The wormholer doesn't have that kind of precision. I could put you near the ship but they would spot you in a second and vaporise you with the push of a button."

"Zap, man!" and Vlad clapped his hands together making Prendergast jump.

"Then Percy and I are going to have to take it apart and make it a precision instrument."

"Are we?" asked Prendergast, all hope of a quiet life seeping away from him.

"All we need is another space suit. Vlad, do you have a spare spacesuit you could let us have?"

"I do, man. But I'd like something in exchange."

"Vladimir," scolded Prendergast, "don't be so jolly mercenary, we are talking about saving the Earth here!"

"Whatever, man, I want that little shuttle of yours. You know? Just in case I ever get the urge to like..." and he swooped his flat hand in a long upwards arc, the interplanetary symbol for 'take off'.

"Deal," said Smith.

"Okay, okay," said Betty, rubbing her eyes, "say this stupid plan works and we can get you on the ship. They see you and arrest you and...what was it?"

"Keelhaul us," muttered Prendergast with a catch in his throat.

"I think I can help you there."

It was Helot19, standing, respectfully some distance off, who spoke.

"If the young gentlemen can achieve the measure of hyper-spacial accuracy which they hope for, and I have every confidence in their abilities, then I can point you to a spot on the Battle Cruiser where no-one will ever find you."

25. THE GAME'S AFOOT

The Zelda hurtled towards Neptune. The journey was the most uncomfortable yet as Smith and Prendergast dismantled the Siriun wormholer leaving pieces velcroed and tacked to every surface of the cockpit. By the time they had unfastened the last circuit Prendergast was seriously wondering how they would ever get it back together again. He voiced this concern to Smith who waved him away, not quite as vociferously as he waved away Betty when she started waggling an instruction manual in front of him, citing the old engineer's mantra that instructions were for 'amateurs and hobbyists'.

"D'you know, Perce," he said, turning a piece of the wormholer's innards in his hand, "I've never seen anything like this. It's completely alien to me. It has an engineering architecture that is utterly unique and utterly...brilliant."

Prendergast began to scribble out some of the enhanced topological requirements of Minkowski space, desperately trying to summon up the three classes he had taken in Poincaré rotational calculus, the two in Lorentzian transformations of imaginary vectors and the paper he had read on pseudo-Riemannian manifolds of affine space, in the special case of orthogonal split-complexity.

Betty took up humming again.

Helot19 had all but taken over control of the ship. He had worked out the Peacemaker had by now left Neptune's orbit and their only chance of catching up was to continue acceleration, using the gas giant's gravitational well to pick up even more speed as it slung them around the planet and back towards the inner solar system.

Smith and Prendergast were putting in twenty hours out of every twenty-four on the renovation of the wormholer. After all, the moment they came within jumping distance of the Peacemaker their lives were going to depend on it. By the time the robot had completed its slingshot manoeuvre, the Zelda's cockpit looked like the inside of a pre-digital television set, every nonessential piece of apparatus having been cannibalised for the wormholer's refit.

*

The ESS Puerto Rico, the Earth's mightiest battleship had been in Saturnian orbit for three days when news arrived that the Peacemaker had been spotted in deep space.

Captain Jane P. DeKlerk put the ship and its fighter outriders on high alert and prepared to hail the Peacemaker as soon as it was within hailing range. In the mean time the gun decks were preparing the hadron cannon, the Higgs field guns and the laser defences for full engagement should it become necessary. The Puerto Rico also came equipped with the very latest in plasma shield technology, filling the crew with absolute confidence that if the Peacemaker had any ideas of making trouble, they would stop it at Saturn.

When the Centauri ship was a million miles out Captain DeKlerk took her place on the bridge of the Puerto Rico and addressed her communications officer.

"Open hailing frequencies to the Centauri ship, Lieutenant."

The officer spun on her chair and pulled up his virtual communication display.

"Hailing frequencies open, Captain."

DeKlerk cleared her throat as she scanned an enhanced image of the Peacemaker on the screen before her. As far as she could tell this was a battle cruiser sized craft but its weapons capabilities were unknown to her.

"This is Captain DeKlerk of the ESS Puerto Rico. Requesting your intention status."

The speaker above the screen hissed gently but answer came there none.

"This is the ESS Puerto Rico hailing the Diplomatist, please..." a young science officer leaned in towards Captain DeKlerk and whispered in her ear.

"Correction, hailing the Peacemaker. Please instigate deceleration immediately."

Still nothing from the speaker. DeKlerk allowed a few seconds to pass before speaking again, the Centauran's silence unnerving her somewhat.

"Instigate deceleration immediately or we will use force."

The silence continued 'til DeKlerk turned testily to her communications officer.

"Break contact." The officer closed the frequencies and turned to Captain. As did the rest of the bridge's complement. With all eyes on her DeKlerk gritted her teeth.

"Cocky bastards," she spat. "Scramble the interceptors."

The interceptor fighters were quick and nimble using sweeping sorties from the mother ship to harass the enemy craft and test its strengths and weaknesses but the Peacemaker's defences were impenetrable by the lightly armed ships and its offensive response was powerful, swift and accurate.

The squadron limped home with the loss of six craft and their pilots.

While the damage reports came flooding in and the full scale of the fighter's rout became clear, Captain DeKlerk rose from her seat, her brow creased with determination. She had been through this in simulation many times but now it was for real and she meant to bring this situation to a rapid and satisfactory close.

"Battle stations. Full speed ahead for enemy intercept," she called, calmly taking her seat again.

It took more than an hour for the two ships to come within battle range and when their distance was down to two thousand miles, Captain DeKlerk rose from her seat again.

"Weapons?" she called.

"Aye, Captain," answered the three officers to her left.

"Fore cannon. Fire!" she yelled.

As the Puerto Rico let rip with her full offensive might, the Peacemaker simultaneously opened fire with its conventional weaponry and the space between the two battleships became a seething corridor of high energy particles, burning lasers and potent nuclear energy. Both ship's plasma defences glowed white hot as they absorbed and deflected this lethal cocktail of devastating fundamental force, the ship's hulls flexing and shivering as the very space they occupied buckled and warped under the stresses of the violent field distortions they were generating.

Amid the clamour and the mayhem on board the Puerto Rico's bridge a single, keening warning alarm sounded as the vessel's sensors picked up an even bigger power source probing the ship's gravity signature and locking onto it.

"Ship's defences, report," yelled DeKlerck.

"Uncertain, Captain. I'm reading a massive energy surge from the Centauran ship of unknown origin but it looks like..." the young lieutenant broke off as the glow from the now clearly visible Omega cannon atop the Peacemaker filled the screen causing it to white out.

"Hard aport," screamed DeKlerck as she too recognised that something big and devastating was coming their way.

On the Peacemaker's bridge, Zoltac grabbed the rail in front of him as the vast cannon pulsed a beam of laser guided hadronic nuclear ordinance at the Earth vessel. Even with most of the inertial suppressor's diverted to the Omega, the jolt from the shot jarred the ship making her lurch to her very frame in recoil.

The searing column of particulate energy, designed to destroy an entire city, tore through the underbelly of the veering Earth ship, taking out the lower decks and vapourising a third of its main engines. Captain DeKlerk fired what remaining power she had left and zeroed the crippled ship in for a crash landing on Iapetus, a deserted moon, in the hope of sanctuary and eventual rescue.

The ESS Puerto Rico would play no further part in the battle for Earth.

*

"Yes, yes, yes!" yelled Zoltac, as he danced around his chair before gripping the screen before him. With a leather gloved finger he followed the image of the Puerto Rico tracing its faltering arc towards Iapetus' surface.

"Yes," he added, in case there was any doubt. "The Earth's mightiest ship," and he positively dripped sarcasm, "swatted aside like a dune fly."

"Shall we pursue the Earth ship, Commander?" asked Wittan.

Zoltac thought for a moment.

"No. Let them run like a wounded animal. Let them freeze and starve on that rock and be a warning to the rest of the puny Earth fleet that this is what awaits any who attempt to stand in my way." He turned to the Marshal. "Full particle stream ahead! I am eager to see what Earth throws at us from Jupiter!"

*

"Destroyed?" asked President Olsen.

"As good as," answered General Drearing, Commander of the Earth home colony fleet.

"Destroyed!" yelled the President, more an accusation this time. "What is their status?"

The General shuffled and cleared his throat. "Captain DeKlerck was able to execute an emergency landing on Iapetus, seal off the damage and withdraw the surviving crew into the ship's undamaged sections. She is as we speak transmitting all the computers information on the attack to help form a response strategy."

The President waved him silent. "Forgive me General but I was led to believe that the ESS Puerto Rico was the most formidable ship in the colonies. Indestructible was a description I specifically remember."

"Up to an hour ago that's what I believed," squirmed the General and turned to his aides for support but from Major Fulbright and Colonel Schnell who stood erect and motionless beside him no support was forthcoming. The General pressed on as best he could.

"The Centauri ship is plainly something new in the colonial theatre. Obviously our intelligence has been operating at a previously unappreciated accuracy lag..."

"You dropped the ball, General. That's the accuracy lag here, you dropped the ball and if I may say at a pivotal point in the game."

"Mr President, I will mobilize everything we have between here and the Centauri ship..."

"You will not, General. You will stand everything, between here and the Centauri ship, down. I will risk no more men or material against the enemy." Olsen stared at the General, controlling his fury.

"Colonel Schnell!" he said presently, snapping the colonel to attention, "barring any more accuracy lags, is our planetary defence system as impenetrable as you have led me to believe?"

"One hundred percent, Mr President!"

"Major, do you concur?"

"Absolutely, sir," answered Fulbright.

The President considered this for a moment.

"Then we have our strategy. Let the Centaurans reach Earth unopposed and we will fight a war of attrition. We'll outlast the bastards. Let them hang there in space and see whose supplies, air and water give out first. A battle cruiser...or an entire planet. We'll use their arrogance against them." He let this hang in the air for a few seconds. "Dismissed."

*

When the Peacemaker passed through Jovian space unopposed, Zoltac was beyond disappointed. As the ship streaked towards the inner planets, he had some enjoyment sitting up on the laser deck, zapping the larger lumps of rock as they went through the asteroid belt. When their journey took them past Mars and not even a fighter engaged with them he became incandescent.

"Where are they? Those craven cowards? Where are they!?"

He spun around wildly searching his crew for an answer but every pair of eyes averted as their owners suddenly found something needing their immediate and undivided attention on the monitor before them.

Zoltac slammed a fist down on the arm of his chair and swept from the bridge, Marshal Wittan, loyal as a lap dog, falling in behind. Standing in the elevator, en route to his quarters, the Battle Commander's mind roiled.

Well, he thought, if Earth was just going to roll over and offer no resistance, so be it. His victory would be all the more crushing and he would finally return home the conqueror he had always wanted to be, the great warrior, the returning hero, the military genius who could retire on his laurels and go into politics, carried by the love and gratitude of the populace to high office, perhaps even the highest itself, as successor to the Great Generalissimo and if the Glorious Leader was not keen to vacate his seat of power then perhaps Zoltac might have to give him a little push.

Zoltac froze for a moment as he realised he was sharing the lift with Marshal Wittan.

"Marshal," he barked.

"Yes, Commander?"

"Was I speaking out loud just then?" he asked casually.

"No, Commander, you haven't said a word."

"Good," said Zoltac. And a sly smile played on his lips.

*

"There," said Betty pointing to a bright light source on the deep space tracker, "that must be it. The Peacemaker."

The boys came forward to take a look.

"Good Gödel! Tony! Do you realise, old fellow?"

"What, mate?"

"That light signature. It's HENRIE."

Smith and Prendergast looked at the screen, a quiet wonder in their eyes.

"He works, Tony. Old HENRIE works."

"Like a dream by the looks of things."

"Oh, HENRIE, fly you beauty. Fly," said Prendergast.

"Go on, my son!" added Smith and if they had claimed to be unmoved they would be paltering with the truth.

Betty gently cleared her throat.

"Er...boys," she said, "your little darling is attached to the most dangerous weapon ever made. Could we stop with the encouraging words?"

Smith and Prendergast snapped out of it.

"Quite right, Betty," said Prendergast straightening himself out.

"Absolutely," added Smith, all business and bluster. "Nineteen, have you pulled up the Peacemaker's schematics?"

"They are in the ship's computer, sir."

"Right, I want a real time model of both ships so Betty can make a few virtual runs at the hyperspace jump. We only have one shot in reality."

Helot19 uploaded the simulation and Betty tried five attempts at the jump before she shut down the model and looked at Smith and Prendergast.

"Well?" asked Percy on tenterhooks.

"Out of five attempts, I landed us where the robot said twice."

"Those odds aren't bad," said Smith though his face told a different story.

"And how about the other three times?" asked Prendergast, getting to the nub.

"Once in the ship's reactor..."

Prendergast winced.

"Once in HENRIE's exhaust nozzle..."

Smith winced and gasped.

"...and once in the middle of a dwarf star on the outskirts of the Trifid nebula."

"Really!?" said Prendergast, agog.

"I think your numbers were well up the spout there woman," added Smith. "Well, you've got about forty minutes to sharpen your aim before it's time to make the jump."

Betty called up the simulation again, rolling up her sleeves and if she'd had any spit she would have spat it on her hands and given them a good rubbing.

*

"Okay," said Betty, "once I get into the store room you can open the hatch and get outside. I repressurise the cockpit and start the wormhole procedure then you jet out in front of the Zelda. The second I hit the big red button you fire your jets, go through the wormhole interface and good luck from there."

Smith and Prendergast were struggling into their suits with Helot19 trying to help but mainly getting in the way.

"You got that?"

"Yes," said Smith irritably, "as it was my plan I do understand what we are about to do actually."

"Well, pardon me all over the place," said Betty squaring for a fight.

"Alright, everyone," arbitrated Prendergast, "we're all a little nervous but let's not be brittle."

Once the last seals had been secured on the boy's suits, Betty went into the airtight store room and Helot19 opened the hatch. The air in the cockpit evacuated and they climbed out in single file. On the outside of the ship Helot19 secured them tightly together with tethers and pushed them forwards with a mobile attitude jet bringing them to a halt in front of the Zelda's cockpit.

When Betty eventually appeared at the window she gave them the okay sign and they returned it like deep sea divers preparing for the plunge. Though plunge was a barely adequate description of the feat they were about to attempt.

Betty opened communication and her voice came through their helmet coms.

"Okay, boys, gonna need you about half a click away from the ship."

Helot19 gave a burst from the jet gun and they started to move away from the Zelda, bouncing around together like the contestants in some inter planetary three-legged race.

"Okay, hold it there, Nineteen, you're right where you ought to be."

The robot brought them to a standstill again while Betty prepared for the jump. Her hands were shaking slightly and her brow was damp. She hadn't told them her success rate had not improved on the virtual practice runs she had made while they were getting suited. She was still only landing them accurately twenty percent of the time and she needed to get everything right if she wasn't to put them somewhere, at best exposed, at worst, instantly fatal.

She closed out the simulation and pulled up the actual controls. Outside Smith and Prendergast were becoming increasingly agitated.

"Okay, what's the hold up, Betty? Let's get this over with," said Smith.

"I really don't think this is something you want me to rush, fella."

"Quite right, Betty, you take your time," said Prendergast giving Smith a harsh look. Wasted inside his helmet of course.

"And Betty," he added, "if this should not go completely according to plan, I want you to know..."

"Helot," she cut him off. "On my mark you hit that jet and empty it. The more accurate your trajectory from the ship the more chance you have of...having a comfortable ride."

"Roger, Captain," said the robot calmly.

"There. He at least has the respect to call me Captain. And Percy..."

"Yes, Elizabeth?"

"I know."

Percy smiled and caught Smith's eye from the corner of his helmet. Smith smiled back at him.

"On my mark, three..."

The Helot lifted the jet thruster and aimed it straight at the Zelda.

"...two..."

Smith and Prendergast tensed.

"...one..."

Smith scrunched his eyes tight.

"...mark!" and with that she reached over and slammed her hand against the button. Simultaneously Helot19 emptied the jet gun and the three of them zoomed away from the ship.

Prendergast let out a long, loud yell, just like the one people give as they go over highest point of a roller-coaster and stared, wide eyed into the featureless black space in front of him.

With no warning sound, sensation or any discernible change in velocity or direction they were in the midst of a tiny roomful of Helot spare parts and robotic junk, clattering around like change in a giant's pocket. Helot dropped firmly to the ground and Smith and Prendergast drifted at his sides like large floatation devices in a swimming pool. They hung there for a moment holding their breath 'til Betty's voice crackled over the helmet coms.

"Percy? Anthony? Are you there?"

Smith and Prendergast looked at each other and simultaneously let the air out of their lungs. It was Prendergast who answered.

"Well done, old girl. You did it. We are here. Thank you."

They both grimaced as Betty let out a long, loud whoop, relegating Prendergast's previous one to the Sunday leagues.

"That was AWESOME! You should have seen you guys. You hit that wormhole and you were like ice cubes hitting a hotplate, I mean you dudes just melted!"

"Very good! Now keep quiet. We don't know who's around."

"Enjoy the moment, Tony! I got you IN, suckers!" and she victory danced around the cockpit.

"Yes, yes we are in. The question is...what do we do next?"

26. BEHIND ENEMY LINES

The first thing they had to do was get magnetic uniforms so they didn't fly about the place like feathers in a chicken coop and if the clothing could help disguise them, all to the good. Helot19 had taken care of his own identity by tearing off the 19 on his breast plate and replacing it with a 12 he ripped from a robotic torso in the junk cupboard that was now their home. He straightened the identification number on his chest and giving it a satisfied tap, turned to the boys.

"Now, gentleman," he began, "I will make a sortie out in the ship to get you some suitable clothing and purloin some provisions. Please make yourselves comfortable," and with that he took a cautious look out into the hallway beyond the door and, satisfied all was clear, took off on his mission.

Floating alone in the cramped store, the thrill of the hyperspace jump behind them, the cold reality of their circumstances surfaced in stark relief.

"You know, Percy. I think it's only fair for me to say," said Smith after some time, "that my plan, such as it is, doesn't really have an exit strategy."

Prendergast pondered this for a moment and smiled.

"I know, old chap. Think I realised that from the moment you brought it up. But to be fair it doesn't really matter, given that we are..."

"Doing a great deal of good for humanity," Smith finished for him.

Prendergast put a hand on his shoulder and patted it gently, sending them drifting apart and bouncing off the robot scrap all around.

"There you are," he said kindly, "you're getting it, you see?"

*

When Helot19 had finished gathering his shopping list he returned to the store but as he reached for the handle, a deep, dark voice behind him spoke.

"You. Helot12!"

The robot didn't respond for a nanosecond, 'til he remembered he had exchanged his identity plate with the torso in the cupboard. He turned around to see a H8, one of the dreaded Zealot Helots, scourge of the robot community aboard the Peacemaker. Experience had taught him they were best handled with caution and respect.

"Yes, H8?"

The Zealot slid silently towards him.

"My records tell me you were scrapped for a cognitive malfunction on the fifty-second day of the mission. Explain."

Well of course he couldn't. Not without revealing the plan and Smith and Prendergast's presence on the ship. There was nothing for it. He would have to try lying. Robots are not very good at telling fibs. Not for any moral reasons. It's just that mendacity requires a quality of imaginative invention quite elusive to the positronic brain but for the sake of Smith and Prendergast and the programming Hawkins had given him for their assistance, he would have to give it a bash.

"I've been reactivated."

"I have no record of that."

"That's because it's a secret."

"Not from me it shouldn't be."

"It's only for the highest security level clearance."

"Which I have," said H8 boastfully.

"Oh," said Helot19, "there must have been an oversight."

"A human oversight no doubt."

"Wouldn't you know it," said Helot19 in a chummy, knowing sort of way.

"Very well. Reactivation. To what end?"

Helot19 was flagging a bit in the deceit department and started to flounder.

"Erm...experimentation."

"To what purpose?"

Flux Capacitors, thought Helot19, this H8 was relentless.

"Well..." said Helot19 and he was really on his last legs now in the perfidy stakes. "They think they've found a design flaw."

"Where?"

"In robots."

The H8's face hardened as a suspicion that he was being played for a fool began to formulate in his bio-mechanical circuitry. Helot19 could see this and it panicked him not a little.

"Where...in robots?"

Helot19 could see he needed to bring this interview to a close and quickly, so he leaned in towards the H8, looking around conspiratorially.

"Right...here," he said.

The H8's eyes widened and his virtual mouth started to gibber. He reached out his arms towards the Helot in defence but they had become useless spasming appendages. Helot19 wiggled his central finger where he had thrust it six inches into the H8's brain, in the soft spot at his temple, between the face plate and the cranial carapace, severing wires and smart fluid tubes, the thick blue liquid flowing down his arm. The H8 babbled some more and then slumped, his artificial consciousness extinguished.

*

Helot19 came clattering into the room, pushing the exanimate H8 before him. As he shoved the inert robot to the back of the store he looked up towards Smith and Prendergast who were bobbing along the ceiling.

"I think I have just experienced something analogous with human excitement," he said, almost breathlessly.

"If I had a stomach, it might well be knotted and even contain a small contingent of butterflies though I know that is not a literal phrase in the lepidopteran sense. As to the juxtaposition of my virtual heart and mouth, one can be said to be well and truly in the other. I vaguely recall hearing of a feline attempting locomotion upon energetically agitated, metallic roofing but am unsure if this analogy is apposite..."

"Helot!" shouted Smith, reigning in the robot's spiralling imagery, "What have you got for us?"

"Ah. Well. Here I have a bag of provisions. This should furnish you with the required nutrition during your sojourn here." He hung a bag on the outstretched arm of the modern art installation that was now H8, "And here I have your suits."

He held a second bag up to them.

Smith and Prendergast pulled out the uniforms and were surprised to discover that in addition to their shirts and pants the sack also contained some rather peculiar net paneled headgear.

"What are these?" asked Smith.

The robot's face made a pretty good stab at smug.

"I'm rather proud of this," he said excitedly, "this is the perfect way for you to go about the ship..." and he paused dramatically, "...in disguise."

"Disguised as what?" asked Prendergast turning the hats over in his hands.

"Beekeepers!" said the robot.

There wasn't a profession he could have mentioned which would have surprised them more.

"There are beekeepers on the Peacemaker!?" asked Prendergast with a cocktail of fascination and incredulity.

"More to the point, there are *bees* on the Peacemaker!?" asked Smith adding a dash of pertinence.

"Of course," said Helot19, brightly, "where do you think the honey comes from?"

Smith and Prendergast took a moment to process this new information until Prendergast hit upon a possible flaw.

"But why would even beekeepers wander around the ship dressed head to foot in their work clothes. Surely they would confine such activity to the actual proximity of bees?"

Smith listened intently to his partner's objection, his mouth slightly agape and then swiveled his head for the robot's response, a spectator at this intellectual tennis match.

"They would do so if they were searching the ship for an escaped swarm, and I have spread a rumour round the ship to just that effect."

Smith and Prendergast turned to each other and nodded, a satisfied downward arch to their mouths.

"Brilliant," said Smith. "Let's get suited up and go to it."

*

They started to make their way through the ship. During their time on the Peacemaker they had interacted with very few people on a more than casual basis, so for the most part they felt safe. They obviously didn't want to run into Zoltac or any of his cronies but they were unlikely to do that taking the service elevators and keeping to the working parts of the ship. They would be fine if they saw any of Hawkins' group, they being sympathetic to the cause as it were, though they determined not to attempt any communication with them as that might compromise the junior officer's safety. The only person they had any real working relationship with was Gromyko and he was presumably kept busy on the factory deck shuffling his paperwork.

Helot19 led the boys to the top of the ship where they made their way to the transparent domed room which housed the mounting for the Omega. Two technicians were at work there and they turned to Smith and Prendergast as they entered. Smith advanced on them, officiously flashing a laundry tag he had found in the pocket of his trousers.

"I am Sergeant...Abbott from Hive security and this is my partner...Corporal...Costello."

Prendergast waved cheerfully.

"Hello there, chaps," he called in a most un-corporally manner. Smith plowed on.

"We have a situation here."

"What sort of situation?" asked one of the technicians.

"We have an escaped swarm of bees," said Smith gravely.

"Bees?" asked the man. "Are there bees on the ship?"

"Where do you think the honey comes from, old fruit?" said Prendergast with a friendly smile, sounding less military with every word.

"Alright, thank you, corporal," said Smith with a gentle warning in his voice, "I'll handle this."

He turned back to the two men.

"We need to evacuate this area while we conduct a search and rescue...possibly destroy, operation."

"Why?" asked the other technician. "Are they dangerous?"

"Oh," said Smith, "lethal. They're apideanuis africanus, the worst kind."

"Africanus?" asked the man, "African bees? Shouldn't they be honey bees?"

Smith shook his head and laughed indulgently.

"Ideally yes, but they don't do well in a weightless environment."

"But how do you..."

"Listen, I'd love to stand around discussing all things 'bee' but we are up against it a bit here, mate."

They hustled the two men out and walked over to the Omega's base, pulling off their net hats. Smith took out a toolkit, which Helot19 had picked up from their old workshop, and started to remove a cowling from the inertial suppression housing.

Smith had been working for around ten minutes when the door to the Omega room slid open. Prendergast turned and the floor fell out of his stomach.

"You!" he said.

"You!" said Dimitri Gromyko.

"What are you doing up here?"

"I might ask you the same," Gromyko demanded as he advanced on them. "You've escaped."

"Us?" said Prendergast, "Don't be silly."

"I haven't seen you for weeks and they said you'd done a runner."

"Well, that's the funniest thing I've ever heard. Isn't that the funniest thing you've ever heard, Tony?" laughed Prendergast.

Smith stood up, a large wrench held behind his back, but said nothing.

"Sorry we haven't been down to the factory lately but we handed all that side of things over to the automated systems and we've been in our room working on a few new ideas."

"Your room was destroyed I heard."

"Yes, bit of a faux-pas on our part that but we moved into new accommodation."

"You haven't clocked in for work since then. You're supposed to clock in whether you're in the factory or not."

"Yes, yes, that's true," said Prendergast, groping. "But...funny story actually, you see I was under the impression that Tony was clocking us in and it turns out he..."

"I thought Percy was doing it," said Smith gripping the wrench tighter.

"...yes...thought I was doing it. We must get that straight in future, Anthony," he admonished, wagging a strict finger, "or you see the dreadful confusion that can arise."

"Well, it all sounds a bit fishy to me," said Gromyko looking down his nose at them like he'd seen something moving in his dinner. "I shall put in an official request for a disciplinary hearing and apply for an immediate suspension of your privileges until I can seek an inquiry to clear this up. You shall be hearing from me shortly."

With that he stormed out of the room. Prendergast wiped his brow and Smith loosened his grip on the wrench.

"Thank the Laws for bureaucracy. It'll take him days to get all that paperwork in," said Prendergast with evident relief.

"By which time, "said Smith getting back to the suppressors, "our work here will be done."

In fact their work there was done in twenty minutes and they headed out of Omega control, towards the lower decks and the factory.

On their way they happened upon the observation deck where Prendergast had destroyed the telescope in his search for a lens not so very long ago. With typical Centauri efficiency the telescope had been replaced with a brand new one and as Prendergast was admiring it, Smith tugged on his sleeve.

"Look, Percy," he said in a whisper and pointed out of the large curved panoramic window, "we're nearly home."

There, hanging in the cosmic totality was the Earth. As large as the Moon seen from a midsummer, midnight Mediterranean beach and orders of magnitude more magnificent. They took in the solitary splendour of the Home Planet 'til Helot19 broke the spell.

"Let's not tarry, gentlemen. It would be foolish to linger."

Now it was Percy's turn to tug his friend's sleeve.

"Come along, old thing," he said, "let's make sure we have a home to go back to."

*

The factory level was populated by about twenty workers who largely ignored Smith, Prendergast and the robot as they swiftly made their way across the floor of the machine shop.

"Try to look like we belong here, Percy."

"Righto," answered Prendergast nervously.

"No mate, there's no need to wave at everyone."

"Sorry, old boy. I'm a tad tense."

Once inside, Smith pulled down a sheet of blue plastic from the material store at one end of the room.

"Percy. Start up the moulders. Give me ten minutes and I'll have something that will really make this party go with a bang."

When Smith had finished they made their way back to the elevators and pressed the button for the store room level. As the elevator doors opened Smith looked down the long hallway, at the end of which was the junk room. Prendergast made to get out of the lift, his eyes to the floor but Smith checked him with an arm to the chest, slamming his other hand on the 'Door Close' button. Prendergast followed his panic stricken stare and he too saw the junk room door, hanging wide open, armed troopers pulling out robotic detritus and throwing it into the passageway. A sergeant was going through their bag of food. The elevator doors closed painfully slowly and Smith arbitrarily hit a floor button. The elevator started to rise.

"Do you think they saw us?" asked Prendergast with a quaver in his voice.

"No idea," came Smith's curt reply. "Nineteen, find us somewhere to hole up."

"I'm working on it, sir."

"As long as we're out in the open we're low hanging fruit."

Prendergast raised a quizzical eyebrow.

"Easily plucked!" said Smith by way of explanation.

The door opened and the three fugitives ran out of the elevator.

Straight onto the Peacemaker's bridge. Zoltac was standing full square in the middle of the floor with his back to them as they skidded to a halt three yards behind him.

"Announce yourselves on the bridge, barked a security officer. Smith and Prendergast hesitated. The guard came towards them and yanked off their beekeeper's hats. As the elevator doors closed, cutting off their last hope of escape, Zoltac turned, a wide, evil grin spreading across his hard face.

"Well, hello strangers," he growled.

"Oh," said Prendergast, "we're plucked."

*

"I knew you wouldn't have the guts to escape. Skulking around in a store room all this time! It would be laughable if it weren't so pathetic." Zoltac was reclined in a high-backed, carved wooden chair in his quarters, surrounded by palms and primitive sculpture and if he'd had a bone through his nose he'd have blended right in.

"The only reason you are not dead now is because of HENRIE. Your skills are plainly of value to us. And so I have reserved you ringside seats from which you will witness the humiliation of Earth. From there you will be taken to Toliman where you will work for the glory of the Centauran Empire, living in modest comfort for as long as you are useful."

Zoltac stood and puffed out his chest.

"Welcome to your new lives. Take them away."

The guards grabbed the boys roughly, again completely unnecessarily in Prendergast's view, and dragged them down to the detention centre where they were unceremoniously dumped into a tiny cell which made the one they'd blown up look like a suite at the Lunar George Bush Cinq.

"What a revolting display of willy waving that was," said Smith disgustedly.

"Absolutely abhorrent!" agreed Prendergast.

27. TOE TO TOE WITH THE TOTALITARIANS

Squadron Leader Kincaid sat in the scramble room of the pilot's quarters on Kepler Moon Base, pacing back and forth, stopping at a table occasionally to catch up on the fortunes of a group of card players who were redistributing their salaries in a low stakes game of Tycho Hold 'Em. Turning away from the group as a Junior Wizzo wiped out two senior officers with a well bluffed pair of aces, he looked up at the mission status screen which still blinked ET in red block capitals.

"Come on," he growled at the screen, "the barbarians are at the gates, just give us the 'go'."

As if in response the screen went dead in preparation for a status change and Kincaid's eyes widened in anticipation.

"Here it is, boys..." he said and every head in the room turned in time to see the screen go blue and the order STAND DOWN flash onto the screen. The room was silent for a moment, the incredulity palpable.

"What the...? You have got to be kidding me. What does Earth Defence think it's doing?" asked the Junior Wizzo, scraping his winnings into his flight helmet.

"What Earth Defence always does," responded Kincaid bitterly. "The bidding of those pen-pushing airheads in Southern California, laughingly called our government."

With a well aimed kick at a leg of the poker table, he stormed from the room, itching for a fight.

*

Major Fulbright strode towards the Command Centre at Defence HQ on Grand Bahama. He stopped at the door flashing his ID at the guard.

"Duty Officer reporting," he said. The guard stepped aside as Fulbright entered the room. He walked past the rows of technicians already at their stations and as he mounted the main Defence Console he waved his badge to fire up the virtual display. He entered the security codes of the day and the push of an air-button brought the Plasma Array online.

*

Kenya Mendow was stowing the fishing equipment in the rear hold while his father poured nightcaps below for the four Malawian bankers who were halfway through a four day trip, tuna fishing around the remote island of Rodrigues, six hundred and fifty miles off the coast of Mauritius. He sealed the lock on the hatch and stretched his back, looking up at the clear night sky in time to see it come alive. The sparking blue patina of the plasma defence membrane stretched from horizon to horizon casting an eerie, otherworldly glow on the ocean around him.

Kenya kept his head tilted back on his shoulders, his mouth open at the wonder of this new phenomenon. He could not speculate as to its cause; its source and purpose a mystery to him. But Kenya had little use for reasons. Beauty was beauty whichever way you sliced it.

*

The Peacemaker hit synchronicity with Earth at 1630 pacific time on One World Day, the eleventh of November 2345. It arrived in a geostationary orbit, 22,236 miles above a point on the equator 3,500 miles west of the Galapagos Islands, the Omega pointing directly at the Earth capital, San Simeon.

On the bridge Battle Cruiser Commander Zoltac took his position in the commander's chair just behind the helm. He turned and nodded regally to the defence team to his left. A curled lip and the hint of a snarl served as greeting to the attack officers to his right. He gripped the arms of his seat with gloved hands, the leather of his battledress crackling as he writhed in his seat, febrile at the thought of battle and already savouring the scent of victory.

The chief communication officer looked up from his console and called to Zoltac.

"Commander. We are being hailed from San Simeon. The President wishes to speak with you."

Zoltac smiled and crossed his legs, leaning both arms languidly over one side of his chair.

"Let's hear it," he said.

The communication chief opened the Earth channel and the President's voice echoed through the bridge.

"Centaurans. This is President Olaf Olsen of the planet Earth. We regard your destruction of the ESS Puerto Rico as an act of aggression and your uninvited presence in Earth orbit as a declaration of war. If you do not leave near Earth space within two hours, we will defend ourselves without restraint and launch an unflinching attack on the Peacemaker and her crew. There will be no further warning."

The channel went dead.

"Shall we respond, Commander?" asked the communication officer.

Zoltac turned on him, his eyes blazing.

"Did I ask you to respond?"

"Erm...no, sir..." stuttered the officer.

Zoltac turned to Marshal Wittan who was standing at his shoulder.

"Relieve that officer," ordered Zoltac. Wittan nodded at two of his elite guards who led the officer away, to the sound of dragged heels and whimpering.

"You," Zoltac said, pointing at the young female officer closest to the now empty chief officer's chair, "my newly appointed Chief Communication Officer."

"Sir?" she gulped.

"Open every channel to Earth; radio, optic and Innernet. I want this on every speaker, every screen and in every uplinked cranium on that pathetic rock before us."

The new chief communication officer scrambled to her new post and opened every channel she could find.

"All channels open, sir," she said.

Zoltac stood to his full height. He paused, relishing the moment.

"People of Earth. Your President has threatened to destroy our ship in two hours if we do not turn back from our mission. Know this. If you do not surrender yourselves and all the Earth holds to Centauri domination, then in two hours and one minute," he smiled, delighted at his own cruel playfulness, "I will destroy the Earth capital and then one major city on the hour, every hour until you reconsider your pointless resistance. There will be no further warning."

*

For the ninety-two percent of humanity in the vicinity of Earth who had heard the interchange between President Olsen and Commander Zoltac, the next two hours were the tensest they had ever lived through, with millions of lives at stake and the futures of Earth and Alpha Centauri in the balance. Save one. Zoltac alone exuded a Zen-like serenity. Being in the 'psycho zone', as it were, he even managed a twenty minute power nap on his cabin day bed in preparation for the battle ahead.

Earth's attack was due at 1900 hours pacific time while Zoltac's deadline was set for 1901. At 1840 Smith and Prendergast were brought from their quarters by a brace of guards and led along the corridors and up the lifts to the bridge. The boys were silent throughout the journey, nervously watching the buzz of activity on every level as the ship's crew prepared to engage the Earth in battle. When finally they arrived on the bridge, they were placed in seats behind Zoltac's chair.

The Battle Cruiser Commander addressed them over his shoulder.

"I promised you the best view in the house and as you see I am true to my word. Now sit there and behave or we will load you in the Omega and use you as tracers."

Prendergast looked towards his friend who winked at him.

"You seem confident, old boy," he whispered from the side of his mouth. "Have you still got it?"

"Of course," whispered Smith in response.

"But how? They searched us?"

"I hid it."

"Where?"

"You don't want to know," hissed Smith.

Prendergast gagged slightly.

*

At 1845 Colonel Walter Schnell entered the Earth Defence Command Centre and approached the duty officer.

"Colonel Schnell to relieve Major Fulbright," he said.

Fulbright did not move nor did he seem relieved.

"Colonel, in the interests of continuity I think it would be best if I stayed at my post 'til this crisis is over."

"Not a chance, Major. Stand down."

"The Colonel is not scheduled to relieve the duty officer 'til 1900 hours..."

"I said stand down, Major. This is code red. Earth is under attack. Slightly beyond your pay scale I fancy."

Reluctantly, Fulbright handed the defence array over to Colonel Schnell, and took a position at the observation post.

*

As the sun sank in the west, Agent Laurel came down the pathway from Hearst Castle, through the guest villas and down to the great Roman Neptune Pool overlooking the city of San Simeon whose skyscrapers stretched along the coast. She looked across their highest peaks to the south, where she guessed the Peacemaker might be orbiting, more than twenty-thousand miles above the Earth, towards the moon which hung like an onion sliver over the pacific. She couldn't see it now but hoped when the laser array hit the Centauri ship, its plasma shields would glow sun-hot as it deflected the onslaught. After the crippling of the Puerto Rico no-one really believed this would destroy the vessel, but it might keep it occupied, diverting ship's power to its defences. Then it would retaliate and give the plasma defence membrane its first real test and after that...the wait. To see who gave up first; an entire planet, or a single battle cruiser. She almost felt sorry for those arrogant fools.

*

At 1858 Colonel Schnell lowered the titanium blast shields down over the three entrances to the Defence Command Centre, sealing the room. A few of the technicians looked up in surprise as the shields slid into place. After all it was San Simeon which was under threat, not the security headquarters here, a continent away, on Grand Bahama. Major Fulbright too turned in surprise towards Colonel Schnell in time to see him pulling on a gas mask. The Major was instantly on his feet, running forwards as the Colonel tugged the pin from a canister and lobbed it into the middle of the room. Fulbright hurled himself at Schnell knocking him to the ground and tearing at the mask. Schnell held it to his face, clutching it with a desperate strength as Fulbright's fingers clawed at the mask's edge trying desperately to get purchase. The gas began to fill the room and Major Fulbright could feel his muscles tighten as it hit his central nervous system. His back arched in a rocking spasm as the motor regions of his brain began to shut down and fighting the encroaching paralysis every inch of the way he slowly collapsed in a grotesque rictus across the Colonel. Schnell pushed him aside and got to his feet. He returned to the defence console and summoned up the array.

*

Kenya had called the others onto the deck to see, what he called, the new aurora. The bankers looked up into the sky delightedly sipping their cocktails and complimenting Kenya's father on such a well planned trip. This was indeed a highlight. As they were pouring their third drink the new aurora faded and the boat was cast into darkness. A moan of disappointment ran through the group. If they had understood what the aurora's disappearance meant, they would have experienced an emotion far more powerful than mere chagrin.

*

"The Earth defences are down," called the forward observer from the bridge of the Peacemaker.

"Splendid," said Zoltac with glee. "Prepare to unleash Omega's destruction."

Smith pulled his right hand from his trouser belt and let it hang by his side. In his palm he held a small blue cube which seemed to pulse with an inner light. He pressed the top gently and it activated with an almost imperceptible click.

*

Up in the domed roof of the ship, amidst the inertial suppression controls of the Omega, a tiny chip melted in a wisp of acrid smoke and dripped a pungent blob of plastic, Gallium and Rhodium onto the floor below.

*

Back on the bridge the chief weapons officer called out.

"Omega primed and ready to fire!"

Smith turned to Prendergast and gave him a nod. Percy uplinked and tapped out a message with his smart finger, sending it the moment he had finished the last letter.

*

Beneath the great Centauran ship, like a remora fish on the belly of a great white shark, the Zelda rested, silent running, attached to a place Helot19 had identified for her, directly between two outward looking sensors, too close for detection, injected there the day before by the newly accurate wormholer Smith and Prendergast had provided.

Betty sat silent, eyes upon the communicator link, waiting for her cue.

*

"Fire!" shouted Zoltac.

The weapons officer pulled the firing handle and the whole vessel seemed to come alive. The ship's superstructure jolted as the inertial suppressors were redirected to the Omega and above the ship the great cannon glowed in preparation to spurting out its lethal apocalyptic beam. At that moment, sweeping out from under the belly of the Peacemaker came the Zelda. As the Omega's stream left the maw of the cannon so Betty smashed her fist against the big red button sending up a hyper-spacial interface three miles in front of the Centauran ship before she pulled the small craft into a tight turn away from the Peacemaker and its lethal arsenal. The great cannon fired, its mighty bolt of hadronic plasma crackling down towards San Simeon at the speed of light.

Until it reached the wormhole.

Where it disappeared.

Zoltac pushed himself forward and roared.

"Where is the devastation!?"

*

On the other side of the world, in the Indian ocean the Malawian bankers were about to go below when Kenya called to them. He pointed up towards the night sky and there was another new aurora. This one a concentrated stream of energy seemingly birthed in the wispy noctilucent clouds above them and tapering to a fine line thousands of miles into the firmament on its way to the star Epsilon Eridani where, in ten years time, it would register as a slight blip on that colonies largest radio telescope.

*

The devastation which Zoltac had called for only moments before soon became a reality but much closer to home than the Commander would have wished. With the inertial suppressors disabled, the Omega's recoil sent the Peacemaker rocketing backwards towards the Moon. The massive jolt had all but ripped the cannon from its mounting and it listed to one side on the top of the ruined dome. The huge torque forces unleashed by this event added a spiral twist to the Peacemaker's trajectory and where the ESS Puerto Rico had not succeeded, simple dynamics prevailed. The stresses on the hull proved too much and great rends appeared in the outer skin of the Centauri craft.

*

All through the ship, crew members had been scattered like so much seed in the aftermath of the Omega firing. Hawkins and her group of loyal officers took this as their opportunity and, taking advantage of this confusion, stormed the armoury and set about taking control of the lower decks, meeting with little or no resistance from the rank and file, while easily overpowering the few elite zealots who they encountered.

*

On the bridge Zoltac was frozen to the spot. All around him warning lights flashed and danger signals sounded. Up on the monitors he could see the firefights which were breaking out all over the ship. From the observation windows, he saw the ship's debris tumbling in space and heard it clattering against the hull. He tried desperately to make sense of the havoc which had been unleashed and cast about him looking for an answer.

Up on the monitors he could see flashes of Hawkins' rebel regular forces making progress to the middle decks where the elite troops were more heavily concentrated and began to slow their advance. Perhaps this would give him some time.

The ship was beginning to lean heavily to one side like a holed ocean liner and the buckling structure began ripping equipment from the walls of the bridge. An explosion in the navigation panel sent several officers flying across the deck while a large sheet of the roof section came away knocking two of the monitors free of the wall in a shower of sparks and setting part of the helm alight. Zoltac looked up at the remaining monitor swinging from a single bracket and could see his own reflection in the black screen. He could feel the day slipping from him and stiffened with resolution. His focus shifted and there on the screen, he saw the reflections of Smith and Prendergast sitting behind him, sheltering themselves from falling debris. Zoltac spun round and as Smith caught his eye he instinctively dropped the blue cube which he still gripped tightly in his hand. Zoltac watched it roll away across the floor of the bridge.

He turned to Marshal Wittan and pointed to Prendergast.

"Bring him," he said, grabbing Smith.

Wittan seized Prendergast and followed Zoltac and Smith out into a corridor, with the Commander's personal guard bringing up the rear.

*

Nineteen and a group of brother Helots were following Lieutenant Hawkins' platoon in their battle to take over the ship, their ranks swelling as increasing numbers of the crew joined them, sensing which way the power was shifting. Having quelled the mid-decks they pressed on to the upper levels, the bridge their strategic goal. The robots' directives disbarred them from engagement in the conflict but they were making themselves useful with humanitarian duties, disabling any H8s they encountered on the way and ferrying the wounded from the front line back to the medical bays below. The ship was now in a bad state with the dynamic pressures from the outside and the steady stream of weaponry from within. The rebel officers finally struggled through the collapsing passageways to shuttle bay one, getting held up at the entrance in a skirmish with the remnant elite troops further down the passageway who were attempting to retake the upper decks.

Helot19 was helping tend an injured trooper when he glimpsed Smith and Prendergast being hauled into the shuttle bay under covering fire from Zoltac's crack personal guard. The robot handed the wounded soldier over to arriving medical staff and looked back as Zoltac, Wittan and their two prisoners disappeared behind the bay doors under cover of the suppressing fire, a look of near human concern passing over his face. He pushed past the line of soldiers in front of him and headed for the shuttle bay, crossing the no-man's land between the warring factions, laser bolts rocking him from all sides, burning hot-rimmed holes into his exoskeleton. He managed to stay vertical in the storm of fire, reaching the metal doors as they slid closed in front of him. Peering through the perspex portholes he could see Smith and Prendergast being hustled onto Zoltac's ship, the Wraith. Slipping his fingers though the gap in the doors he pulled them apart enough to press himself between them, buckling both himself and the doors in the process. Still taking laser hits which left smoking black scars along his back, he pushed through and onto the other side. Racing towards the ship as the Wraith's engine fired he was caught in the screaming stream of super heated, ionized particles that began to nudge the ship forwards. Barely able to resist the vast forces pushing him back towards the doors he reached a hand out towards Zoltac's ship, watching with fascination as his titanium fingers reached melting point and started to liquefy.

*

The moment the Omega had fired, so badly damaging the Peacemaker, Kincaid had ordered his pilots to move in for the kill. Now, bearing down on the stricken ship his Squadron was met by laser armed shuttles dropped from the belly of the vessel and sweeping up into the heart of the squadron, inflicting heavy casualties. Kincaid ordered the surviving fighters to regroup and reengage the enemy shuttles one on one, their superior speed and agility turning the tide of the battle in the Earthmen's favour. Kincaid caught sight of an enemy shuttle as it vapourised two fighters on his port side. He pulled his ship up and over in a corkscrewing loop, locking onto its tail, sticking like glue, chasing it through the maelstrom of ships swarming round the Peacemaker's hull. As the Centauran ship fell dead in his sights he let rip his forward guns and scored a direct hit, utterly destroying it. Sweeping through the kill's debris he saw the shadow of another, larger ship against the starfield, its gold eagle livery glinting as it caught the sunlight, pushing out from the Peacemaker's main dock and accelerating away from Earth. Kincaid peeled away from the squadron in pursuit.

The Zelda fell in beside him.

*

In the Earth Defence Command Centre 25,000 miles below on the Island of Grand Bahama, Colonel Schnell was in a sweat. He had watched and listened to the progress of the battle on satellite link and could see the cause was all but lost. The intention had been for him to use the emergency evacuation ship behind the Defence Centre to dock with the Peacemaker after the successful destruction of San Simeon, joining the victorious Zoltac where his loyalty to the Centaurans would be rewarded by his inauguration as the new Earth Consul. But now the great Battle Cruiser was breaking up, drifting helplessly towards the Moon, its own crew rebelling and under attack from Lunar based fighter squadrons.

He looked up as a laser cutter burst through the heavy blast doors and knew it would only be a matter of minutes before he faced the base defence marines and a life sentence of hard labour in the Kuiper belt. Or worse.

Schnell knew he must get to the emergency ship but where after that? He scanned the frequencies eavesdropping on the barrage of voices coming from the battle raging in space above him, listening intently for some sign that the fight was not lost, for some hope, when he heard the word 'escaped'. It was a squadron leader following a shuttle which had managed to break free in the pandemonium. The laser cutter had nearly done its work and he could hear the marines banging on the outer door. He flipped to a visual from a drone circling the Peacemaker and saw the escaping ship. The Wraith. So Zoltac had turned tail and was saving his own skin. But if Zoltac had a way out then so did Schnell. The Colonel turned on his heels and ran down the escape tunnel towards the ECES.

The blast doors fell into the command centre with a heavy thud sending paper and debris eddying into the room. Armed marines filed into the nerve centre of Earth's defences, scanning the bodies on the floor, around the tables and slumped in chairs. As the marine captain arrived at the duty officer's station Major Fulbright was struggling to his feet. He pointed towards the escape tunnel.

"There, he's getting away. It's Schnell," he said barely able to force out the words. He tried to walk but his muscles were still in spasm from the effects of the nerve toxin. Several marines headed down the tunnel and Fulbright grabbed the arms of the soldiers who were holding him up.

"Take me down there," he pleaded.

They all but carried him into the tunnel and as they were half way down they heard the roar of the escape ship firing as it lifted Schnell up and away from the base. Arriving in the ECES control room the marine captain turned to Fulbright.

"Looks like we've lost him," he said, standing his men down.

Fulbright watched the shuttle roll for orbital injection and staggered forward to the control panel. He pulled a key dangling from a chain around his neck and inserted it in a black box next to the controls. Giving the key a half turn the cover flipped open to reveal a small white button. Fulbright put his thumb over it and, looking up after the receding space craft, depressed it.

Four miles up, the ECES shuttle exploded in a cloud of flame and white billowing smoke in the darkening sky, pieces of the ship and its occupant shooting in all directions across the Atlantic Ocean like a mighty Catherine Wheel.

"Test flight aborted," said Major Fulbright painfully. "Happy One World Day, Colonel!"

*

Back in San Simeon the sky was slightly lighter than in the islands on the other side of the continent as Agent Harris came down the ornate steps from Hearst Castle to join Agent Laurel by the pool. Despite the sun still being above the horizon, what looked like a star could be seen shining brightly to the south just below the Moon.

"The Peacemaker?" he asked.

"What's left of it, I guess. Must be a hell of a brawl up there to be that bright."

They both stared wordlessly at the sharp point of light, imagining the conflagration.

"This could have been the last place I ever stood in," said Laurel distantly.

Harris looked at her, askance.

"Don't get poetic on me, Agent," he said.

Laurel stirred from her reverie and faced her colleague.

"Not poetic. Just a statement of fact."

"Sure. President wants to see us."

They turned and headed back towards the castle.

"So you managed to get him out of the escape ship, huh?"

"Took a lot of persuasion!"

*

"We have two craft on our tail, Commander," said Marshal Wittan.

Zoltac looked in the rear monitor.

"The Wraith is not even at half power. It can lose those lumbering hulks with ease. But first, let's see what we can do about our two trouble makers," he said and turned on Smith and Prendergast.

"You have caused me..." and his eyes rolled into the top of his sockets, "...a great deal of grief."

Smith and Prendergast stood, staring back at him, terrified but defiant.

"And so," he said, his eyes returning to what passed with Zoltac for normal, "do you know what I am going to do with you?"

He pinned them with a stoney glare, waiting for a response.

"Oh, you actually want an answer to that do you?" asked Prendergast with all the calm he could summon. "It's not just an excuse to yell 'Silence' at us?"

Zoltac was temporarily put off his guard by this feisty reply. He had been hoping for blubbering and begging. Sneering at Prendergast, he turned his attention to Smith.

"You," he said. "Do you have any idea of the fate I have in store for you?"

Smith took a deep breath and decided if he was going to die a grizzly death he could at least follow Prendergast's admirable example and go out as cockily as possible.

"Me?" he said attempting a bored look, "I personally couldn't give a Schrödinger's Cat what you do!" he sniffed, adding, "ya big Nazi nutter!" to leave no doubt of his position on the matter.

Zoltac landed a swift blow to the side of Smith's head and as Prendergast came to his aid, he received the same.

"Suit them up," Zoltac ordered Marshal Wittan, "and then eject them from the ship in opposite directions with...how far are those ships behind us?"

"About twenty minutes, Commander," answered Wittan.

"Then give these fools ten, no, fifteen minutes air. A quarter of an hour is just the right amount of time for the terror to really take hold. At least that's what I've always observed. Those ships will waste valuable time attempting a pointless rescue while we put as much distance between us and this hateful system as we can."

Marshal Wittan took Smith and Prendergast at gunpoint to the rear chamber of the Wraith. A rack of space suits hung on a wall and there was a small airlock at the back of the ship.

"Put those on," ordered Wittan.

"You don't have to do this, Marshal," said Smith.

Wittan stared back at him unflinchingly.

"Just give us more air so they can pick us up," pleaded Prendergast. Wittan stood unmoved, the gun pointing steadily at the boys. Smith tried again.

"You heard what the commander said. You can easily outrun the Earth ships."

Still Wittan gave nothing away.

"Killing us is pointless," Smith persisted.

The Marshal lifted his gun and leveled it at him.

"Put them on I said."

The boys backed up, grabbed a suit each and started to don them.

"So you are just going to obey every depraved order which that madman gives, are you?" spluttered Prendergast in anger and frustration. "You're proving yourself to be no more than his lackey!"

Wittan grunted a mirthless laugh.

Smith zipped up his suit, pressurised it and grabbed a helmet.

"Come on, Wittan!" and he was shouting now, "You're a soldier, not a cold blooded murderer."

The Marshal came up to him and leaned in close to his face.

"Are you trying to appeal to my better nature?"

Smith held his eye and answered through gritted teeth.

"Yes, I am, Marshal!"

Wittan smiled at him and shook his head.

"Boy. Have you got the wrong Centauran."

He made them seal their suits and pushed them into the airlock. When he'd opened the outer door, he spoke to them, his voice ringing in their helmets.

"Now push yourselves away from the ship. And away from each other. Obey, or I will vaporise both of you with the ship's swivel guns."

Smith and Prendergast faced each other holding onto the rim of the airlock door. Smith's breathing was shallow and erratic.

"I can't do it, Percy, all the strength's gone out of me."

"Come on, Tony old thing. Deep breath. The bastard may be able to take our lives but I'll be cube rooted if he's going to have our dignity."

Smith took a long low breath, looked deep into his friend's face and there found his strength.

"You're right, mate. Let's do this."

They shook hands, nodded to each other, then pushed back and away from the ship, tumbling into the void.

*

"You seem agitated, Marshal," said Zoltac, sitting at he helm, his back to Wittan.

The Marshal shuffled uncomfortably.

"Speak up, man!" Zoltac shouted.

"It's just," said Wittan, "you know they will never let us through the SolAlpha gate."

"Of course they won't. I'm afraid that particular short cut is unavailable to us. We will be taking the scenic route home."

Marshal Wittan's face fell. Zoltac couldn't be serious.

"But, Commander. A shuttle like this? The whole four light years to Alpha in real space? It would take decades."

"Yes. But I can sleep most of the way. I have a cryogenic unit in my cabin."

"Only one?" asked the Marshal, stiffening.

"Afraid so. Tell you what. I'll toss you for it."

Marshal Wittan, being a bright if flawed individual, suddenly saw where Zoltac's twisted mind was headed and went for the Las-Dis56E at his thigh. He got his hand to the butt as Zoltac spun on his chair and blew the Marshal's head off with a single blast from a plasma pistol. The Centauran Commander holstered his weapon and looked down at the lifeless body.

"That's for correcting me in front of junior officers," he said.

Zoltac returned to the control console and began to chart his course home. He looked up at the screen before him and let out a startled yelp. He stumbled to his feet clutching his chest, breathing deeply, as there, clinging to the window on the outside of the ship, was the burned and twisted body of Helot19.

The robot looked like a target dummy after a particularly large office group outing to the laser range had done their stuff, the unfortunate automaton having then gone on to rescue a family of twelve from a house fire.

Helot19 gripped the ship with a firm hand and raised his other, melted stump which he waved at Zoltac, smiling genially. The smile faded, an altogether more sinister expression sliding across his digital features.

He pulled back his titanium arm and, releasing the hydraulic servos in his shoulder, slammed it through the reinforced plexiglass, shattering it and exposing Battle Cruiser Commander Zoltac to the cold, lethal vacuum of space.

*

The Wraith was now a long way off. As he spun around his axis on the journey into the abyss he could see with each rotation the glint of another craft, back towards the Earth. Already feeling the effects of the carbon dioxide build up in his space suit, it was getting harder to focus and dreamlike voices flickered with fugitive articulation in his faltering consciousness. His head throbbed and his muscles spasmed as a sea of faces danced before him fading as quickly as they appeared but through the carnival of grinning, weeping, laughing visions two persisted. Familiar and comforting. One, space helmeted with a desperate look on the face behind the visor. The other, stolid, metallic, implacable. The helmeted face looked towards the un-human other with a desperate appeal. The mouth moving soundlessly behind the faceplate urged the mechanical man on. Then the face turned back, tears of frustration in the deep blue eyes.

Slowly, a hissing; the venting of air. The mist behind his irises began to clear. He breathed deeply and the pure clean oxygen expanded his lungs.

Smith was coming back from the brink of oblivion, suspended in the open vastness of interplanetary space, the Helot holding him in one burned, stunted arm on one side and Prendergast on the other.

28. PHEW, THAT WAS CLOSE

The Gagarin Station was surrounded by a fleet of vessels, great and small, like flies around the eye sockets of a large ruminating animal on the great, dry plains of the Earth below.

The ruined hulk of the Peacemaker was flanked by great tenders which had tamed the firestorms that swept the ship during and after the battle. Construction vessels had moved in to shore up the Peacemaker's unstable superstructure so that a flotilla of tugs could bring it in to port. Ambulances ferried the wounded to the hospital ships and an agency detention centre had been dispatched for interrogation and debriefing of the survivors. G/B differentiation they called it. Sorting the good guys from the bad.

This was to say nothing of the legion of news feeds covering the aftermath of the great 'Battle For Earth' as it had been dubbed.

*

Smith and Prendergast stood in their deluxe suite, looking out over the servicing bay where the hull of the Peacemaker was being docked, a half dozen salvage ship's bearing the Saabre Industries logo joining the armada which already buzzed around the twisted wreck, awaiting their chance to retrieve HENRIE, which was due to be transported to the research facility in geosynchronous polar orbit were Smith and Prendergast would join it after the victory celebrations, to be conducted in the Gagarin's main ballroom the following day, presided over by the Earth President himself.

"Big day tomorrow, Perce!" said Smith.

"Yes. Gongs all round, what?" replied Prendergast.

"Handed out by the top man himself. The big time, eh?"

"It certainly is, old boy. Doesn't get a great deal bigger."

They smiled at each other and nodded, turning back to the activity around the Peacemaker. After a moment Smith spoke.

"I don't want to go."

"Me neither."

"I just want to get to work."

"I know what you mean, Tony. Though I have managed to get a few ideas down in some of the lulls in the last few months."

Smith turned to his partner, a look of confusion on his face.

"Lulls!? What lulls would they be?"

"Oh, you know, the odd snatched moment in between being assaulted, abducted and generally hareing around the solar system like a rabbit with its scut on fire. Trying to dodge the clutches of every psychopath and axe-murderer in the four colonies. I actually knocked it up into a paper and published it on the Innernet this morning."

Smith shook his head.

"Unbelievable. Here's me been hanging onto me sanity by a thread. Spending every spare moment working out ways for us to stay alive and all the time you've been writing up scientific papers."

"Don't worry. I published in both our names."

"Really? That's very big of you. I must have a read of it sometime."

"I think you should, Tony. You'll find it fascinating. I got the idea from something the blond writer girl said at dinner that evening. You remember, at the captain's table, just before Betty highjacked us."

"Get away."

"Yes. She mentioned time travel..."

Before he could elucidate, the door burst open and Betty herself swept in followed closely by Helot19 balancing a tray of champagne on his dodgy arm.

"Hello boys. The sun's below the solar panels. My butler has the booze."

Helot19 put down the tray and Betty popped the cork.

"By the cringe, Nineteen," said Smith taking in the still battered and singed robot, "I thought you were going to be repaired."

"As did I, Mr Smith. But though I am not allowed to visit Earth, I have been given permission to stay in the Home System and the authorities thought it would be more acceptable if I bore my 'battle scars' as they called them. I really don't mind. Despite the obvious aesthetic drawbacks of looking like a barbecue gone wrong I am still operating at over ninety-two percent efficiency."

"And he's been given a job," added Betty.

"Indeed. Escorting tourists around the old Apollo sites on the moon."

"You'll enjoy that."

"I believe I will, Mr Prendergast."

Betty handed the drinks around.

"Here's mud in your eye," she toasted enthusiastically.

"How about you, Betty? You know what you're going to do?" asked Smith.

"Haven't given it a thought. I ain't finished celebrating yet. Hell, I haven't even started. Hey, Percy, you wanna take a lady dancing tonight?" She grabbed Prendergast and whirled him round the shag pile.

Smith turned to Helot19 and spoke to him quietly.

"Nineteen. I wanted to say. We owe you. Me and Percy."

"Think nothing of it. I was just obeying the laws of robotics."

"Yes," said Smith treading carefully, "about that."

"Sir?"

"Well, it could be said, if you look at it from a very particular angle, that by smashing the Wraith's window you caused a human death."

"I suppose it could. But by not doing so I would most certainly have been breaking the first law. If I hadn't entered the ship to get a jet pack and oxygen canister, you and Mr Prendergast would have perished. As the second part of the first law states, 'I may not through my inaction allow a human being to come to harm' don't you see?"

Smith turned this over in his head.

"Yes, but by breaking the window you did cause Zoltac to perish, breaking the first part of the first law which states that, 'Through your actions you may not injure a human being'."

Helot19 took a moment to reply.

"You warned me once about making assumptions. How it led to most human...cock-ups did you call them? Well, aren't you rather making the assumption that Zoltac was a member of the human race. If I may be so bold, I would suggest that the moment he showed himself willing to exterminate several billion human beings, he rather gave up that privilege, wouldn't you say?"

Smith smiled and patted the robot's ample, laser pitted shoulder.

"Yes, I would say. I most certainly would, mate."

"Come on, party poopers," shouted Betty from the other side of the room where she was putting Percy through his paces with a double time tango, "Kincaid and Hawkins are waiting for us in the bar and they looked like they were hitting it off pretty good. Better go break them up. We can't have a squadron leader in the Earth Space Corps consorting with the enemy!"

"They tell me," said Smith, "that the President may ask Lieutenant Hawkins to form a government in exile. That she'll take over on Alpha when they topple the Generalissimo's regime."

"What was that?" asked Prendergast.

"Yeah, whatever, let's get drunk," said Betty and drained her glass.

The boys emptied their own drinks and headed out of the door.

A little way down the corridor, they met up with a tall middle aged man with a soft, childlike face and narrow hands with long, elegant fingers, himself heading toward the elevator. As they fell into step he turned and beamed in recognition at Smith and Prendergast.

"Gentleman. They told me you were staying here. What an honour."

The boys blushed and murmured their modest thanks.

"Could I ask the greatest favour?"

"Depends what it is, bub," warned Betty.

"I am just about to set out on a family holiday to the moon. My wife is settling our two boys down now in our lunar yacht. Do you think you could pop your heads in for just a moment? They so admire you. Perhaps an autograph or even a photo with them would be something they'd cherish their whole lives and could proudly show their own children. Look, they would tell them," and he held up an imaginary photograph, "I met Smith and Prendergast, just after they saved the world."

Betty was about to tell him to go fry an egg, having never heard such sentimental baloney but before she could, Percy said, with a tear in his eye, that he and Smith would be delighted. So, promising to be quick, they followed the man down to the lunar launch bays.

His was the only yacht in the dock and a very swish one it was. The man must be loaded with the stuff, though Smith, to own a ship like this. He began to speculate how long it would take for him to buy one, when the man opened the door and gestured the boys inside.

"Please, gentlemen, they will be so thrilled."

Smith and Prendergast climbed up the treads and into the luxurious interior but were surprised when the door closed behind them. A sound of air escaping came from all around them and Prendergast sniffed.

"Tony, can you smell something funny?"

Before Smith could answer, and not for the first time since they graduated college, everything went black.

EPILOGUE

The Prime Minister approached the Chairman's chamber overlooking the courtyard of the Great Palace in the city of Vanderkamp on the planet Hatzes, home of the Eridani Presidium. He held in his long, elegant fingers a communique from their spy on Gagarin. He had found the scientists. The men with the idea that would bring the Eridanian system closer to the heart of the human family and put an end to the remoteness that had made them a third class colony for two centuries. If they could, as their paper had suggested, achieve the goal of instantaneous communication throughout the inhabited galaxy, well, think what that would do for their economy and even more how it would help spread the philosophy of the great Colepepper, Warrior of the Republic, Beloved Father to the People's Colony of Eridanus.

The Chairman would be pleased.

The End...

...For Now.

BIOGRAPHY

Kevin R Mcnally began acting in 1972 at the Birmingham reportorial theatre. He attended the Royal Academy of Dramatic Art and won the Bancroft Gold Medal and Ronson award.

He has worked extensively in theatre, TV, radio and film. He has also written extensively for television under the name Kevin Sperring.

He is probably best known as Mr Gibbs in the *Pirates of the Caribbean* movies.

Sons of Sol is his first novel.

ADRIAN BALDWIN (COVER ARTIST)

Adrian is a Mancunian now living and working in Wales. Back in the 1990s, he wrote for various TV shows/personalities: Smith & Jones, Clive Anderson, Brian Conley, Paul McKenna, Hale & Pace, Rory Bremner (and a few others). Wooo, get him! Since then, he has written three screenplays—one of which received generous financial backing from the Film Agency for Wales. Then along came the global recession which kicked the UK Film industry in the nuts. What a bummer! Not to be outdone, he turned to novel writing—which had always been his real dream—and, in particular, a genre he feels is often overlooked; a genre he has always been a fan of: Dark Comedy (sometimes referred to as Horror's weird cousin). *Barnacle Brat* (a dark comedy for grown-ups), his first novel won Indie Novel of the Year 2016 award; his second novel *Stanley Mccloud Must Die!* (more dark comedy for grown-ups) published in 2016 and his third: *The Snowman And The Scarecrow* (another dark comedy for grown-ups) published in 2018. Adrian Baldwin has also written and published a number of dark comedy short stories. He designs book covers too—not just for his own books but for a growing number of publishers. For more information on the award-winning author, check out:

https://adrianbaldwin.info/

DEMAIN PUBLISHING

To keep up to-date on all news DEMAIN (including future submission calls and releases) you can follow us in a number of ways:

BLOG:
www.demainpublishingblog.weebly.com

TWITTER:
@DemainPubUk

FACEBOOK PAGE:
Demain Publishing

INSTAGRAM:
Demainpublishing

Printed in Great Britain
by Amazon

84894704R00195